BEC BENSON

STRAIGHT TO YOU

ISBN: 978-1-968356-00-2 (Print)

ISBN: 978-1-968356-01-9 (Kindle)

Book Cover: Anna with The Bloodied Soul Creative

Editor: Editing by Gee

Proofreader: Brittany at Campfire Edits

Character Art: @conceptsbycanea

STRAIGHT TO YOU

BEC BENSON

CONTENT WARNINGS

This is <u>not</u> a dark romance, thriller, or mystery, but it does explore darker themes.

The following contains spoilers. If you feel comfortable going in without reading the warnings, please feel free to skip to the next page.

Content warnings include: mentions of homophobia, stalking, violence, kidnapping, privacy invasion, home invasion, hospitalization, non-consensual recording, one main character is outed, blood and injury, confinement, mental health themes, vulgar and offensive language, explicit sex scenes (18+), and emotional distress.

For a more detailed list, please visit: https://becbenson.com/ straight-to-you

To everyone who has supported me on this journey, thank you.
I hope you love Logan and Ryder as much as I do.

1

RYDER

"*You make me feel so good, baby.*" My voice is breathy, and I add a little grunt for good measure to sell the moment. "*Oh,* fuck. *I can't wait to get my cock inside your tight little hole.*"

I pause for a second to make sure the words land with the right kind of heat.

If there's one thing I've learned from narrating romance novels, it's that the more I immerse myself in the scene, the more it connects. I've been narrating audiobooks for years now—mostly gay romance novels, which tends to surprise people since I've always identified as straight.

When I was first getting started after college, I'd take any job I could, but the first time I had a request to do a queer romance novel, something clicked for me. That one job turned into more, and now it pretty much fills my entire calendar, and I wouldn't have it any other way.

Love is love, and I love this genre. There's so much tension and vulnerability, and the sex scenes are always fun to record. Let's just say I've learned *a lot* about what you can do with two dicks over the years.

When people ask what I do, I always keep it simple; I'm an audiobook narrator. But if they ask for specifics, I tell them —and it almost always leads to the inevitable question: "So… are you gay?" Like, my sexuality is something I owe strangers.

I've never understood why people feel so entitled to that answer. As if who I'm attracted to somehow affects how well I can do my job. But honestly? Their opinion of me and what I do isn't my problem or my business.

All that matters to me is doing these stories justice and, hopefully, helping readers connect more deeply with themselves.

I glance at the time and realize I should probably call it a night. My focus isn't where it needs to be, and if I do this scene half-distracted, the delivery won't land, and I'll end up having to redo it tomorrow.

Plus, I'm already late to meet Logan.

Logan's been my best friend since we met freshman year in college, and no one loves to give me shit more than he does. But for all his relentless teasing, he's also my fiercest defender. Logan is bi, so if anyone so much as breathes a negative word about my career, his hackles instantly go up. It's only happened twice, but both times he shut the conversation down so fast, the people in question were practically tripping over themselves apologizing, swearing up and down they weren't homophobic—as if that somehow erased whatever ignorant joke they'd just made.

Of course, his protective streak doesn't stop him from giving me shit every chance he gets. Mainly about the fact that despite narrating steamy queer romance, I've never been with a man myself. According to Logan, that means I'm 'depriving myself of essential research.' He always smirks like he knows something I don't, which, frankly, is infuriating.

He's also constantly on my ass about my complete inability to be on time for literally anything, which I know he'll remind me of tonight.

I turn my mic off and shut my laptop before heading into my bedroom to grab a clean shirt and hoodie from the pile of folded laundry I have yet to put away, and decide the jeans I'm already wearing are good enough. I brush my teeth, lather on deodorant, text Logan I'm leaving now, and grab my wallet and keys before heading out the door.

As usual, I make the six-minute drive to Logan's apartment, park, and walk the rest of the way to the bar. We usually just meet there, mostly because of my habitual lateness. I always get caught up in recording, while Logan is ready to socialize and grab a beer the second he leaves the office.

Before I know it, I see the familiar neon Pine Bar sign. The green 'N' occasionally sputters out, but that only adds to its charm. It also makes me chuckle because at this point, they really should serve pie.

As soon as I walk in, I catch Mia's eyes behind the bar and give her a wave. Mia is the unofficial queen of Pine Bar; there's no way this place could function without her. She's also a complete badass who always wears her signature red bandana over her dark curls. I swear I've never seen her without it. She waves back at me as I make my way over to Logan, who's waiting for me in our usual spot.

If I could describe Pine Bar in a word, it'd be eclectic.

There are antique amber sconces mounted on the walls, mixed with posters and local sports memorabilia. It has a very 'locals-only' vibe that's familiar to us. There's also an ancient jukebox in the corner that somehow still works, and the place holds the faint scent of smoke from the wood-burning stove that's tucked into the back corner of the restaurant.

Logan looks up as I make my way to him and smirks. He's got a half-empty pint glass in front of him, and another full one waiting for me.

"You're late," he says, as expected, kicking the chair out for me on the opposite side of the table. "What's the excuse this time? Wait, wait, let me guess. You got all hot and bothered narrating again? Got lost in the moment?"

I snort, reaching for the beer he ordered for me. "You say that like you don't swoon over the same scenes when you read them."

"Guilty as charged," he laughs. "What can I say? Good writing is good writing, and those authors write damn good books."

I smirk into my glass, shaking my head. "You ever gonna give up on ribbing me about being late and just let me show up when I show up?"

Logan shrugs. "Probably not, I like watching your panic texts roll in. It's my form of entertainment before you get here."

"I don't panic-text."

"*Dude.*" He sets his beer down and holds up his phone. "Shit, leaving now! Five mins! Okay, actually leaving now for real." He grins at me like he's waiting for a reaction. "You realize I see you typing before you even hit send, right?"

"Maybe I just want to build suspense."

"Uh-huh." He chuckles. "You're basically the unreliable

narrator of your own commute. Good thing you don't get paid for that."

I laugh, shaking my head at him. This right here is why he's my best friend. The easy back-and-forth, the teasing, the way he knows exactly what to say to get under my skin, but never pushes too far. It's familiar and comfortable in a way I can't put into words.

I look around the bar to see who else we know here, and I immediately regret it when my eyes find Pete's.

"Logan! Ryder! You're up next. I need some real competition," Pete calls out, pointing dramatically at us with a dart in hand. That man loves darts. He's here every night just to play, and he always beats everyone who dares compete with him. I've played a few times to appease him, but most nights I try to stick to talking to Logan instead of getting my ass handed to me.

Logan shakes his head, setting his glass down. "Not happening. My hands are for designing, not darts."

I grin, leaning forward. "You sure that's what your hands are for?"

"Wouldn't you like to know?" Logan shoots back with a wink. "Plus, watching you embarrass yourself is way more entertaining. Go on now. Pete's waiting."

Mia chimes in as she slides a beer to a guy in flannel. "If you two spent half as much time playing as you do running your mouths, Pete might actually have some competition around here."

"Exactly!" Pete shouts, loud enough to make a few heads turn.

"We're good tonight, man. Maybe next time," I call back.

"I'm holding you to that!" Pete yells, smiling as he turns back to the board.

When I turn back to face Logan, he starts talking about work and decompressing from his week. Every time he complains about his job as a graphic designer for a local company, it sounds like hell to me. I guess you don't naturally decompress by talking about the good, easy-going clients, though.

"She told me she wanted a logo that was *approachable yet exclusive*," Logan grumbles. "Explain that to me, Ryder. How can something be both? It's like saying, *make it hot, but cold at the same time*."

"Sounds like a winning brand strategy to me," I declare to rile him up.

"Shut up. You're lucky your audience doesn't get to tell you how to sound," Logan reasons, pointing his beer at me.

I smirk, leaning back in my chair. "That's because I already give my audience *exactly* what they want. The person-alized fan mail and five-star reviews prove it."

Logan rolls his eyes. "How could I forget, you're just out here stealing hearts through a microphone."

"Damn right I am," I smirk. "And yours was free before I ever hit record."

He groans. "I set myself up for that one."

"Sure did." I wink at him—mostly for the bit, but also because this is just how we are.

We've always had this kind of easy banter. Maybe it's just the years of friendship. Or maybe it's because Logan's bi and doesn't seem to mind it when I toe the line between teasing and flirting. It's never serious—we both know that—but it makes the playful back-and-forth more fun.

Logan drains the last of his beer before waving Mia over for another round. I let my gaze wander around the room again to see who else is here while we wait, and that's when they land on a guy at the end of the bar I've never seen before.

He looks a little older than us, in his thirties, with dark hair that's clean cut, wearing a worn-in leather jacket. The thing that really catches my attention, though, is that his dark gaze is locked right on me. It's not a passing glance, either. His eyes seem to linger on me, and he doesn't look away when he notices I'm looking back at him. Most people would break eye contact the second they're caught staring, but he seems unfazed, and something about it feels off. Strange enough to make my skin prickle and for discomfort to set in.

"Earth to Ryder," Logan sighs, nudging my foot under the table. "You good?"

I look away from the man at the bar and turn back to him, shaking off whatever *that* just was. "Yeah, sorry. Zoned out for a second."

He looks at me for a beat longer than usual, like he's making sure I'm truly okay, but drops it a moment later. "Don't scare me like that, man. You're the only one who listens when I spiral about work shit."

I open my mouth, but before I can say anything, Mia appears with two fresh pints.

"Another round for the dynamic duo," she says, sliding the glasses onto the table.

"Thanks, Mia." Logan grins, nudging one toward me. "Maybe now he'll focus."

"My bad," I mutter, giving him a faint smile as I lift the glass. "Cheers."

I try to focus on the drink in my hand and what Logan is saying, but it's so hard because I can't ignore the feeling of someone staring at me. It feels like this guy's eyes are burning a hole into the side of my head.

Ignore it, don't look at the guy who's obsessively staring. Does he not understand social cues? I mean, seriously, dude.

But after a few more seconds of pretending I'm not hyper-aware of the feeling, I give in. And sure enough, his eyes are right where I predicted—on me. And once again, he doesn't pretend to look away; he just holds my gaze.

2

LOGAN

Ryder's being weird. I can tell he's distracted by this rando at the bar, even though he's pretending not to be. He's half listening at best, keeps saying "what" when I stop talking, and he hasn't laughed at a single one of my jokes, which is very unlike him.

I'm not sure what's going on or why this guy suddenly has him so captivated, but I do know I don't like it. *At all.*

I nudge Ryder's knee under the table again. It feels like the tenth time I've tried to pull his attention back from whatever is happening in the bar. Before the guy he's been making eyes with walked in, he was his usual, happy self. Now, it's like he's completely checked out. The shift was so sudden and makes no sense. I've never seen him do this before.

"You sure you're good?" I ask.

Once again, he blinks like I just pulled him out of his head. "Yeah, sorry. Just spaced out again."

Right.

Ryder's not one to zone out like this, especially when it involves another person. He's never shown that much interest

9

in dating, nor spent much time making eyes with people at the bar. He's also straight, which is why it's throwing me off. *Why is this guy holding so much of his attention?*

Friday night is usually *our* night without distractions to decompress and catch up from the week, and right now, this guy is ruining it.

I try to draw him back in, wanting his attention on me instead. I comment on the couple behind us, who've clearly just met on a dating app, and are doing their best to look engaged instead of pretending they aren't both waiting for their best friend to call with a fake emergency to end their misery. That would usually get a smile, maybe even a laugh. But tonight, I get a distracted "hmm" as he taps his phone screen to check the time.

Tonight sucks.

"Think I'm gonna head out," he says. He's barely touched his second beer, and he's already grabbing his jacket from the back of the chair before I even respond. "Feeling kind of off tonight. You ready?"

"Oh." I try not to sound disappointed, even though I don't want the night to end yet. I wish we could rewind to before that guy walked into the bar. "You okay?"

He hesitates for a moment, like he's debating whether to say something more or pretend he's fine. I rack my brain, trying to figure out if I did something to throw him off tonight, but I know in my gut it's got nothing to do with me and everything to do with the stranger in the leather jacket. We've been friends for years, close in a way most people never get, and I've never seen him pull away like this. It's making me feel uneasy because I can't tell if I'm missing something major going on with Ryder right now.

Is he into that guy?

He reluctantly sighs, meeting my gaze. "Don't look right now, but that guy at the bar keeps staring at me, and I don't like it. Every time I glance over, he's still looking. Doesn't even try to look away, like most people would. It's creeping me out."

"I know who you're talking about," I confirm. "I saw you looking over there a few times. Weird he keeps staring at you. Wonder what it'll take for that guy to take a hint you're not interested."

He's probably trying to flirt and doesn't know Ryder is straight. But, honestly, if this is his version of making a move, it's seriously backfiring. The lingering, borderline obsessive eye contact is not a turn-on for anyone.

"Yeah, I'm not sure, but I'm ready to get out of here."

I nod, draining the last of my beer. We both close out and head outside, making the walk to my apartment. When we reach my building, I slow down and he stops to look at me.

"You sure you don't want to stay?" I ask, hoping he'll change his mind. It doesn't happen often, but when he heads home on a Friday, the loneliness hits harder. This night's always been ours, and without him, it just feels empty.

"I don't know, that guy put me in a weird mood. Think I want to go home tonight and decompress," he says. "Next week, promise."

I force myself to nod, but I hate that he wants to process tonight alone. I'm the one he's supposed to turn to when something's bothering him.

"Alright. Text me when you get home."

"I will," he says, giving me a small, forced smile before turning and walking the few more steps toward his car.

That guy at the bar clearly rattled him, and I can't help but wonder if it's because he was staring at Ryder like he was waiting for an invite to approach him, or something else entirely. Ryder has never had an issue with queer people. If that guy was into him—and it sure seemed like he was—I know that wouldn't be the problem. But something about tonight was different, and whatever it stirred up, I've never seen Ryder react like that before.

Turning and heading inside my building, I make my way to my apartment. The door swings shut behind me, and the sound echoes, reminding me that he's not here despite how many pieces of him are scattered around my apartment.

It doesn't even bother me that his hoodie is still sitting on a kitchen chair or that he bought a second charger for his laptop, which he leaves plugged into my wall. Sometimes I'll even find his socks under the coffee table. He's always around and I never get tired of him, which is telling because if anyone else pulled the shit he did, I'd probably never invite them back over.

I think that's what's worrying me so much. I've known him for almost a decade, and not once have I ever wanted space or needed a break from him, and he's never mentioned wanting space from me, either. Not until tonight anyway, and I know for most people that's unthinkable, but that's just our norm.

I used to joke that it was because we were really compatible and that he got me in a way most people didn't. But lately, I've started wondering if maybe the reason none of my relationships ever stuck is because I already give the best parts of myself to him.

It's dumb, probably. We're just friends. Best friends. Practically attached at the hip, but sometimes, when he's not here, it feels like a piece of me is missing.

Why am I feeling so needy right now?

We've been friends since freshman year of college after we met in Introduction to Environmental Science, a random gen-ed that didn't make sense for either of us to take, but that's college. Ryder was a communications major with a minor in performing arts, and I was a graphic design student.

On the first day of class, Ryder dropped into the seat next to mine and immediately started making jokes about how boring this class would be, and that's what pulled me into his orbit.

I'll admit it—at first, I had a crush. How could I not? Ryder is *hot* with his thick, unruly brown hair that always makes him look like he has perfectly styled bedhead. He's got a sharp jawline and a short beard that really works for him, and his smile completely draws you in. It makes you feel like you're the only person in the world. At least, that's how I felt. And I especially like that he's two inches taller than me. Being six feet tall, I'm used to being the one people lean on. But with him? I wanted to shrink into his arms and let him hold me close.

Then there's his voice. It's deep and confident, and the kind that commands attention without trying. It's no wonder he became a narrator right after college. His voice could convince anyone of anything.

He's the perfect package. The perfect *straight* package. And once I learned that, I buried my crush as deep down as it would go and moved on. Or at least, that's what I've always told myself, and I think I've done a damn good job.

Starting junior year of college, we moved in together off-campus and didn't separate until last year, when we finally decided, mostly for the sake of other people, that maybe twenty-seven was the age to get our own places.

Truthfully, it's the worst decision we've ever made. I've

never felt as lonely as I have in the past year, and it always makes the rare Friday nights we don't spend together even harder.

It's just one night, I remind myself. It's not like he said he doesn't want to spend time with me anymore.

I don't know why my mind is spiraling so hard. Maybe the problem is that it's been too long since I've let myself want anything—or anyone—outside of work and spending time with him. Maybe it's pent-up tension and loneliness I didn't realize I was experiencing until Ryder's attention shifted elsewhere. Maybe I need to hook up with someone and get this feeling out of my system. Something low stakes. Just...something that reminds me I still exist outside of this friendship I've built my whole damn world around.

All I wanted tonight was to spend time with my best friend, and it felt like all he wanted to do was check out and go home.

Realistically, I know it has nothing to do with me, but my thoughts have a way of making it personal anyway.

My phone buzzes in my pocket, and I pull it out, seeing a text from Ryder.

RYDER:

Home. Night Logan

That was brief. Clearly, he doesn't want to talk more tonight, and I don't want to push him if he's already feeling like he needs space.

LOGAN:

Night Ry

I toss my phone down on the couch next to me, but don't

move away. I wish he'd stayed, and I wish I'd asked more questions because my mind is running wild.

I try to tell myself it's nothing, and that he promised next week he'd be back on my couch with me, stealing the blanket, and falling asleep halfway through a movie. I think about turning on the TV, but instead, my eyes drift to a picture of the two of us at the county fair a few years ago. Ryder's arm is slung around my shoulders, both of us laughing, and he's holding a giant stuffed bear he won at one of those rigged basketball games. I still remember how he handed it to me with a huge grin and said, "I won it for you, obviously. For the nights I'm not there."

I wish I knew where that thing went because I'd snuggle the fluff out of it tonight.

Yep, it's time to open up my dating apps. Tomorrow, though, I need to get a grip first.

This level of neediness is new for me, but it's clear I need to redirect my attention to someone I could actually have a future with, or who could at least make me come so that I can take my mind off my best friend.

By the time I head to bed and I'm almost asleep, I hear my phone buzz on my nightstand. Groaning, I reach for it, and my eyes widen when I see Ryder's name.

Huh, that's odd. Maybe he wants to talk about tonight after all.

I swipe to answer, putting it on speaker. "You're not usually a late-night caller. Everything okay?"

He pauses for a second before responding, and I'm immediately worried.

"It's probably nothing," he says quietly. "I thought I heard something outside my window, but it's probably a raccoon or something. I don't know. I'm being paranoid."

"Did you check?"

"Yeah. Didn't see anything. Just...tonight's been weird, I guess."

"You want me to come over?" I ask, already halfway out of bed. "Or did you just wanna talk?"

He hesitates. "Just talk. I don't know, I think I needed to hear you tell me it was probably nothing. I'm sure you were almost asleep. Sorry."

My chest tightens.

"Don't be sorry. You can call me anytime. But seriously, if anything else happens, you call me back and I'll come over."

"Okay. Deal."

The line goes quiet for a few seconds, but I don't want to hang up. I know he doesn't either, probably still wired from whatever freaked him out.

"You remember that night junior year," I start, "when we locked ourselves out of the apartment and had to sit on the porch wrapped in the car blanket until the locksmith showed up?"

He lets out a short, soft laugh.

"Yeah. You wouldn't stop complaining that your ass was freezing."

"Because it was! And you were no help. You kept reading random facts off your phone like that was gonna warm us up."

"I was *distracting* you. That's called being a good friend."

I smile to myself. His voice already sounds a little steadier. "You still do that, you know," I say.

"What, read facts?"

"Distract me. Settle me down without even realizing it," I say with a soft smile into my pillow.

He doesn't say anything right away, but I hear the way he exhales like he's finally letting some of the tension go.

"Thanks, you just did that for me," he murmurs.

"Mmmm, I did, you caught me."

"And thanks for picking up, I knew you'd talk some sense into me."

"Any time," I tell him, meaning it. "Now go to sleep. I'll talk to you tomorrow, okay? But don't hesitate to call me again if you need me."

"Okay, thanks. Night, Logan."

"Night, Ry."

As soon as I hang up, I can't help but wonder if waiting until tomorrow is too long. I let my thumb hover over his name in my phone, but I shake my head and set it back down. He said he's okay, and I need to believe him.

But just in case, I turn my volume all the way up.

3

RYDER

I told Logan I was fine, and I meant it.

Probably.

He distracted me and pulled me out of my head, the way he always does. If I hadn't called, I'd probably be up all night letting worst-case scenarios eat me alive.

I should've stayed over like I usually do. Curled up on the couch with him, half-watching some awful movie, falling asleep to the sound of his breathing like I've done a hundred times until he tells me to get in bed. But tonight felt weird in a way I couldn't shake, like something underneath the surface had shifted, and I'm the only one who felt it.

Ever since I saw that guy at the bar sitting there, watching me, I've felt off. I didn't have the words to explain the creeped out and borderline suspicious feeling to Logan yet, mostly because I'm pretty sure there isn't any logic behind it. There was just *something* about the way the guy looked at me. His gaze was heavy, disturbing, and he wasn't trying to be subtle about it either, which somehow made it even worse.

I'm sure I'll never see him again, but it hasn't sat right with me all night.

Then, when I got home, I swore I heard something outside my window that sounded a lot like breaking branches. When I first heard the noise, I peeked through my blinds and half expected to see the guy from the bar standing there. Well, that or something straight out of a bad horror movie with a masked man in the front yard, or a figure under the streetlights.

But there was nothing.

Realistically, it was probably just my neighbor's kid sneaking out again and diving into my bushes to avoid getting caught. That would make the most sense, especially since he's done it before.

At this point, I can't tell if I'm paranoid because tonight's been so fucking strange, or if something is actually wrong, and I hate that I can't tell the difference. Paranoia isn't my style. If anything, I'm usually the opposite—carefree and laid-back to a fault—which is why tonight's rattling me so much.

No wonder Logan was two seconds from driving over here. I was acting weird at the bar, basically blew him off when we usually spend every Friday night together, and then called him late at night because I heard a noise outside my window. I've probably totally freaked him out, and I'm definitely gonna need to make that up to him.

I'm sure it's probably stress from work and deadlines building up that's exacerbating everything. That's gotta be it. I just need to shut my brain off and get some sleep so I can make some real progress recording tomorrow. Then I'll feel better. All of today's paranoia will evaporate, and I'll be able to laugh at how dramatic my reaction to this whole thing was.

AT SOME POINT, I MUST'VE FALLEN ASLEEP BECAUSE THE NEXT thing I know, my alarm is blaring in my ear and I really hate that fucking sound.

I turn off the alarm and check my notifications, spotting a text from Logan.

LOGAN:

The rest of the night go okay?

RYDER:

Yeah, just woke up. Feel better already.

I set my phone down and force myself to get out of bed. If I'd stayed at Logan's, I'm sure the coffee would already be ready and waiting for me.

I should've just stayed there last night. It would've made way more sense than coming home to stew in my thoughts.

Despite wishing Logan were handing me a cup of coffee, I accept my fate as I pour water into the coffee maker, scoop in the grounds, and flip the switch. While I wait, I grab a mug from the cabinet that says, *'No coffee. No talkie.'* It was a gift from Logan, and it's annoyingly spot-on. I'm sure he laughed to himself when he picked it out, though I've never had a problem talking to him first thing in the morning. Just everyone else.

Mugs with silly sayings on them became our thing in our senior year of college. It started during a white elephant gift exchange one Christmas, when I ended up with a hideous mug that read, *'I cannot brain today. It has the dumb.'* Seriously, who comes up with this stuff? But Logan thought it was hilarious, and from that moment on, he started buying cheesy mugs every time he saw one. Now both our houses are full of them, and it's the one thing he doesn't mind not matching.

Once the coffee's done, I pour myself a cup and head to my recording booth—a small room I built off the corner of the living room. It's nothing fancy, but it's big enough to comfortably fit a desk, a chair, and all my equipment. Plus, it's soundproofed, windowless, and way better than trying to record in a tiny closet like I used to. I told myself I'd outgrown spending all day in the closet.

The manuscript I'm narrating is open to where I left off last night, and I already know I need to be in the right headspace to kick things off with a sex scene first thing in the morning. If I'm going to get this done—and do it right—I need to be fully dialed in, layering in the right inflection, pacing, and tone. Narration isn't just reading out loud. Not if you want it to feel authentic.

I exhale through my nose and roll my shoulders to loosen up, mentally walking through the scene and thinking through the shifts in cadence, the emotional beats, and where the tension needs to land. With one last breath, I shake out my arms, adjust the mic, clear my throat, and drop into character.

"You're shaking for me, baby."

I keep my voice low and pause to let the tension stretch before shifting my tone slightly for the other character.

"I've wanted this for so long. Wanted you for so long."

I smirk, even though no one can see it. I always treat these scenes like I'm in them—well, within reason. I'm not gonna whip my dick out or anything, but the feeling has to be real.

"Mmm," I moan into the mic, closing my eyes and letting myself really feel it—

BANG.

A loud noise cuts through my headphones, shattering the moment and yanking me straight out of the scene.

What the fuck was that?

I rip off my headphones, heart pounding. The room's insulated and soundproofed, so for a sound to break through, it had to be loud. Really loud. Like someone just knocked over a bookshelf in my living room, loud. But I don't hear anything else, and not being able to see out of a window only makes it worse.

As much as I want to ignore it, I know I need to check around my house. My pulse kicks up as I open the door and step out of my office, but everything looks untouched from where I'm standing. The front door's still locked, and nothing's out of place as I make my way through the house.

I let out a breath and rub my hand over my scruff, trying to compose myself. I wait a few more minutes before deciding it was probably something outside, and head back to the booth. I take a few deep breaths and focus on getting back into character before pulling my headphones back on and pressing record.

"Show me how much. Be a good boy and take out my cock," I say, slipping back into the scene.

4

LOGAN

This week sucked big time, so thank god it's Friday.

Ryder came over on Tuesday and brought homemade cookies that his mom had mailed to us. Well, technically mailed to *him*, but we both know she expects him to share. That woman loves to bake, and even though we live three hours away, she still sends us care packages like we're college kids and not twenty-eight-year-olds.

She remembers everyone's favorite treat, and while there's typically a variety in her packages, there's always an extra batch of peanut butter blossoms because she knows they're my favorite. Ryder likes to joke that she does it to bribe me into looking after him, but I know it's because she enjoys making people feel loved. Not that I'd ever need to be bribed to take care of Ryder.

Unlike Ryder, I grew up only twenty minutes from where we live now. This is the only place I've ever known. People always talk about how important it is to get out of your home-town, and I get it, I do. My older brother, Michael, always talks about how great life is in Baltimore and how I should visit more often. I always thought I'd leave after college, but once Ryder said he wanted to stay, any plans I had to leave just...evaporated.

And I don't feel bad about it. Nor do I feel like a failure.

I know it probably sounds co-dependent, but all I've ever wanted since I met him is to be where he is. He's my person, and when you find that, you don't just walk away from the thing most people spend their whole lives searching for.

It's the reason I buried my crush all those years ago, because Ryder's friendship means more to me than getting caught up in any romantic feelings I know won't be returned. Whatever this is between us, it isn't about romance. It's about knowing someone inside and out. He's home, and I'm okay with our relationship staying exactly as it is, because having him in my life at all is enough.

Sure, staying limited my job options, but I like my job, even if I complain about it frequently. It's the only marketing agency in town, and I got hired right out of college after a successful internship with them, and I'm proud of that. Maybe someday I'll apply for a job at a larger company, or go all-in on freelancing—the thought crosses my mind every now and then when I see old classmates posting their fancy promotions online. But the truth is, I'm not in any rush to trade the life I have for a longer commute or a pile of new stress.

Right now, I'm happy with what I have: Ryder and our Friday night rituals, a steady job that lets me live a comfortable life, and my parents living close by.

This week, though, has been a grind with multiple last-minute call requests and too many emails marked 'urgent' that weren't even close to it.

Usually, I'd head to the bar and start decompressing solo until Ryder eventually showed up. But tonight, I'm not in the

mood to drink or socialize without him. I just want to see him
—let him help me loosen up just by being around before I
have to deal with anyone else, even if I do pretty much like
everyone in there.

Plus, I've missed him this week. It feels like we've barely
had a chance to catch up, aside from the few hours I saw him
on Tuesday.

When I finally make it home from work, I drop my bag on
the floor and decide to hop in the shower. Knowing Ryder,
he'll probably still be another twenty minutes or so, but I send
him a quick text anyway to let him know I'll wait for him.

LOGAN:

Waiting for you tonight instead of heading
to the bar. Just come in when you get here.

He replies instantly.

RYDER:

Cool, heading over soon.

I bring my phone into the bathroom, put on my favorite
playlist, and turn on the shower. Undressing as I wait for it to
heat up, I light the candle on my vanity. As soon as I step
under the water, it feels like some of the tension from the
week starts to melt away. *God, I needed this.*

I grab the bar of soap and run it over my chest, working
my way down. When I reach my dick, my hand lingers a little
longer than necessary. I wasn't planning to jerk off, but after
the week I've had—and the fact it's been months since
anyone else has touched me—it's hard not to think about it.
Just the thought of someone else's hand on me and a body
pressed up against mine is enough to get me hard.

Ever since last weekend, my thoughts have continued to

drift back to Ryder, no matter how much I try to remind myself to keep him in the friend zone. I can't shake how protective I felt. Or how jealous.

Fuck it. He's probably still at least fifteen minutes away, and my dick's fully hard now from thinking about him.

I wrap my hand around myself and start stroking—and *fuck*, it feels good. I let my head tip back and try to focus on the sensation, but my mind keeps drifting back to Ryder.

Fuck, why can't I stop thinking about him?

I give in to the thoughts because I'm already too far gone to stop them.

I imagine Ryder standing there, broad shoulders that draw my eyes to his pink nipples, then lower, to the faint trail of hair leading down his stomach, guiding me exactly where I want to go. His chest rising and falling, lips parted, as he watches me drop to my knees in front of him. God, I want to touch him. Taste him. Hear him. His skin would be warm under my hands, and I bet if I touched him right, he'd let out one of those breathy little moans that would wreck me.

My strokes get faster, and a low moan slips out as my body starts to tense. I'm close, so fucking close—

"Uh, Logan?" Ryder's voice hits me like a lightning bolt, and I freeze.

His voice came out so soft, like he wasn't sure if he should speak or disappear out of the bathroom door without a word. My heart is pounding as I turn toward the glass door of the shower, making eye contact with him. Even though I wasn't facing him, he knew what I was doing.

"Ryder—" I manage, my voice surprised and my cock still hard in my hand.

"I...um," he starts, "Logan…"

He doesn't finish but the way he says my name feels like a zap straight to my dick. It was breathy and so fucking sexy.

He stands there completely unmoving, not looking away. His eyes are locked on mine—or at least, I think they are. It's hard to tell through the steam. They could be locked on my cock, which seems less likely, but not impossible, I suppose. The glass is just foggy enough to blur the details, but not enough to hide the way his lips part slightly or the flush rising in his cheeks. He *is* looking. He must be. And I've never wanted to turn the shower to cold faster.

He seems to be stuck in place, waiting for me to do something, and my cock is throbbing from whatever is happening right now. I love the feel of his eyes on me, the blush on his cheeks, the way his lips are parted. *Just like I imagined.*

His hesitation feels like a dare. So, I take it. I'm way too turned on to be thinking clearly right now.

I start stroking myself again as I keep my gaze focused on him. I want to know what's going through his head right now. *Is he hard? Does he like what he sees? Does he want to take his cock out and stroke himself? Strip naked and get in the shower?*

Fuck. The thoughts circle fast, heat winding in my gut quickly, and I'm close again. Just from him standing there, watching me, and I can't help but let another moan fall from my lips.

That sound must snap Ryder out of his trance because he quickly lets out a nervous little laugh and steps back from the doorway. "Um...sorry," he gulps. His voice sounds nervous now, like he doesn't know what the hell to do. "Guess I'll, uh...wait out there. Try not to take all night," he says on a breathless laugh.

I open my mouth to say something, anything, but the

words are stuck in my throat as he walks out the door and shuts it behind him without so much as a backward glance in my direction.

Why the hell did I do that? Did I just fuck up our friendship? What is wrong with me?

The silence he left behind is deafening and I let out a shaky breath, unsure what the fuck just happened.

But…he didn't act like he hated it.

He didn't storm out. He didn't cover his eyes or pretend he hadn't seen anything. If anything, I'm pretty positive his eyes *did* drop to my cock before snapping back up like he wasn't sure if he was allowed to look.

I don't know what to do with that, but my hand is still stroking my dick, caught between adrenaline and desire.

The way he said my name is still replaying in my head, all breathy and unsure. I've spent years stuffing those kinds of thoughts into a box and pretending they didn't exist. Anytime something slipped through the cracks or Ryder got overly flirty with me, I'd slam the lid shut. But right now, I don't have that much willpower.

My vision from earlier shifts to him on his knees for me, looking up through his lashes with that same dazed expression on his face, is so vivid. I imagine his lips parting and his face flushed and wanting. Him sticking his tongue out waiting for me to slide my dick between his lips, and before I can stop it, I'm coming hard with a strangled grunt. The water quickly washes my bad decisions down the drain with it.

I stand there a minute, chest heaving, trying to collect myself because Ryder is my best friend. *Only* my best friend —I seem to need to remind myself of that more and more these days—and I have to hope I didn't just fuck up the best friendship I've ever had.

By the time I'm dressed and stepping out of the bathroom, I see Ryder stretched out on the couch, scrolling through his phone. He doesn't look up right away, so I clear my throat and run a hand through my damp hair.

"Uh, sorry about that," I say, trying to keep it light. I don't know what he's thinking. Hell, I don't even know what *I'm* thinking. This is brand new territory for both of us, and I know I crossed so many lines in there.

Ryder just smirks at me, clearly knowing I'm feeling awkward about this conversation. "Don't worry, I'm not scarred for life or anything."

I bark out a laugh, surprised by how relaxed he seems, but then again, it *is* Ryder, and that's kind of his whole vibe. I take a deep breath, feeling better about this conversation already. "The one time you actually show up on time, huh?"

"I told you I was heading over," he shoots back, and *fair*, he did. But usually that means he'll still be another fifteen minutes, at least. It's really his fault for being so bad at being on time and giving accurate updates. "Not my fault you were…occupied."

"Oh, we're calling it 'occupied' now?" I grin in his direction and throw up some air quotes around the word.

I drop onto the couch and leave a cushion of space between us. Usually, I wouldn't worry about that, but I don't want to make him feel uncomfortable after what just happened—whatever *that* was.

But then again, he did walk in without knocking, and he knows the bathroom has a glass shower door, which makes me wonder why.

I try to push the thought out of my mind because Ryder's straight. He always has been, and whatever feelings I'm trying to project onto him need to stay buried. I've made it this long without slipping, I know I can lock it all back up and do it again because no matter what, I'd rather have him in my life as my best friend than risk losing him.

"THERE YOU TWO ARE!" MIA CALLS OUT AS WE WALK INTO the bar, a little later than usual.

"Yeah, yeah. Blame Logan tonight, it's actually *his* fault," Ryder responds, and I know he's thrilled I'm the reason why we're late. "I was on time for once." He smirks my way, and I can't help but shake my head at him. He's eating this up.

"Mark it down as a once-in-a-decade occurrence," I shoot back with no heat.

"I'll grab your drinks and bring them over to ya," Mia confirms. We make our way over to our regular table, saying hi to some of the other regulars as we pass them.

Mia walks over with two frosty mugs filled to the brim with beer. "I still can't believe Ryder was on time for once."

Ryder shrugs and shoots me a quick look before saying, "Yep, showed up right when things got interesting, too."

I nearly choke on a laugh and shoot him a warning look. He's not going to tell people our business, but still. He's pushing it. Instead of saying anything more, though, he just takes a sip of his beer, looking way too pleased with that little crumb he dropped for Mia.

She raises an eyebrow before waving it off. "I'm not even gonna ask."

"Probably for the best," I murmur.

She walks off shaking her head, and I can only imagine the things that woman has heard from patrons in this bar.

"What's wrong with you?" I laugh, asking Ryder as soon as she's out of earshot.

He licks his lips and grins. "Nothing, I just appreciate good timing."

I snort, and I'm grateful he's not being weird about this, but he also seems a little extra...flirty? Don't get me wrong, he's always a little flirty with me, and I know we have a unique friendship compared to most guys, but he's acting so *normal* about finding me jerking off in the shower. I guess I expected him to want to bury it and move on.

Maybe this is a good sign.

Not wanting to push him too far, I decide to move the conversation back to safer territory. *And to stop myself from thinking too deeply about this potential shift in him.*

"You ever think we spend too much time here?"

Ryder tilts his head like he wasn't expecting the question. "Nope, it's the perfect amount. I like being a regular. I like walking in and having Mia pour my beer without even having to ask what I want."

"You're so predictable," I laugh.

Before he gets another word out, the door at the front of the bar swings open, and I watch Ryder's face drop. I turn my head to see what caused the reaction, and it's the same guy he couldn't stop glancing at last Friday.

Of course this asshole had to come back and fuck up our Friday night ritual two weeks in a row.

Ryder hasn't brought up last Friday at all, and I assumed if he did want to talk about it, he would have said something on Tuesday.

"Did something happen with that guy?" I ask, unable to stop myself now.

He shakes his head, eyes still glancing at the guy. It's like as much as he wants to ignore him, he'd rather know where he is at all times. "No, nothing happened. Just gave me the creeps."

I nod, glancing over at the guy, but right now, he doesn't seem focused on Ryder at all. Maybe it was a one-time thing, and he realized Ryder wasn't exactly giving off a 'come flirt with me' vibe and decided to move on.

"Wanna leave?" I offer. I don't particularly want a repeat of last weekend with Ryder getting all withdrawn and broody. "We can go somewhere else. Or grab takeout and crash at mine."

Ryder finally looks at me. "No. It's fine. I don't even think he's noticed me this time. I'm sure I was overreacting. Last weekend was just weird; I was really in my head."

I nod, but still, something about the way this stranger is causing Ryder to react unsettles me.

Realistically, though, the guy probably thinks Ryder is hot because, as we've already established, *he is.*

Mia hands the man his drink, which looks like a whiskey neat, and he turns to scan the room. His gaze lands on us, and he pauses, looking at us long enough that it feels deliberate. And now I get why Ryder felt so on edge last week. There's something *off* about the way the guy's looking at us. It's not a friendly gaze, or even curious. It's the kind of look that makes your stomach tighten even if you can't explain why.

"Uh, Loge," Ryder whispers.

"I see him," I confirm, as I watch him get closer and closer to our table. "I'll deal with this."

He's tall, probably around our height. He's got a broad chest and shoulders; the kind of build that makes you wonder if he played football. He's wearing a worn leather jacket, and there's something about the way he moves that immediately puts me on edge.

He stops at the edge of the table with his whiskey in hand. "Mind if I join you?" he asks.

"You always invite yourself to other people's tables, or is tonight special?" I ask, tilting my head.

His lips twitch like he finds this funny. "Thought I'd introduce myself."

I glance at Ryder, who is looking only at me, and I don't want to make him more uncomfortable, but maybe this will help both of us feel more at ease if we exchange a few words. Feel him out.

"Okay," I grumble. "And you are?"

"Kyle," he offers.

"Logan," I reply.

Then he turns expectantly toward Ryder and offers him a big smile, which I certainly didn't get.

"And you're Ryder, right?"

My head snaps in his direction. How does he know who Ryder is, and what kind of person doesn't just ask someone's name, even if they do already know it somehow?

"Uh," he hesitates. "Yeah."

"How do you know his name?" I question, completely uncaring if I come off as rude. The only person I care about at this table is Ryder.

"Oh, the bartender told me."

"Hm," I hum.

He nods at me, and I can't help but wonder if there's more to it. Maybe he already knows who Ryder is and is trying to play it off like he doesn't.

Ryder does have a public Instagram account for his narration, and he has a decent following. All of his accounts are tied to his name. Even if he doesn't post his face all that often, it's out there. We've joked more than once about listeners falling in love with his voice. Hell, I've seen the DMs.

So maybe this guy isn't just some rando who wants Ryder. Maybe he's a fan and trying to hide it, which almost makes it worse.

"You two live around here?" he asks, looking at Ryder, sliding his drink onto the table like he plans to stay a while.

"Yep," I say before Ryder can respond, not wanting him to feel pressured into talking to this guy. "Grew up in the area. Small town, everyone knows everyone." I try to insinuate to him that strangers stand out here.

Kyle shrugs, unbothered by my comment. "I like places like this, easier to meet people." His eyes drift back to Ryder.

"What brings you here?" I ask.

"Construction."

I see Ryder nod slightly, but he hasn't said a word since confirming his name, and I know it's time to wrap this conversation up. Ryder usually isn't this quiet, and his disinterest in joining the conversation tells me everything I need to know—this isn't helping.

"Well, cheers to that," I say, lifting my beer in a half-assed toast. Trying to make him realize it's time for him to go.

But he doesn't lift his glass from the table, and he doesn't leave. He just watches Ryder for a second and says, "You ever get the feeling you're supposed to meet someone? Like you're in the right place, at the exact right time? Almost like your meeting is fate?"

The hair on the back of my neck prickles. *Yeah, it's time for him to go.*

"Can't say I've had that particular epiphany," I reply, setting my beer down.

Kyle huffs out a little fake laugh, and I hate the sound. "Maybe you will," he replies, looking right at Ryder, who's doing his best to avoid eye contact.

"Well, it was nice meeting you, Ryder. Maybe we can talk some more soon," he says, as he lifts his drink from the table. Then, as if he remembers I'm there too, he turns to me with a quick nod. "Logan."

As soon as he walks away, Ryder lets out a big exhale like he's been holding his breath for minutes.

"What the hell was that?" I ask quietly.

Ryder shakes his head slowly. "I don't know, but I didn't like it. He seems weirdly into me."

I nod in agreement. That whole fate thing? It rubbed me the wrong way, and I make a mental note to ask Mia about that guy later to see what he really said about Ryder.

"You wanna go home?" I ask.

Ryder's eyes flick to mine, and I see the way his shoulders relax, just a little. "Yeah," he nods. "Let's go."

We pay and head outside. Mia commented that we've been dipping quickly over the last two weeks, and I told her we'd talk later. This guy's construction project needs to wrap up soon so he can go back to wherever the hell he came from. I hate that he's making Ryder feel uncomfortable in *our* spot.

As soon as we start walking home, the tension that clung to us at the bar begins to loosen, and I'm already feeling a bit better. When we get inside my apartment, Ryder kicks off his shoes by the door and collapses onto the couch. Nights like this always remind me of when we lived together, and I hate that we tried to be 'mature adults' and get our own places. We only live a six-minute drive apart now, but that still feels too far.

"You're staying over tonight, right?" I confirm as I grab a couple of bottles of water from the fridge.

Ryder glances over at me, one arm slung over the back of the couch like he's weighing his options. "Eh, I'll stay. I'm too comfy to move now."

"Too comfy already?" I laugh, raising an eyebrow as I toss him a bottle. "You've been here all of sixty seconds."

"That's all it takes for your couch to work its magic," he chuckles, cracking the bottle open. "Plus, I know you'd miss me."

He scoots over to make room for me on the couch as I plop down beside him, turning on the TV.

"Pretty sure I survived last Friday night when you went home."

"Yeah, but I was giving you some alone time to appreciate how much you need me," he teases.

"You know I always need you," I admit, not even pretending to hide the truth. Last weekend sucked without him and I want him to know just how much I want him here with me.

"Me too," he says quietly, before glancing at me. "Thanks for doing all the talking with that guy, Loge."

"Of course. The whole conversation was bizarre. I don't know how to explain it."

Ryder nods. "Yeah. I don't know what that guy's deal is, but he was giving me weird vibes last week, too. Except then he was just watching me from across the bar."

I nod. It makes a lot of sense now that he's explaining it. "He's not exactly hiding how into you he is, either."

"Tell me about it," he groans.

I was right about that guy being into Ryder, but Ry's definitely not into him. That should make me feel better, but it doesn't, mostly because I hate seeing him this tense. It's not like him at all.

We stay on the couch watching TV for a little bit about a new blind dating show called *Love Without Labels* until I can't keep my eyes open anymore, despite how entertaining it is.

"You coming to bed or you wanna stay out here?" I ask, getting up off the couch.

"Yeah, let's go to bed."

I stand up first and hold my hand out to Ryder to help pull him off the couch. He grabs it, but he lets go as soon as he's upright. Part of me wants to reach out and slide my fingers through his and keep holding his hand, but I don't.

He follows me down the short hallway, and we both head into the bathroom to brush our teeth. When we're done, we strip down to our boxer briefs and get into bed. Ryder lets out a contented sigh as he burrows under the blanket, his arm brushing mine, and something about the casual closeness nearly undoes me, even though this is very standard for us.

I want to reach for him, pull him closer, and wrap him up in my arms because that's how needy I feel tonight. And if I did, he wouldn't think twice. We've cuddled more times than I can count. Honestly, platonic cuddles should be more of a thing between friends.

But I know tonight if I let myself reach for him, I'll want more. Not just a sleepy shoulder to lean on, or the kind of casual cuddle that means nothing. I'll want him to wrap his arm around me like I matter.

And I can't want that.

Ryder shifts onto his side to face me, fingers brushing my

arm as he gets comfortable. A few seconds later, he drapes an arm across my chest, and I don't move. I just smile to myself and let it happen.

5

RYDER

Holy shit, it's hot.

Logan's always been a human furnace and, if I'm being honest, I love it. I think that's why I always end up gravitating toward him in my sleep. Even if we don't start the night curled up together, I somehow manage to have wrapped myself around him by morning. My arm is still draped over his chest, and my face is buried in the pillow just inches from his shoulder, which is pretty on par for us.

We've been doing this for years. Seven, to be exact. Ever since that night junior year in college, when Logan's girlfriend at the time, Jenn, dumped him publicly and brutally. As soon as she finished making a scene at the party we were at, I grabbed Logan and told him we were going home. He didn't argue, and he didn't say much of anything on the walk back to our apartment, which is how I knew what happened had really gotten to him. Neither of us is usually quiet unless something is wrong, and that was the quietest I'd ever seen him, until we got home, and it all came spilling out.

"She's right, you know," he'd started, leaning forward on

the couch with his elbows on his knees. "I didn't prioritize her, I couldn't. I didn't care the way I knew I was supposed to."

I'd gone over to sit next to him and comfort him. "Logan—"

"No, seriously, Ry," he'd cut me off, and I'd hated seeing him beat himself up. "I did screw this relationship up. She wanted more, and I couldn't give it to her. I couldn't even make my girlfriend a priority. And you know what? I don't even care! I don't. I really don't think I do. I still would have picked you to hang out with all those times. I don't care if that makes me a bad boyfriend." He scrubbed his hands down his face and then laughed to himself before continuing. "She'd always get so mad at me when I'd show up to class and bring you a coffee, but forget her order. Whatever, it's probably better this way."

I remember feeling so mad at her in that moment for making him doubt himself. Sure, Logan wasn't perfect. No one is. But he's kind, generous, and loyal. The idea that he wasn't enough was ridiculous. He did kind and thoughtful things for me all the time, he still does, because that's just the kind of person he is. And maybe we spent a lot of time together, but he *did* make time for her. I don't know what she expected, because we were in college, lived together, and were best friends, so of course, we spent a lot of time together.

"Hey," I'd said softly, nudging his shoulder with my own. "That's not true, okay? You're one of the best people I know. Screw her if she can't see that."

He scoffed out a bitter laugh, his gaze fixed on the coffee table. "You're biased."

"Maybe," I admitted, nudging him again with a small grin. "But I'm also right."

Logan didn't argue, but he didn't look at me, either. He sat there beside me, staring at nothing, with his shoulders hunched. His tears were silent when they fell, and I didn't want to push him to talk, so I'd run my thumb over his cheek every so often to wipe them away. I wanted him to know I was there and he wasn't alone.

Finally, after what felt like hours of us sitting on the couch together, he turned to look at me.

"Can I—" He stopped, clearing his throat. "Can I sleep in your bed tonight?"

I was caught off guard by the question because we'd never shared a bed before. "What?"

"I just..." He ran a hand through his blonde hair, looking down at his lap, and I hated that he was nervous to ask me this. "I don't want to be alone right now. I'm sorry if that's weird."

Something in his voice broke me. He sounded so lost and so unlike himself that I didn't even hesitate. If he needed someone to sleep next to, I wanted that person to be me.

"Yeah," I said, standing and holding out a hand. "Of course you can. Come on."

He looked up at me then, and there was something so vulnerable in his eyes. Part of me wanted to pull him into a hug and never let go. Instead, I waited with my hand outstretched until he finally took it. He didn't say anything as I led him to my room; he just climbed into my bed, pulled the blankets up to his chest, and waited for me.

I slid onto the other side of the mattress and for a moment, we laid there side by side, until I finally reached out and pulled him into me. I didn't think about it, I just did it. It felt right. And I'm glad I did because he melted right into me with a long exhale, snuggling closer like he'd been waiting for that moment, too.

"Thanks," he whispered.

"Anytime," I said, meaning it.

And I did, because that night when I felt him curl into me, I knew I'd never say no to him. I'd let him crawl into my bed every night for the rest of our lives if he needed to. That night, I realized how much space he took up in my heart.

We didn't talk about it when he woke up, but the next time he was sad, or tired, or lonely, or even had one too many drinks, he'd ask again. And again. Until he no longer needed to ask, and it was just...us.

Now, when we stay the night at either of our places, we always sleep together, and if we cuddle or wake up wrapped around each other, it's not a big deal. I love being his person and his comfort, just like he's mine.

Logan's phone buzzes on the nightstand, pulling me out of my thoughts, and he stirs beneath me. His hand brushes against mine, where it's still draped over him. "Morning," he says, voice groggy.

I smirk, but don't move away from him. I'm not ready to untangle our bodies and face the day yet. "Morning, sunshine."

"You're heavy," he grumbles, eyes still closed.

"Haven't got any lighter since last time," I quip back.

Logan cracks one eye open to look me in the eye. "You could at least pretend to feel bad about crushing me in my sleep."

"Crushing?" I laugh. "Please. I'm the perfect size for a human blanket. You're lucky to have me."

"Lucky, sure," he repeats dryly. I smile at him and move so he can get out of bed.

I watch him as he walks to the bathroom and realize I should stop ogling my best friend in his tight boxer briefs. Jumping out of bed before he comes back into the room, I grab a hoodie from the chair in the corner of his room and pull it on as I head to the kitchen. "Coffee?" I yell out to him.

"Please," Logan responds from inside the bathroom.

I head to the kitchen and start the machine, but as I wait for the coffee to brew, my thoughts drift right back to Logan. I've been trying not to think about him in the shower, but my mind won't quit. It shouldn't have been so hot. He's my *best friend* and a *man*, but I can't get the image of him stroking his cock out of my head.

I shouldn't have walked in, but I had to piss. Which is ironic considering I didn't even end up going after that. *Completely forgot about it, to be honest.*

For once, I was actually trying to be on time, and in my rush, I didn't use the bathroom before I left. But still, I know I could've knocked—or just waited. Instead, I stepped inside without thinking twice, because it's Logan. We've been in the bathroom together more times than I can count. Sure, it's usually just brushing our teeth, but back when we had an actual shower curtain and only one bathroom, he'd be showering while I shaved, and it was never a big deal.

But when I walked in and saw him jerking off, it felt like the air was knocked from my lungs because I didn't expect to see *that*. I should've apologized and gotten the hell out of there.

But I didn't.

I *stared* at him, completely rooted in place.

I've never looked at another man and wondered what it

would feel like to touch him. Not even Logan. Not in all the years we've been friends. Not during our college years when we shared everything. Not when we were drunk, half-asleep, and barely dressed. I've never questioned how I felt about him —until now.

There's no way he didn't notice me staring, even if he hasn't said a word about it since. I couldn't get myself to move. I stood there, completely caught up in watching him stroke himself like he didn't care I was there. Or maybe like he *wanted* me to be.

And I don't know why I liked it so much. I only know that I did.

I stood there so long that he continued stroking himself again, and it felt like he was daring me to make a choice: leave, watch, or join. My brain was screaming at me to pick one, and part of me wanted to stay, to watch.

Maybe even touch.

I liked the way he touched himself, the little breathy grunts and moans that slipped out, and the way he didn't hold back, even with me in the room. That level of confidence was sexy as hell. But as much as I wanted to listen to him, I panicked and left because that's what I thought I *should* do. It turned me on, and I didn't know what to do with that.

Because why *now*? Why *him*? Why like *this*?

Why did I get hard watching my best friend jerk off in the shower like it was the hottest thing I'd ever seen?

The whole thing felt...intimate. Like I was seeing something I wasn't supposed to. I run a hand down my face like that'll do a damn thing to unsee it. I need to get it together and stop trying to imagine what my best friend looks like when he comes. Or how he sounds.

"Earth to Ryder," Logan calls out, already holding a steaming mug of coffee in his hand.

I blink, snapping out of it. "What?"

"You've been staring at the coffee like it'll brew faster if you glare at it long enough, but it's done. Back to zoning out, huh?"

I roll my eyes and grab a mug for myself that says, *'Blow me. I'm hot,'* and roll my eyes as Logan laughs to himself.

"Just tired. This'll help," I say, motioning to the coffee.

Once it's doctored up, I take a sip, hoping the heat will jolt me out of the not-very-innocent daydream I was having about the way Logan's hand moved in the shower.

6

LOGAN

Yesterday was strange.

I don't know how to explain it, and I'm still sorting through it all. I *thought* I'd buried those feelings for Ryder for good, but now they're louder than ever, pressing in from every side, and I have no idea how to quiet them. But I'll figure it out. I have to, before I say, or do, something I can't take back.

"What's the plan for today?" I ask.

Ryder's face lights up like he's been waiting for me to ask that. "What do you say we get out of here?"

I glance over at him, already guessing where this is going. We tend to be creatures of habit, so while we have our Friday night ritual, we also do the same thing every Saturday morning when it's in season and we're not busy.

"Farmer's market?"

"Yup," he says with that familiar spark in his voice. "It's supposed to be sunny today, so I was thinking we could do our usual. I'll even buy you a new candle."

"You want to buy me a new candle? Well, I'm not turning that down," I say with a grin.

"Just let me brush my teeth and change," Ryder says casually, brushing past me and heading toward the dresser drawer I cleared out for him a few months ago. He opens the top drawer and pulls out a gray t-shirt.

"You're really leaning into this whole 'drawer' situation," I say, reaching for my sweatshirt from the hook by the door.

He snorts, tugging the shirt over his head. "Would you rather I keep raiding your closet? 'Cause I can do that too. Happily."

"Don't pretend you don't still do that anyway." I don't mind, though. I kind of love it. It stirs up a possessive feeling in me, knowing he's walking around in *my* clothes. I know I shouldn't have those thoughts about my best friend, but I'm only human, and if it were up to me, he'd wear them every day.

"Yeah, well, your stuff's comfortable," Ryder acknowledges, pulling his shirt down. "You buy the good cotton."

"Glad I can keep you in luxury. Anything else you need? Slippers? A monogrammed robe?" I deadpan.

"Don't tempt me. I'd rock the hell out of a monogrammed robe."

I shake my head at him, knowing he so would.

Twenty minutes later, we're in Ryder's car heading toward the market. His phone is connected, playing some chill alternative music I've grown to like over the years.

The market is already in full swing by the time we get there, with tents stretched down both sides of the block.

"Let's see if they have those honey sticks again," Ryder says, shoving his hands into the pocket of his black hoodie as we start walking through the booths.

"You're obsessed," I snicker, falling in step beside him.

"They're good!" he shoots back with a big smile on his face.

Ryder would spend hundreds of dollars every time we came if I didn't reel him in. I love his enthusiasm, but there are so many things we don't need.

The first twenty minutes or so pass in a blur as we browse the booths. We've managed to turn the farmer's market into a whole experience by chatting with all the vendors, sampling their products, and talking about their booth branding.

Once we reach the candle booth I usually buy from, Ryder turns to me with a grin. "How about that new candle?"

"Let's see what they've got," I say, trying to reel in my rapidly beating heart over such a small gesture. *Fuck, this is not good.*

There are sampler candles lined up with the lids off, stacked neatly along the display. Ryder picks one up and reads the label out loud, clearly amused.

"'Cozy Forest.' Wow. A scent and a vibe." He gives it a sniff, then scrunches his nose. "Nope. Smells like a car air freshener."

I let out a little laugh, then quickly glanced to see if the candle vendor I've bought from many times had heard him, but thankfully, she's deep in conversation with another customer.

I reach for a different candle, lift it to my nose, and breathe in deeply. It smells like fresh rain mixed with something smoky; it's unique, but I think I like it.

"I like this one," I say, holding it out to Ryder. "Thoughts?"

He leans in and sniffs. "Hmm, yeah. I like it enough to smell it in your apartment for the next month."

My stomach does a stupid little flip at that. "Glad it meets your incredibly high standards," I say, pretending it doesn't affect me.

Shit, I need to get it together.

Ryder swaps it for a non-sample candle, then takes out his card. After he pays, we grab the candle, say thank you, and turn to head to the next booth. It's mostly bins of old posters, and as expected, Ryder starts flipping through them. I can't relate to the people who peruse the market from the middle of the road because Ryder always wants to be up close and personal, which is also why we always leave with so much.

As I turn to look at the other booths ahead of us, I still.

The guy from Pine Bar, Kyle, is here, and he's looking right at Ryder. I turn to see if Ryder's noticed him yet, but he's still flipping through posters, completely unaware.

The same angry feeling from last night coils in my gut.

Why the fuck does this dude keep showing up where we are?

"Logan," Ryder calls out to me. "Come look at this poster."

"Uh," I say, hesitantly. Unsure if I should address Kyle being here, or ignore it with the hope he'll leave. The last thing I want is a repeat of the last two Friday nights, where we've had to cut our plans short because Kyle doesn't understand social cues or boundaries.

But he must see the concern etched on my face because his smile falters. "What's wrong?"

I tilt my head slightly, and his gaze follows mine. It takes only a moment before he sees Kyle looking right at him, and, just like last night, Kyle starts walking right toward us as if one glance after staring someone down for minutes at a time is an invitation.

49

Ryder shifts beside me, his body going still in a way that makes every instinct in me go on alert. He doesn't say anything, but I can feel the tension radiating off him. *Here we go again.*

Kyle stops in front of us. "Hey, didn't think I'd run into you here."

Ryder forces a polite smile. "Small town," he says, voice neutral.

"Right," Kyle nods, then glances over at me. "I was told strangers stick out around here. Isn't that right, Logan?"

"Just a fact," I reply flatly.

Kyle smiles again, but there's no friendliness behind it. If anything, it feels disingenuous. He breaks eye contact with me and turns his attention entirely to Ryder now.

"If you ever wanted to show me around, I'd be into that. Assuming you're not too...busy." His eyes flick between us like he's trying to decode something.

I shift slightly, stepping to put myself between them, so that if Kyle wants to talk to Ryder, he'll have to do it through me. My stance is casual, but I'm fully aware of how close I am now. And so is Kyle.

He isn't deterred, of course. Instead, he takes our silence as an invitation to keep pressing.

"Unless you two are...?" He lets the question hang in the air like he's leaving room for Ryder to laugh it off and say, *"God, no, we're just friends,"* then invite him to grab drinks later. But I know he's not asking if we're together, he's *hoping* we're not.

Ryder doesn't take the bait. "Listen, man," he starts. "I don't know if I somehow gave you the wrong idea, but I'm not interested."

Kyle hums, seeming completely unfazed by Ryder's

response. "Another time, then." He lingers a second too long with a smirk on his face before turning and walking away.

Ryder exhales slowly. "What is with that guy? He's everywhere, and he won't quit. I don't know how much clearer I could've been."

"No kidding," I mutter, still watching the spot where Kyle vanished.

I glance at him and notice he's tense again, like he's still processing whatever just happened.

"Wanna grab bagels and coffee and head down to the lake?"

When he finally looks at me, the tension in his face eases just slightly. "Yeah. Yeah, let's do that."

"Cool. Let's grab them and get out of here before he comes back asking for directions to our front doors."

That earns a faint huff of laughter, barely there, but I'll take it.

7

RYDER

When we arrive at the lake, it's almost empty, and I'm grateful for the space to be with Logan. He grabs a blanket from the trunk, and we walk over to a grassy spot on the shore for him to spread the blanket out.

"Think Kyle's gonna follow us here, too?" Logan says dryly, tilting his head toward me as he drops down.

"Not unless he's got some type of GPS tracker on us." Though I wouldn't put that past him, honestly.

I hand him the coffee and bagels as I move to sit beside him. He takes his bagel out of the bag, then hands mine to me. The silence settles as we start to eat, and I let my gaze drift out over the water, trying to make sense of the way everything in me still feels scrambled from the last twenty-four hours.

Something's shifting in me, and that scares me almost as much as it thrills me. The feelings I'm having toward Logan are new, and I'm not sure what to do with them because I've never looked at another man this way before. Not once. Not even with how much my work has tried to sell me on falling for your best friend over the years.

I've been straight my whole life—or at least I've always *thought* I was. So why am I so aware of every inch of space between us on this blanket? Why did watching him in the shower make my whole body light up like it was wired for *him*? The reaction had been instant.

He's still staring out at the lake, and I catch the way his thumb brushes slowly up and down the side of his coffee cup. It's such a small, meaningless motion, but for some reason, it makes me want to reach for him and pull him into me.

I don't understand what's happening to me.

But instead of pulling him into me, I shift slightly, leaning back beside him, letting our bodies press together from shoulder to ankle. He doesn't move away. If anything, he leans into me slightly, and the voice in my head screams; *I don't want him to pull away.*

How could I have missed something so significant about my sexuality my entire life?

It probably has something to do with my asshole dad. I always swore I wouldn't be like him, and I don't think I am, but he always scoffed at men who seemed a little too close.

He'd hate me if he could see me now.

He'd always make comments about things being 'not right' or about how 'real men didn't do things like that,' whatever *that* means. He was a hateful prick, and I'm glad he left when I was young. I haven't seen or heard from him since, and I don't care to.

After he left, my mom seemed much happier and gave me room to be whoever I wanted. But even without his presence, I've never thought about other guys the way I'm thinking about Logan now.

I guess it's possible I unconsciously learned to avoid anything that might have made him angry or unpredictable, and that would've included feelings about other guys. But apparently, all it took was watching Logan stroke his dick in the shower last night to make me hard and wake me the hell up. I wasn't confused—maybe about what it means for *us*—but I'm positive I was turned on by him jerking off.

I'm *very* aware that if I'm into him, then I must not be straight after all, and I'm perfectly okay with that. Plenty of people discover their sexuality later in life—I'm just another one added to the list.

The thing I can't wrap my head around, though, is that these feelings are crossing a line we've never touched before, and if we do cross it, there's no going back. We'd never be the same Logan and Ryder we are now. Especially if he didn't feel the same way, which I think is what I'm most afraid of.

I can't ruin ten years of friendship for feelings I've had for less than twenty-four hours.

If Logan ever felt anything toward me, I think I'd be able to tell. He's always been open with me about his sexuality and dating interests. He told me he was bi almost as soon as we met, and I told him it was cool and didn't change anything because it didn't. I was glad he felt comfortable enough around me to say it out loud.

After that, dating stories and casual hookup talk became a regular part of our friendship. Neither of us had much going on that first year, but once Logan did start seeing people, I wasn't a fan. Not that he was dating, just that he was spending time with someone else. Anyone else, honestly.

He only dated Jenn and a guy named Nick, who sucked, so that relationship didn't last long. But I remember how it felt when he spent more time with them than with me. I told myself it was just a matter of being best friends, and it made sense to feel a little left out. However, looking back, I can see now that maybe it was more than that. When he wasn't around, I didn't know what to do with myself. It always felt like something was missing.

Holy shit, I think I was jealous. How did I never notice any of this before?

I shift to take a sip of my coffee, pressing even closer to him, and it hits me. I've never felt more at ease being this close to someone, but that ease is exactly what unsettles me. Because it shouldn't feel this natural to want more from my best friend when I've never wanted to be with a man before. There's an ache in my chest that won't go away—the kind that whispers *you want more.*

And I do. God, I do.

But what does that mean for the version of me I've always known? The one who never second-guessed myself or my sexuality? The one who's always been so sure I was straight? The one who never once wanted to hop in the shower with my male best friend?

That version of me was clearly missing something. But now that I know, I can move forward the right way. I've always picked Logan, maybe this means choosing him in a different way.

If he ever wants me back, that is.

Because what I feel for him doesn't feel like some identity crisis. It feels right and natural, almost like something that's always been there, waiting for me to catch up.

I glance at Logan, and something in me settles.

"You good?" he asks, noticing me looking.

I nod. "Yeah. Just glad we came out here."

He smiles at me before looking back out toward the water. "Me too."

Logan is my comfort, my safe place, my person. Even if that's all we'll ever be, it's enough. He's always been enough.

We spend another fifteen or so minutes at the lake before we pack up and head back to Logan's. As soon as we walk in, he drops his keys by the door and heads straight to the bathroom. I take out my phone to look at my emails because I need something to focus on that's not him alone in the bathroom.

My inbox is mostly filled with newsletters I don't remember signing up for, and some I'm almost positive I've already unsubscribed from. There's also a new audiobook inquiry from an author that's in demand, which I'm stoked to see. Plus a few responses to work emails I've sent, which I flag for later.

Then I spot what I assume is fan mail, but the subject line is a little odd, and so is the sender's name.

a78iejhr5454@gmail.com: You make it sound so real.

I hover my thumb over the delete button for a second, but curiosity wins, and I open it.

"I wonder if you know how many nights I fall asleep to the sound of your voice."

Huh, that's odd. There's no greeting or sign-off, just a single line of text sitting there, staring back at me. I'm sure it's harmless, though, even if the sender's name looks downright spammy. Plenty of people get really into books—rightfully so—and it's not the first time I've gotten a weird message like this. I'm sure it won't be the last, either. Just a passionate fan who forgot how emails are supposed to work, I'm sure.

"Everything okay?" Logan's voice cuts through my thoughts as he makes his way over to me from the bathroom.

"Uh, yeah," I say. "Just a weird email is all."

"Weird how?"

"It's vague," I shrug, but I know he's waiting for me to say more. "Like, 'you make it sound so real,' that kind of thing. You know, fans get attached to books. I'm sure it's nothing. Happens frequently enough."

His face looks cautious, as if he thinks I'm downplaying something.

"Let me see," he says, holding out his hand expectantly.

I hesitate for a second before handing him my phone. It's just an email, it's not a big deal, and it's not like I have anything to hide. Watching as his eyes scan the screen, I feel a twinge of unease that he's going to say something I'm not going to like.

"Uh, Ry, this isn't normal," he says, and I try to ignore the unease it's causing.

"It's not *that* weird," I argue, though the words feel hollow even as they leave my mouth. "Fans get invested. It's part of the job."

And it is, at least, that's what I've always told myself. I mean, I have public social media accounts tied to my narration work. It's not like I post anything crazy. It's mostly just behind-the-scenes recording stuff, book promos, and the occasional photo of me. But yeah, my real name's attached to it. *Maybe I should've used a pseudonym.* We've even joked about the 'in love with your voice' fan comments before, so an email like this isn't *that* weird.

Logan crosses his arms and levels me with a look that can

only mean, *who are you kidding.* "Do fans usually send creepy messages like this? They didn't even include a name or any context. It's weird, Ry. I feel like none of your other ones have given this vibe. This one's just got a strange feeling to it. I don't know how to explain it."

I shrug again. "I mean, no, but people like my voice, right? It's why I keep getting booked. It's a compliment, really."

Logan doesn't look convinced as he hands me back my phone. "Still. I don't like it."

"Same, but I doubt I'll hear from this person again," I counter. The last thing I want is for Logan to worry about me even more.

And now this is another layer of things I don't know how to deal with.

He stares at me for a long moment, his lips pressing into a thin line before nodding. "Just keep an eye on it, okay? And tell me if you get any others."

"Yeah, yeah," I say, slipping my phone into my pocket. "I will. Promise."

Logan turns back toward the kitchen, when all I want is for him to come back and join me on the couch. I want his warmth and comfort, but I don't want to explain the mess that's going on in my head.

At this point, I don't even know what to focus on—the creepy guy from the bar, the strange noises at my house, all the shit with Logan, and now this short, anonymous email that is for some reason leaving a bad taste in my mouth.

How has all of this managed to happen in the span of eight days? I haven't even had time to fully sit with one thing before the next rolls in. I guess this is the Universe's way of saying I complained way too much about my life being boring because *what the fuck*, this is a lot at once.

"You know what?" Logan calls out from the kitchen. "You should block them."

I'm not convinced blocking some spammy, throwaway email will actually do anything, but I'll do it anyway to give us both more peace of mind.

"Yeah, that's not a bad idea," I say, pulling my phone back out and hitting *block sender*.

He comes back into the living room and eyes my screen, giving me a small nod before dropping down next to me on the couch.

"Want to put something on?"

"Sure," I nod. "Something funny."

He grabs the remote and clicks through the options until we land on some action comedy we've both seen multiple times. Logan settles in next to me, and at some point, we start to sink further into each other.

I try to focus on the movie, but my body is more aware of him than it's ever been. He must have a magic dick or something because what's always been platonic between us has completely shifted for me.

I'm trying to keep it together, but it's all too easy for me to imagine Logan with his head tipped back, hand moving up and down his shaft, and his open mouth letting out little grunts and moans. *Fuck,* it was hot, and it felt like there was tension between us—I just can't tell if it was sexual, or if I'm reading into it because I want it to be.

When the movie finally wraps up, I glance over at Logan. He looks perfect with his sleepy face and disheveled, dirty blonde hair. I should probably offer to go home, just to see if he wants some space, because while I don't want to leave, I want to know if he wants me to stay.

"I should probably head home," I say casually, testing the waters.

"You don't have to," he reassures me.

Relief hits harder than it should, and I try to control the smile threatening to take over my face. "You sure?" I ask, trying to sound like it's no big deal.

"Yeah." He nods. "Stay. You know you'll sleep better here. It's been another weird day, and I'd rather know you're safe in my bed with me."

My heart stumbles over that last part. *In my bed. With me.*

"Okay," I say, pushing to my feet. "If you insist."

I head toward the bathroom, and Logan cuts in front of me and throws a smirk over his shoulder. He got what he wanted —and so did I.

In the bathroom, I grab my toothbrush—the blue one sitting beside his green one in the holder—and start brushing. Logan slides in next to me and does the same. It's such a small, ordinary thing we've done countless times, but it makes something in my chest flutter tonight. Even if I never tell him how I feel, I'd be happy with just this. With him. Forever.

When we're done, we head into the bedroom and undress. I climb into bed and snuggle into my usual spot with my favorite pillow—the one Logan bought for me after I kept complaining his pillows were too firm.

He pulls back the covers on his side and slides in next to me, and I reach for him instantly. I'm not even pretending I don't need him close tonight. I don't want to think about anything else, I just want him.

He shifts onto his side, settling in as the little spoon, and my dick is pressed right against his ass. I adjust slightly, trying not to draw attention to it, but then he wiggles back into me even closer. I stop breathing for half a second, but he doesn't pull away. If anything, I swear he's pressing into me on purpose.

He's warm, all muscle and comfort, and clearly unbothered by the fact that he's making me hard. Despite all the years we've slept together, this has never been a problem. Sure, I've woken up hard on multiple occasions, but it's never been a conscious thought to have to force my dick to behave because of the feel of him pressing into me.

He continues shifting, and I try to hold back a groan because at this point, he must be torturing me on purpose. He reaches back and threads his fingers through my hair, rubbing soft circles into my scalp, knowing I love that—and I can't help the quiet sigh that escapes me.

"Go to sleep," Logan murmurs. "We can deal with whatever we need to tomorrow."

He leans down to press a light kiss to my hand that's wrapped around him, and it jolts something awake inside me because that's unusual, even for us. I squeeze him tighter in response, holding on until sleep slowly starts to pull me under.

"Logan," I say, nudging him lightly. "Your mom."

He groans, peeling his face away from my shoulder and cracking one eye open. "You talk to her. I'm sleeping," he mumbles, shoving his face back into my arm.

"I'm not ready for that conversation," I huff a little laugh as I shove the phone into his hand.

Reluctantly, he sits up and swipes to answer the call. "Hi, Mom," he says, his voice still groggy.

I try not to listen, but it's impossible not to hear the warmth in her voice as she speaks. Logan's parents have always made me feel like part of the family since my mom is a few hours away, and I love them more for it.

"Yeah, I'm fine," Logan says. His voice starting to soften and lose the edge of sleep. "No, I wasn't asleep—well, not really…Yeah, Ryder's here."

At that, he shoots me a look, one eyebrow raised as if he's daring me to say something about being in bed with him. I bite back a laugh and flop back against the pillows, letting my eyes drift shut again. Logan keeps talking, and I have a feeling this call will lead to something.

"Yeah, I'll tell him…Okay…Love you too," he says finally, hanging up with a sigh.

"What'd she want?"

"She wants us to come over today," Logan says, stretching his arms over his head, and I try not to stare at his body, but damn does he look good.

"Something about Dad fixing the back deck and needing an extra set of hands," he adds.

"Us?" I ask, already knowing the answer.

"Yeah, and if I'm going, you're not getting out of it," he says with a side eye glare. "And she's not above bribing you. She told me to tell you she's making dinner."

"She's evil. She knows I can't say no to a home-cooked meal I don't have to cook."

"She's smart," Logan corrects, grinning. "And she misses you. Apparently, I'm not entertaining enough on my own. I think she's missing Michael. He hasn't been home since Christmas."

"Alright, let's go," I say with a sigh. I didn't expect to spend my Sunday working on a deck project, but there's no way I'm saying no to spending another whole day with Logan.

We make the drive to Logan's parents' house. It's a drive we've done more times than I can count, and it always reminds me how lucky he is to have them so close, and how I should call my mom more often. The last time I spoke to her was when I called to thank her for the cookies she sent last week.

When we pull into the driveway, Logan's mom is already on the porch, waving us in like she's been counting down the minutes until we arrive. "Hey, you two!" she calls out, her voice full of that warm motherly energy that somehow makes everything feel right in the world.

She wraps Logan in a hug first, holding him a little longer than necessary to make him squirm. "Mom," he groans, but there's more affection than annoyance in his voice.

Then she turns toward me. "Ryder, sweetheart, you look too thin. Are you eating enough?" she asks, pulling me into a hug that smells like she's already been baking.

"Yes, Mrs. Hart, I'm eating," I laugh as she releases me.

"Don't you worry, I'll make extra tonight so you boys can each take some food home," she says with a wink, ruffling Logan's dirty blonde hair as he lovingly swats her hand away.

Inside, the house definitely smells like she's already got something in the oven, and I see Logan's dad already outside through the window. We walk out to meet him, and he waves when he sees us, his smile so much like Logan's it always throws me a little.

"Hey, finally! I took on way more than I could handle with

this deck by myself. Should've known, but that's what I've got you two for," he says with a chuckle.

"Yeah, yeah, we're here," Logan says, smiling as he grabs a pair of gloves from the pile on the table and tosses me a pair too.

"Don't worry, Mr. Hart, Logan's just here for moral support. I'll do the real work," I say, slipping the gloves on, shooting Logan a smirk.

"Ha-ha," Logan deadpans, nudging me with his elbow as we head over to where his dad is. "Don't let him fool you, Dad. Ryder can't hammer a nail without nearly breaking his thumb. Happened at our last house. It was kinda funny though, so maybe we'll get some free entertainment today."

I level him with a glare, but he beams back at me.

"You two are ridiculous," Mr. Hart laughs, handing us a few tools. "Hopefully, no one breaks anything today. And quit calling me Mr. Hart, Ryder. You know it's Jim."

And then, we get to work, trying to spend the next few hours keeping up with Jim's requests. He's been measuring and cutting the boards while Logan and I work on screwing them into the base. It feels good to have a regular day with Logan and his family after all of the strange things that have been happening recently.

"Look at that," I say, looking at the board I just screwed in. "That's what I call craftsmanship."

Logan comes up to stand beside me and hums. "Alright, I'll give you that one. Not bad."

I raise an eyebrow. "Not bad? That's damn near perfect and you know it."

He smirks. "Fine. But don't let it go to your head. There's still about twenty more boards to go."

Jim chuckles behind us with a pencil in hand to mark the boards. "You two sound like an old married couple."

Logan's eyes go wide for half a second before he recovers with a grin. "He wishes."

I laugh too, but I don't miss that flicker of something in his expression before the smile. And the comment sticks with me longer than it probably should because maybe I've been missing something this whole time. I've never really thought about our relationship in too much depth, but maybe we are kind of like an old married couple already. We have our weekly *platonic* 'date night' at Pine Bar, we shop at the farmer's market together, and we've got a favorite spot at the lake where we always end up watching the water and talking. We cook together, know how each other likes our coffee, and even sleep in the same bed, cuddled up together. *Have I been treating Logan like we're in a relationship this entire time?*

I used to tell myself that's what close best friends do, but I know that's a lie. I don't think any of our other friends sleep in the same bed together, but I also don't care because I *like* sleeping in bed with him.

I'm starting to see all those 'little' things differently now. Maybe there were always signs pointing to something more, and I wasn't ready to see them.

Logan's parents even know how close we are. Though they don't know we share a bed, Anne did ask if I was there this morning...

Maybe the only people who've been confused about this are Logan and I.

I still don't know how to bring this up to Logan, either, but that's a problem for future me to deal with. I've never wanted to hang out with a girlfriend the same way I want to hang out with him. My ex from a few years ago would always get mad that I wanted Logan to come with us to the farmer's market, and at the time, I didn't understand why, because the farmers market was *our* thing before I'd ever met her, just like Pine Bar. She was joining in on an activity that was usually reserved for Logan and me. I wasn't just going to uninvite him from something we always did together.

By the time we're done, the deck looks good as new, according to Anne. She came outside a couple of times to bring us drinks and snacks throughout the day. The first time she did it, I glanced over at Logan and watched the interaction with a small smile; it's easy to see where he gets his warmth and compassion from.

As promised, Anne cooked more food than we could possibly eat, but I'm certainly not complaining because it was delicious. She also loads us up with containers of food to take home, including an entire container of cookies each.

"Mom," Logan groans as she hands him another container. "We're not starving."

"Well, I don't get to do this for your brother, so I'm doing it for you two," she says, waving him off. "Besides, I know you'll forget to eat the second you get busy with work. Just let me do this for you."

He groans, but I know it's only out of love, then she turns to me. "You make sure he doesn't overdo it, okay?"

"Yeah," I say, barely getting the word out before she's pulling me into a hug. "Of course."

"And take care of yourself, too, Ryder. I'll see you boys soon."

Logan sighs at this whole routine, but I catch the softness in his expression as he grabs the last of the packed-up food. He hugs his mom, then I follow him out the door, our arms full of food.

By the time we get back to Logan's apartment, I don't even make it to the couch before I collapse against the wall near the door, tilting my head back with a sigh. It's been a long time since I've done a full day of manual labor. It felt good, sure, but I'm also completely exhausted.

Logan snorts as he kicks off his shoes. "You're pathetic."

"We built a whole ass deck today. I'm allowed to be pathetic."

He rolls his eyes as he laughs, tossing his keys onto the entry table. "Shower first. Before you pass out right next to the door."

I lift a tired hand in protest. "In a minute."

"Nope. Go." He bends down, grabs my wrist, and yanks me up like I weigh nothing. "See how nice I am? Letting you shower first in my apartment?"

I grumble, but he's right. My muscles are stiff, my back aches, and I'm probably still covered in sawdust despite shaking out my hair multiple times.

Maybe he could shower with me and hold me up right.

Well, shit. Despite how tired I am, it seems like I'm not tired enough to forget this newfound interest in my best friend. Instead of risking opening my mouth, I drag myself to the bedroom to grab clean clothes from my drawer—and I take his hoodie too, just because—and head into the bathroom.

The second the hot water hits my skin, I exhale and feel my body start to relax. Logan was right. I needed this. My body feels like it's been put through a blender, and standing under the spray is the exact kind of reprieve I needed.

By the time I step out, towel-drying my hair, Logan's already claimed the couch and has reruns playing on the TV.

"Took you long enough. Get preoccupied in there?" he asks with a smirk.

I flop down beside him, letting the couch swallow me whole. "Wouldn't you like to know?"

He chuckles. "You staying over?"

I shrug, already sinking deeper into the cushions. "If you don't care. Too lazy to drive home."

"Shocking, with how much energy you have after today," he deadpans. "But I'm not mad about another night of cuddles."

Relief washes through me. Not that I thought he'd kick me out, but after a whole weekend with him, I'm still not ready to go home to my too-quiet house.

Logan gets up with a groan and disappears into the bathroom for his shower. I don't know why tonight feels different. We've done this hundreds of times. We've spent entire weekends together before. But something about this one—something about *him*—keeps tugging at my thoughts. Maybe it's just the weekend getting to me. Maybe it's the way his family treats me like I belong. Maybe it's the quiet comfort of falling into step with him so easily. Maybe it's the way I keep catching myself wondering what it would feel like to kiss him. Or maybe—

I hear the door to the bathroom open, and before I can stop myself, I call out to him.

"Logan."

He looks down the hall, blue eyes curious. "Yeah?"

I hesitate. The words catch in my throat. *I missed you last week. You're my best friend. I love you. Let's live together again. I hate being apart. I want you. I think I have feelings for you.*

"Thanks for today," I say instead.

His brow furrows like he knows I'm not saying everything I want to, but he just nods. "Of course. Thank *you*. I know my parents appreciated it."

He pops back into the bathroom for a moment before coming back into the living room. I'm lying the full length of the couch, and instead of giving me a second to adjust, he drops down right on top of me. His head of wet hair is already soaking my shirt, but I don't mind at all as I embrace him fully and pull the blanket over both of us. We stay like that until he eventually peels himself off me and insists we go to bed before we fall asleep on the couch. I don't want to move, but he tugs me to my feet.

The second we crawl into bed, Logan is against me, pulling me close so we're chest to chest, both of us on our sides facing each other. We don't usually sleep like this. Typically, one of us has our head on the other's chest, or we spoon. This feels far more intimate than any position we've ever been in, and feels harder to chalk up to platonic comfort, but I'm not complaining.

Maybe he felt something shift Friday night, too.

I feel his breath against my collarbone as his arms wrap tightly around my waist. He slips one of his legs between mine so we're slotted together and I can feel his dick against mine. He's not fully hard, but we've never been dick to dick before. I try to keep it together so I don't freak him out by getting hard again.

He leans forward, letting his lips graze the side of my neck and linger there. I don't want to move away, so I stay there and let myself lean into him more because whatever is happening between us, I want it.

69

8

RYDER

Morning comes way too fast, but after a whole weekend with Logan, I feel ready to tackle Monday. Logan's already out of bed by the time I wake up, so I pull on a pair of black sweatpants and head to the kitchen to find him sipping his coffee.

"Morning," he says with a small smile.

"Morning," I reply, rubbing the sleep from my eyes.

"What mug do you want today?" he asks, opening the cabinet. " *'Shh, my coffee and I are having a moment,'* or *'I like big mugs and I cannot lie'*?"

"The first one," I laugh because it's such a ridiculous question. "I don't need *that* much coffee today," I say, pointing at the slightly smaller option. "I feel refreshed after last night. Gonna head home in a few minutes to start work."

"Give the people what they want," he teases, waggling his eyebrows as he hands me the full mug, already made up the way I like.

"Yeah, yeah," I mutter, smirking over the rim before taking a sip.

He grins and grabs his keys. "I'm heading to work. Text me when you're done. And don't forget to lock the door when you leave!"

"Will do," I call after him as he heads to his office.

Logan's always looked out for me, but ever since I started narrating years ago, he's become extra particular about certain things, like locking the doors.

"You've got those noise-canceling headphones on," he's reminded me more than once. "You wouldn't even hear someone come in. I want you to be safe, that's all."

I used to roll my eyes at that, but after last weekend, I completely get where he's coming from. I never mentioned the noise I heard while recording to Logan. Honestly, I've been trying not to dwell on it, especially since I haven't heard anything else. It was probably a neighbor working on a project or another perfectly reasonable explanation, rather than someone inside my house.

When I get home, I drop my bag by the door, flip the deadbolt, make a fresh cup of coffee, and head to my recording room. I'm excited for today's chapters—it's a low-angst hockey romance, which is exactly what I need: good banter and a fun low-angst plot.

I prep like I always do, and once everything is set, I hit record and immerse myself in the story. It's just me, the characters, and a world way less complicated than my own.

I'm making good progress, but I pause at the chapter break to grab some water. When I return to my office, I notice a new email notification. I consider ignoring it—I *should* ignore it—but I've never been good at letting things sit unread. I know I won't be able to focus until I check it.

The second I open it, my stomach drops.

The subject line says: ***You're doing so well.***

I hesitate, dread already curling low in my chest as I click, half-hoping it's some poorly-worded marketing email from a wellness center I never signed up for. Or a spam email that comes off as creepy. Anything other than what my gut reaction tells me it is. The sender's name looks too similar to the one I blocked, and I'm surprised these are even getting through my spam filter.

I let my finger hover over the email and force myself to open it.

"You really are something, Ryder. You know that? I love listening to you read to me. Every line that falls from your lips is perfect, even if you did block me the first time. I know Ryder, I see everything."

I stare at the screen, my heart is in my throat. *What the fuck is happening?*

This isn't the kind of flattery that feels good. Logan was right; it's creepy. This one feels too close to home. They see everything? What the fuck does that mean?

I force myself to recheck the sender's address, hoping for any clue that could tell me who this is. But once again, there's nothing identifiable, just a string of nonsense letters and numbers, like they smashed their finger down on their keyboard and said, 'This works.' It's no more helpful than the first email.

I immediately hit 'block sender' on this address, too, even though I'm sure they'll create another email account.

There's a pressing fear creeping up my spine that whoever sent me this message knows I'm recording right now. With the language they used and the timing, it almost feels like they were waiting for me to take a break from recording so they could hit send.

It makes me feel uneasy, but that's probably ridiculous, *right?*

There's no way anyone but Logan knows what I'm doing right now. This room doesn't even have a window in it, so I know for a fact no one can see me. Whoever sent this probably took a lucky guess that I'd be working right now because it's Monday. They've probably done this before to other people and know they get blocked. Or they have some type of software that allows them to see if they've been blocked. That has to be it.

I look around the room to see if I notice anything different, but it all looks the same to me. Nothing seems out of place, so I'm sure the timing was a strange coincidence.

I swallow hard and scan the email again. It's not an outright threat, but the tone doesn't sit right with me. It's not a usual fan email, and I hate not knowing who's sending these or what they're trying to get at. *Are they really watching me?*

Grabbing my phone off my desk, there's only one person I want to talk to right now. I know he won't like what I have to tell him, but I go to my favorites and hit his name before I can talk myself out of it.

The phone rings once. Then twice. Then a third time.

My stomach twists tighter with each second he doesn't answer because all I want is to talk to him and have him reassure me it's probably nothing. Usually, I'd try not to let it bother me like I did with the last email, but this one feels more personal and makes me feel jittery. It's like my body is telling me something my mind is trying to deny.

Finally, I hear his voice.

"Hey Ryder," he says in a somewhat distracted tone.

I don't even care that he's distracted; I already feel like I can breathe slightly easier just from hearing his voice.

I swallow, trying to keep my voice casual, but it still comes out tighter than I want. "Hey, you busy?"

"Working on design edits. What's up?" He pauses for a second. "You okay?"

I don't answer right away because honestly, I don't know. *Am I?* I can't help but feel like I'm being paranoid. Do I have anything to worry about, or am I about to dump unnecessary stress on him during his work day?

But I promised him I'd tell him, so I do.

"I got another email," I ignore his question and say instead.

The shift in Logan's voice is immediate. "What do you mean, another? Like from the same person? I thought you blocked them."

"I did. It's a different email address, but it's all letters and numbers like last time. It's gotta be the same person from Saturday, though. It had a similar feel, but..." I hesitate, trying to find the right words. "It feels a little more personal, though. Invasive, maybe. Creepy."

"Invasive, how? What's it say?" Logan's voice drops lower. I wonder if he's surrounded by his coworkers, and I realize maybe I should've texted him first.

I don't want to paraphrase, so I read it to him. There's no way to dress it up to make it feel less creepy, and when I finish, the silence on the other end of the line is deafening.

"Send it to me. Right now, Ryder," his tone is firm. He doesn't usually get demanding like this, and it throws me for a second, but I can tell he's concerned about what I just told him.

I do as he asks and silently wait for him to reply, until I hear a muttered curse.

"Alright, I'm coming over now. Don't do anything, just wait for me to get there."

"Logan—"

"Nope, don't argue. I'll be there as soon as I can, and make sure the doors are locked."

My heart rate picks up at that thought, but I'm positive I locked the door. To make sure, though, I get up to double-check anyway while he's still on the phone with me.

"Doors locked," I confirm. I'm positive the back door is locked because it always is. I haven't gone out that door in a while, but I check anyway. And yep, it's locked.

"I'm going to go talk to my boss, then I'll leave," he says.

I let out a little laugh because the last thing I need is him telling his boss that his best friend received a semi-strange email, so he needs the rest of the day off.

"Logan, it's fine. I'm sure it's nothing."

"Nope," he snaps. Then I hear him let out a deep breath, "Just let me do this, alright? It's not like I'll be able to focus on work the rest of the day anyway. And you know I'd never forgive myself if something happened to you just so I could work a full eight-hour day."

"Fine, fine, I'll see you when you get here," I concede, rubbing a hand over my beard.

I think that'll be the end of our conversation, but Logan's next words make my chest ache for a different reason.

"You're my best friend, Ry. I love you, you know I'd do anything for you, right?"

I didn't realize how badly I needed to hear that at this moment. Selfishly, I'm glad he's coming over because I don't want to be in my house all alone, but I do feel a smidge of guilt that he's going to take the afternoon off. I probably should've waited to call him about this at the end of the day.

"Same, Lo. I love you, too. Thanks for this, I'll see you soon."

"No problem."

We hang up, and I decide that instead of spiraling, I should probably be productive. I go around the house to make sure the windows are locked, just in case. I make it through almost all of them when I hear knocking at my front door.

I walk over to it and look through the peephole to see Logan standing there. When I pull the door open, he has a disheveled look on his face, and his dirty blonde hair is a mess. He looks like he's run his fingers through it at least a dozen times on the drive over.

"Hey, you didn't need to come, Loge," I say, stepping back to let him inside. He doesn't respond; he just walks into the house and heads straight toward my bedroom.

I'm unsure what's happening right now, so I shut and lock the door behind him before following him.

"Uh, what's going on?" I question when I see him in my closet.

"Pack a bag," he barks without looking back at me as he pulls one out of my closet.

"What? Why?"

He levels me with a look that says, *this should be obvious.* "Because you're coming to my place. For at least a few days, so pack what you need."

I let out a short laugh, but it feels hollow. I don't want to be alone right now, but I also don't want to impose on Logan's life over two odd emails.

"Logan, I'm fine. I don't need to—"

"Well, I don't like it, Ry." He crosses his arms and tosses the bag on the bed. "Can you do this for me? It'll make me feel better knowing you're not here all alone. Come to my apartment while we figure this out. Please?"

Part of me wants to push back, but the way he's looking at me and the way he said 'please' makes me cave. If he gets sick of me, he'll tell me, although that's never happened before. I'll just need to continue to tamp down my newfound feelings for him while I'm sleeping in his bed indefinitely.

Easy, right?

I give him a nod and try to keep my thoughts PG. Now is not the time to think about him rubbing his ass against my dick while we spoon, or the little kiss he placed on my hand while he was wrapped in my arms.

Think about the email.

"Alright, grab whatever you need then. I'll tell my boss I need to work from home the rest of the week, too. Whoever this creep is, they're already feeling too comfortable with the words they're using, and I'm not gonna leave you alone to deal with it."

He disappears into the bathroom and comes back out with my toothbrush and some toiletries, and I can't help but smile at that.

"You do know I already have a toothbrush at your place, right?"

"Whatever, it's already packed now," he shrugs and keeps moving through the room.

It didn't take long for us to pack everything I needed, including all my recording equipment, my laptop, and a few extras Logan insisted on bringing.

We both drive separately back to Logan's apartment, and

the second we get there, he grabs some of my stuff and leads us inside. As soon as we're in, he locks the deadbolt and starts checking all the windows and balcony door, methodically moving through each one to make sure we're locked in. Even though we have no idea who this person is or if they even know where we live. I'm not going to argue, though. I also want to feel safe.

As I start unpacking some of my stuff, my phone buzzes on the coffee table. I hesitate before picking it up, bracing myself for the worst because there's another email notification staring back at me.

I already know I'm not going to like whatever I see, it's a too-strong gut feeling.

When I click on the icon, it's exactly what I was dreading. The email address is slightly different again, but it's the subject line that makes my skin crawl.

Subject: *Why'd you leave?*

I feel light-headed and dizzy, like I can't breathe. My chest feels tight as I try to suck air in through short, shallow bursts. I press a hand to my sternum to alleviate some of the pressure, but it does nothing to help.

"Ryder?" Logan's voice cuts through the haze. "What is it?"

He comes over, grabbing my hands and pulling me down onto the couch next to him. He keeps his hand in mine, but it's not helping. My throat feels too tight, the panic is hitting me so hard I feel like I might choke on it because someone is *watching* me.

They knew I left.

They were *there*.

At my house.

While I was recording.

The booth doesn't have windows, but what if they were already *inside* my house?

I was away all weekend, and I don't have cameras at my house.

God, what type of home owner doesn't have fucking cameras!?

Then my mind snags on a question that makes me physically sick…

Did they follow us here?

My mind is racing in a million different directions, and I don't know what to do right now, or what to think. If I brought this person right to Logan's door, I don't know how I'll ever forgive myself.

My breathing grows erratic as I try to calm down, but it feels too hard to control until Logan pulls me into him and strokes my back. He's whispering calming words of reassurance to me, but I'm freaking the fuck out.

Fuck, what about the noise?

The one on Friday night sounded like it came from right outside my window.

Were they lurking around trying to find a way in?

The sound I heard the next day while working was so loud it broke through my noise-cancelling headphones, and that's never happened before. *Was it so loud because they were* inside *my house?*

I can't stop shaking. What if I missed something by not checking every room, every window, every inch of my house? Clearly, I've been downplaying the severity of this, but I had no reason to think they were truly watching me—stalking me, by the other emails they'd sent.

I feel so stupid. Someone's been watching me and I've had no idea.

Logan's hand comes up to cup my face now, and I force myself to focus on him. He has no idea why I'm panicking yet, so I unlock my phone and hand it to him. I haven't even opened it yet, but the subject line was all I needed to see to know this has escalated. This isn't just someone from an online fandom; this is someone who wants me to know they're close.

"What the fuck," he mutters and lowers my phone in front of us so we can read the email together.

"I never wanted you to leave, I just wanted you to know how perfect you are. Then he showed up, always trying to be a hero, but he's not, Ryder. He doesn't admire you or care about you to the depths I do. He doesn't listen to you like I do. You're all I hear; all I see. You deserve to be worshiped. I can give that to you."

His grip on the phone tightens, and I can hear his breathing pick up. "This creep has some type of sick fixation on you."

That email did nothing to loosen the panic in my chest. I wish I'd never read it. Every word rings through my head, and I wish I could unsee them.

Worshiped? You deserve to be worshiped?

Who says shit like that?

I try to focus on my anger over this situation instead of fear because I don't want to break down.

"That's it," he snaps, standing abruptly. "I'm calling the cops. This fucker is stalking you."

"Logan, they're not going to do anything," I voice my biggest concern. "It's just an email. We don't even have the name of who's sending them. We don't have anything helpful they could use." I don't know why I'm still trying to be reasonable in this situation when some anonymous person *admitted* to watching me, but I hate the idea of going through a line of questioning and not being taken seriously.

"We need to at least make them aware of this situation. They can document it," he counters firmly. "And that's better than nothing. Maybe they can dig into it. We have to do something, Ryder. I can't sit here and do nothing when I know someone is watching you. Watching you closely enough to know you left your fucking house. It makes things far more dangerous."

I know he's right, even if I'm not convinced it'll help. I'm also scared for Logan because this person doesn't like him being around me, and I could have just led them straight to his door.

If anything happens to Logan because of me, I'll never be able to forgive myself.

He doesn't waste any time pulling out his phone and making the call. He's pacing the room as he relays the details to the dispatcher. I stay rooted to the couch, staring at the email. The words are burned into my brain, and I can't unsee them.

When Logan finally hangs up, he drops back down beside me, his hand resting on my knee, giving it a light squeeze. "They're sending someone out to take a report."

I nod, my throat still tight. "Thanks."

"You don't have to thank me," he says. "I'm not going to let anything happen to you, Ryder. I don't know who the fuck this person thinks they are, but I'm not letting you out of my sight. And we're not leaving this apartment. Okay? Get ready to be real sick of me."

The sincerity in his eyes is almost too much. I look away,

trying to swallow the lump forming in my throat. "I don't know what I'd do without you."

"You'll never have to find out," he says, giving my knee another squeeze.

I try to give him a small smile, but inside, I feel like I'm cracking wide open.

9

LOGAN

The cops come and go, taking their sweet time to tell us the same useless crap Ryder was afraid of hearing: "There's not much we can do right now. We'll file a report and see if there's anything else we can do. Let us know if anything else happens."

Like what? A fucking brick through the window? This creep breaking in?

I want to hit something—preferably whoever thinks it's fun to mess with Ryder. But first, I need to know who the hell it is so I can properly direct my anger.

I pace the living room, too restless to sit down at this point, and Ryder is sitting there silently on the couch, clutching his phone in his hand. He hasn't said much since the officers left, and I hate the withdrawn look on his face.

Ryder's usually the happy-go-lucky one with his bright smile that makes you smile back just from seeing it. He radiates a fun, carefree energy that is absent from him right now. He looks truly defeated after that last email, and seeing him like this isn't right. He's always been one to roll with the punches. He lets things slide off his back, and even helps my stressed-out, color-coded-calendar, everything-in-its-place self truly relax. I've seen him laugh off hate comments, ignore weird DMs, and brush off the judgmental looks a few assholes in this town have thrown his way for narrating queer romance books. He never lets that shit touch him, though. It's like he knows exactly who he is, and nothing anyone says or thinks can shake that.

But this is the first time I've seen him truly rattled. Even when he's talked about his dad, it's like his leaving barely fazes him. Ryder's always been someone who can look at things objectively, understand and accept them for what they are, and move on. So seeing him like this? I'm furious.

I'm pissed at whoever is stalking him, angry for Ryder, and upset that he's going through this. I clench my fists, forcing myself to breathe through the emotions that are surfacing right now as I think more and more about this situation and how it's affecting him. This person wanted to wedge their way under Ryder's skin and make him start questioning everything as he comes undone, and it's working, even though I'm desperate to stop it.

I'll do whatever it takes to help him rebuild those parts of himself brick by brick if I have to, because Ryder is mine. My best friend. My anchor. My whole fucking world. And I'll be damned if I let anyone break him apart.

I walk over to him and drop down next to him, taking his hand in mine. "Hey, you doing okay?" I ask, even though I know it's a pointless question.

His eyes flick up to meet mine, glassy and tired. "Yeah," he murmurs. "I'm fine."

"You don't have to lie to me, Ry. I'm not expecting you to

put on a brave face. It's okay to be scared and upset," I say, my thumb brushing gently across his knuckles.

He huffs out a breath, leaning back against the couch cushions like the weight of everything is finally catching up to him. "What do you want me to say, Loge? That I'm freaked out? That I feel like someone's watching me every second? That I don't know how to make the spiraling thoughts stop?"

"Yeah, Ry," I say simply. "I want you to say all of that. I don't want you to hold this in and let it eat at you alone."

He lets his eyes meet mine, and the distraught expression on his face breaks my heart.

"I just...I don't get it. Why me? I'm nobody special."

My chest tightens at that. "That's not true. You're so special to me, Ry. I care about you more than anyone in the world," I say firmly because it's true. Well, alongside my parents, but we don't need to get technical here.

"As for why someone's doing this," I continue, "I don't know. I mean, I think they're trying to tell you that you're special too, but they're doing it in the most fucked up way possible. We'll figure this out, though. I promise we will. And when I find out who it is, I'll make sure they regret thinking they could ever come after you because this isn't okay."

Ryder swallows hard, and he nods. "I don't even know where to start," he murmurs, and his voice is so small, I want to pull him into me and never let go.

"Well, good thing I'm forcing you to stay here with me so I know what's happening every moment of your life," I say, trying to lighten the mood a little. "Another good thing is that I'm great at overthinking and making plans."

A small smile tugs at his lips, and I feel the tiniest flicker of relief. Humor has always been our default, and it's saved us more than once.

Especially after the whole shower situation.

"Overthinking really is your specialty, huh?"

"Absolutely, and step one of this particular plan is that we stick together. Where you go, I go. No exceptions. Got it?"

He smirks. "Even to the shower?"

I freeze for a second, completely thrown off by the words that left his mouth. Did he just—? In this high-stress situation?

No, no, I definitely heard that right.

My brain completely blanks as I try to come up with a response. Because really, what the hell *do* you say when your best friend, who you've finally admitted to yourself that you're lowkey in love with, makes another casual joke about the shower?

The shower where I jerked off *in front of him,* to *thoughts of him.*

"Uh…" is all I say, and his face breaks into a smile. I'm not even mad because this is the lightest I've seen him all day, despite the blush I can feel crawling up my cheeks. "You don't fight fair," I manage to get out, and he laughs.

I blow out a breath, trying to compose myself, and when he stops laughing after a moment, his face gets more serious. "I had to, but thanks, Logan, for you know…all of this. I don't think I could handle this on my own."

I nudge his knee with mine, not breaking eye contact. "You don't have to thank me. You're my person, Ryder. This is what we do." He smiles, and I try to bring the conversation back to more playful territory without being *that* playful since I have no idea what this means for us. "Besides, you don't really have a choice. You're stuck with me. Rule number one, remember?"

When the first email came, I had a gut feeling something

wasn't right, but I tried not to overreact. I hoped they wouldn't send more emails, that it was an odd one-off thing, but now I know this is just the beginning of something bigger we'll have to face together. This person is here, watching, and they wanted us to know that.

"Do you think they're done? Whoever this is?" Ryder asks, his voice low as his mind circles back to the heaviness of the situation.

"I don't know," I say honestly. But I do know whoever this creep is will have to go through me first, and it seems like they're not my biggest fan in the first place because I have what they want.

He turns his head toward me, eyes meeting mine with something more vulnerable than I'm used to seeing there. "Do you think they followed us here?"

Fuck, I hate this.

I hate how unsure he looks. How afraid he sounds. He has every right to be, of course, but it still cuts deep. The thought that there was a chance someone followed us here had crossed my mind earlier, after the email, but I wasn't going to voice it. I didn't want to add any additional stress to what he's already feeling. At this moment, he doesn't need more theories or fears to be voiced; he needs comfort. He needs me to be strong for both of us so he can break.

"I don't know," I say again. "But we're going to do everything we can to shut them out of your life. Maybe if we keep the curtains closed, you don't respond, and we don't go out, they'll lose interest. And I'll be here, Ry. I'll do everything in my power to keep you safe. I promise."

I squeeze his hand and get up to check every curtain to make sure they're all drawn tight. If that sick bastard is out there, I don't want them to see a goddamn thing.

When I finish, I look at Ryder as he stands up. "I'm calling it a night," he says quietly. "Come on—come to bed with me. I don't want to go alone." Any thought of doing anything else completely vanishes as I follow him down the hall.

We brush our teeth, strip down to our underwear, and climb into bed. I pull him to me like I did last night, burying my face in his neck. His skin is warm, and the way his arms wrap around me makes this the only place I ever want to be.

"I love you, Ry," I whisper, my lips brushing against his throat. It's not sexual, just comforting.

"I love you too, Loge," he murmurs, pressing a kiss to my head.

Whatever comes next, we'll face it together.

Because there is no me without him.

10

RYDER

The worst part about being an adult is that the world doesn't care if your life is falling apart.

Deadlines don't pause just because your life has been hijacked by a psycho. Emails don't stop flooding your inbox because someone is sending you cryptic messages that leave a phantom itch under your skin and make you want to completely erase your online identity. Clients still have launch dates set in stone and, rightfully, need their deliverables on time. The grind doesn't wait for you to catch your breath.

It's fucking exhausting being a person sometimes.

We've spent the last two days holed up in Logan's apartment, and while no new emails have come through, it's still the only thing I can think about. Every time I step into the closet to work, headphones on, mic in front of me, my thoughts spiral. I'm paranoid to the point of second-guessing every sound I hear because that creep made it *known* they're watching. I've never struggled to record like this before. Usually, I can lose myself in the story, but now I have to actively convince myself I can do this at all.

Logan's been hovering in the background, offering coffee, shoulder rubs, and his general presence like a security blanket. He doesn't say much about the stalker, but I catch him glancing at my phone every time it buzzes, watching me for any sign of a negative reaction.

I'm sure he's falling behind on work, too, but once again, he hasn't complained or said anything. His boss told him there's no problem with him working from home as long as he gets everything done, so I know how important it is for him to stay focused.

That's exactly what I need to do, too.

I need to make some real progress on my to-do list before I lose another day with absolutely nothing to show for it. I'm still making my way through the hockey romance, and while it's the kind of book that usually makes me smile while I read, I'm struggling with it. It's hard to read something light and funny out loud for an audience when it feels like the world is crumbling around me.

The thought makes my stomach twist.

These creepy emails about how much this person loves my voice is going to be the reason I lose contracts because I can't manage to pull it together to do my job. That's what pisses me off the most. Not just the fear, but the way it's derailing everything I've worked so hard to build.

I drop down into my chair, dragging my hands down my face. The closet isn't as soundproof as my setup at home, of course, but it'll do. Logan even helped me shove pillows into the corners the other day to help muffle the echo.

A knock at the door makes me jump, and I loathe that everyday things are causing such visceral reactions.

"Yeah?" I call out.

Logan opens the closet door with a coffee mug in one

hand and a plate of toast in the other. "Thought you could use a break since you haven't stopped for lunch," he says, setting them down on the small desk. His hair is a mess like usual, sticking up in a way that makes him look annoyingly good, and he's wearing one of his soft, lived-in shirts that cling to his chest. I feel like I'm seeing Logan in a new light, and despite all the stress I've been under, the nagging new desire I have for him hasn't gone away.

The last couple of nights, Logan's wrapped me up in his arms, and I haven't even pretended to protest because it's exactly what I need. It's one of the only things that's made me feel better, and I dread the moment we have to untangle ourselves for work in the morning.

Now, I spend all day counting down the minutes until I can be wrapped in Logan's arms again. I don't think he realizes the effect he has on me. This is the strangest and most complicated thing we've ever gone through, and he's been my rock. He's made me feel loved and cared for in a way no one else has, anchoring me when I feel like my grip on reality is slipping.

I swallow and turn my attention to the coffee instead of whatever the hell my brain is doing right now. I exhale, wrapping my hands around the coffee mug and focusing on the heat seeping into my skin.

"Thanks," I say, my voice softer than I mean it to be.

"How's recording going?"

I let out a sigh and tell him the truth. "About as well as you'd expect when you're trying to record a rom-com while your life feels like a horror movie."

"Don't be too hard on yourself. You're still doing better than most people would be in your shoes."

"Yeah, well, most people aren't lucky enough to have a

personal assistant-slash-bodyguard-slash-coffee delivery guy on hand," I say, smiling up at him, trying to lighten the mood.

"Don't forget emotional support roommate-slash-best friend," he adds, grinning back at me.

The banter helps a little, it always has. Humor is our way of taking the edge off when things get tense. But as soon as the silence settles between us, my smile falters, and I see Logan's face fall in response. And fuck, I hate that. I hate that I'm dragging him down with me. I know he's just as worried as I am, but he won't let himself show it, not while I'm already falling apart. We can't both break, so he's holding it together for both of us—and I love him more for it.

"Ryder," he says more seriously now. "You know you don't have to push yourself this hard, right? Nobody's expecting you to be perfect. You can take a few days for yourself if you need them."

"I can't," I say, shaking my head. "There's too much riding on this project. I already pushed back the deadline once before shit even got complicated. I can't do it again."

He doesn't argue, just looks at me and nods. "Okay," he says finally. "But don't forget to breathe, alright? And maybe give yourself a little grace. Let me know if there's anything I can do."

I nod, expecting him to turn and leave, but instead, he walks right over, leans down, and presses a soft kiss to my forehead. My mouth drops open at the gesture without my permission, and he walks away, flashing me a small smile over his shoulder before closing the door behind him.

And I feel like my entire concept of reality just shifted.

I'M NOT SURE IF IT WAS THE COFFEE OR THE FOREHEAD KISS, but my evening has completely turned around. For the first time since this mess began, I was able to record a decent amount of work without my thoughts spiraling out of control.

I only have one more scene to make it through tonight before I'm ready to call it a night and head to bed. The scene is, well, spicy as the book world says, so I want to do it while I'm feeling good.

Detailed sex scenes aren't new to me; they're a pretty standard part of my job. I'm sure I've narrated hundreds of them over the years, but these hockey boys are filthy. I quickly skim through the book before I press record, and I feel my cheeks heating at what I'm about to narrate.

As the scene builds, I drop my voice into that low, sultry tone everyone seems to eat up. My words come out thick with tension as I give voice to the character's desires. I add in a few moans, groans, and grunts to bring it to life, and by the time I hit the climax, my face is hot, and I'm grateful no one can see me.

When I reach the end of the chapter, I hit stop, turn off the mic, and drop down into my chair, letting out a deep breath. I rub my eyes and smile to myself because I feel really good about everything I've recorded since this afternoon.

Heading out of the closet, I walk into the bathroom to splash cold water on my face and brush my teeth to decompress before I get into bed with Logan. The last thing I need is to be all keyed up while he rubs his ass into me.

When I walk into the bedroom, Logan is smiling at me. "You good?" he asks, watching me as I settle under the covers.

"Yeah. Really good, actually." I exhale, still a little breathless. "I finally feel like I found my groove again."

He smirks. "Sounded like you found your flow from out here."

My stomach flips, and the casual way he says it catches me off guard. "You...heard that?"

"Bits and pieces," he says, looking at me with a grin. "You get all..." He trails off, "Breathy. Kind of hard to ignore when you're moaning like that in my closet—even if it *is* just for the mic."

"Shut up," I mutter, yanking the blanket over my head to hide the heat rising to my face.

Logan laughs and hooks his fingers into the edge of the blanket, trying to yank it down. "Oh no, you don't," he says, voice full of amusement.

I hold my ground, gripping the fabric tighter, refusing to let him pull it down. Laughter bubbles out of me anyway, and before I know it, he climbs on top of me, straddling my waist to try to pull the blanket down.

"Logan—" I laugh as he yanks the blanket away from my face, triumphantly. His grin is wide and teasing, but the second he looks down at me, something shifts in his expression. The look is so intimate. He releases the blanket and plants his hands on both sides of my head, his weight is pressed into my hips, and I feel my cock start to stiffen beneath him.

Fuck.

He doesn't move, though, as his smile shifts into something unreadable that looks a lot like desire mixed with confusion. The air changes, and I don't know if we're still play-fighting or if...if this is something else.

Can he feel me getting hard?

My pulse is hammering now, and I don't know what the hell I'm supposed to do because the urge to buck my hips up into him is strong. *Fuck, I need to get him off of me before I do something stupid.*

I swallow hard, hoping my face isn't giving away everything I'm feeling. "You win," I say quietly, my voice low. He doesn't respond at first, doesn't move, just holds my gaze as my cock presses into him. Once again, I feel like I have no idea how to act around my best friend, but then he rolls off of me.

"Damn right, I do," he says, shifting onto his back beside me with his grin back in place.

We're both silent for a moment, apart from the sound of our breathing, and my mind won't shut up. My dick is *definitely* hard now just from him straddling me so I think I can rule 'questioning' off my list, as I suspected.

I try to count backwards from one hundred, but that's a pointless tactic because I can still feel the heat of Logan's body next to mine, feel the phantom weight of him straddling me, the look on his face when he was braced over me like he wanted to—

Nope. *Don't go there.*

My thoughts are doing nothing to calm down my rock hard dick that's straining against my waistband. I'm almost positive Logan knows too, there's no way he didn't feel how hard I was while he was on top of me. The blanket's not *that* thick.

Calm the fuck down, body.

I realize there's no use in trying to will my erection to go down on its own. It's not happening because my thoughts won't stop running wild with images of Logan pinning me down. I literally can't think of anything other than *him,* and I let out a frustrated blow.

"Logan," I say, turning my head toward him.

He glances over immediately. "Yeah?"

I hesitate because, what the fuck do I say? *I need to come? Can you leave the room for five minutes? Can you stay? Do you want to watch me touch myself this time? I'm horny, will you help?*

It sounds ridiculous even in my head. I can't possibly say these things out loud. But the pressure is unbearable, and I *need* to touch myself. I should lock myself in the bathroom, but if his hearing me record earlier proves anything, it's that the walls are thin, so I wouldn't be hiding anything from him, anyway.

I lick my lips and try to find the words. "I'm..." I trail off, clearing my throat before trying again. "I'm still, uh, kinda worked up."

His brow furrows slightly. "From the scene?"

"From...everything."

His face breaks into a smirk, gaze dropping pointedly to my staining cock that I knew I wasn't hiding well before coming back up to meet my eyes. "You mean you're hard because of that hot-as-hell flip fucking scene you recorded?"

He's avoiding the real question—the one we're both pretending not to ask. *Am I hard because he straddled my hips?*

So I stick with safer territory, too.

"Something like that." I turn my face away, rubbing a hand over my jaw. "Look, I'll just...go to the bathroom or something. I figured you might hear me, so I didn't want to make it weird by not saying anything." I start to shift, but Logan grabs my wrist, stopping me.

"Wait," he rasps. His voice is less teasing now, more...something else. "You don't have to."

I freeze, my thoughts stuttering to a halt. "What?"

His grip on me isn't tight, but it's enough to keep me stuck in place. Well, that and what he just said. I look at him and realize he's shifted closer to me.

"It's not like we haven't jerked off in the same room before."

"You're serious?" I ask, half-expecting him to make a joke and roll away from me, which wouldn't be like him at all, but it would help me process what's going on.

I mean, sure, we've jacked off in the same room before, but that was sophomore year of college when we didn't have the privacy of our own space in our dorm. But this is different. We're in bed together. Touching. Horny. *Probably from each other.* This feels immensely different from anything we've done in the past, and just the thought of it is building anticipation in me.

"Yeah, sure. It's just jerking off, Ry. Besides, you got to watch me last time in the shower, it's only fair."

I know he's teasing me now, the wink at the end proves it, which only makes it harder to tell if he's serious about letting me stroke myself while he's lying next to me...in the bed we're sharing indefinitely.

It shouldn't be a big deal, though, right? We've both jerked off countless times, and we're best friends. And I *did* watch him the other day. *Guess I wasn't as sneaky as I thought.*

The casual way he's saying this makes me feel like maybe this whole thing isn't such a big deal after all. But with how much I've been dissecting our friendship and my feelings for him lately, it feels like it is, at least to me.

Now that he's planted the seed, though, I can't stop thinking about jerking off next to him. Stroking my dick in front of him, knowing that he'll be watching and hearing every moan I make for real, not just for the mic. I want to see what happens when I touch myself in front of him. I want to know how he'll react, if the sound of me falling apart does anything to him, and if watching me come turns him on. The thought makes my stomach tighten and my cock twitches, begging for freedom because I do want this.

I swallow hard and force my gaze to meet his, offering a small nod in return. My body needs release, and even if I haven't admitted it out loud yet, I *do* want him. This feels like the best way to know if I'm alone in this…or if there's actually the potential for something more between us, and maybe it's worth bringing up.

Slowly, I slide my hand beneath the covers and into my boxer briefs. My fingers wrap around my erection, and I exhale sharply at how good it feels already.

"Not wasting any time, huh?" he teases in a lower-than-usual tone.

"Shut up," I groan, but there's no bite to it. My hand moves more confidently now, stroking myself under the fabric, the pressure making my hips twitch. A low moan slips out before I can stop it, and Logan shifts beside me.

"I can't let you have all the fun tonight," he says.

I glance over as he opens his bedside table and pulls out a small bottle of lube. He squeezes some into his palm and it sounds like the bottle's damn near empty, then he slips his hand down into his waistband and starts stroking himself.

I can't help but turn my head from the pillow to watch, and while I can't see him because he's still covered, his breath hitches just slightly when our eyes connect, and fuck does that turn me on.

"Can I have some?" I ask, the sound of the wet glide of him touching himself making my cock ache.

"Fuck, Ryder," he groans, and I know it's because I waited until after he got started to ask him to pass the bottle over, but the way my name falls from his lips still makes my balls tighten.

He reaches for the bottle, and like I suspected, it's empty. I barely get anything on my hand, and he turns to see.

"Shit, I don't have any more. I'll have to order another bottle tomorrow."

"Fuck," I groan, already dreading having to keep going without it. I bring my hand up to my mouth to spit, but he stops me with a quiet, breathy voice.

"You know, you could just steal some of mine."

I arch my eyebrow, glancing down toward his erection that's still hidden from my sight. *Does he want to, like, high-five me or something? What is he suggesting?*

"It doesn't have to be weird," he continues, eyes locked on mine. "Just stroke me a few times, get your hand slick. Or..." He swallows, his voice dropping even lower, breathier. "I can stroke you. With my lubed hand."

A groan slips out before I can stop it, heat rushing to my face. *Why the fuck does that sound like the best idea I've ever heard?*

Goddamn, this is a different side of Logan I've never seen before—and I can't even pretend I'm not into it. He stops moving his hand now, eyes locked on mine like he's willing me to say yes, and a big part of me wants to. This new part of me that's been stealing glances at my best friend and wondering about *more* for the first time in my life desperately wants me to lean over and wrap my hand around his dick. And I want him to do the same to me. I want to be the reason he's moaning. I want him to look at me the way he did in the shower.

But what if this moment of desire changes everything between us? What if I touch him and realize once will never be enough? What if it's just a one-time thing for him, and it makes me want him even more?

Fuck, what if he doesn't want me the way I want him?

In this moment, though, desire is winning over fear, and my fingers twitch, hesitant to reach out and feel him. His lips part slightly, and—for the first time in my life—I wonder what it would feel like to press my mouth to his. That's when I realize nothing is going to stop me from taking him up on his offer. Whatever's been simmering between us is about to boil over.

I need to do this. I need to find out what this is between us.

Before I can second-guess myself, I move. My hand finds its way into his boxer briefs, and my fingers wrap around his erection hesitantly at first, testing it out. But when I glide my hand toward his tip, his hips jerk into my grasp like he can't help it, a quiet moan slips from his lips—and fuck, that sound goes straight to my dick.

I stroke him again, more confidently now, watching the way his mouth parts and his eyes stay locked on me, like I'm doing something holy. He pushes his underwear down along with the blanket, freeing himself completely, and my eyes lock onto *his* cock that *I'm* stroking. He's thick, flushed, and leaking precum—and I want him. I want to see what else he'll do when I touch him like this.

Then he reaches for me. His hand tugs at my waistband, and I lift my hips without a word, letting him pull my boxer briefs down. Cool air grazes my skin, but then his warm, lubed-up hand wraps around me, and I forget how to breathe.

"Fuck," I whisper, my head dropping back against the pillows.

His grip is firm, rougher than I'm used to, but it's so fucking good. He knows how to touch me and it's like his hand was made to fit around my cock.

We start moving together, stroking each other, breaths shallow and messy between us. We're both still on our backs, side by side, but it feels like we've moved closer. Our heads both turned toward each other. Neither of us makes any indication to stop, completely ignoring the notion that this was just for lube. The way we're touching each other now—this is about want.

The sound of slick skin, quiet gasps, the tension that's been building between us finally breaking open—it's all too much, and not enough. We both shift slightly so we're even closer now, pressing together from ankle to shoulder, as we continue to stroke each other with fervor.

I can't help the moan that falls from my lips—and his echoes mine. I don't even know what's hotter: touching him or hearing him fall apart from just my hand.

His forehead drops to my shoulder, his breath hot against my collarbone. I instinctively tighten my grip around him, and the noise he lets out makes my stomach clench, but I don't want to come yet. I want to savor this moment for as long as I can stave off my orgasm.

"Fuck, Ryder. Oh, fuck," he moans, his voice rough and wrecked like he doesn't know what to do with any of this either. His teeth bite into my shoulder, and I let out the filthiest moan that's ever left my mouth.

But he doesn't stop.

Neither do I.

If I thought I was turned on earlier, it's nothing compared to this. Nothing compared to the fire racing through me now.

My brain's short-circuiting, caught somewhere between

how the hell is this real and *don't you dare stop.* Until very recently, I've always thought I was straight, and now I'm *positive* I'm not, and I'm positive one time with him will never be enough. *I need more.* The thought alone pulls a broken, needy sound from my throat I didn't know I was capable of making, and it rivals the sound I made when he bit my shoulder. Nothing has ever felt this good and he's just giving me a handjob. *I'm totally fucked.*

"Jesus, Ryder, you always sound like that?"

"Like what?" I manage to get out, my breath coming in short pants.

"Like you're about to fall apart. Like you're gonna come with my name on your lips."

My hips jerk involuntarily at his words, heat pooling low in my stomach. Between his words and the sounds he's making, I'm not going to last. The feeling is too overwhelming. The hottest thing I've ever experienced.

"Fuck, Logan. Yessss."

My voice breaks on the last word as his hand moves faster, matching the desperate rhythm I've set on him. The slick glide of our hands and the breathless noises spilling from both of us is overwhelming, and I can tell we're both close.

"Come," Logan urges, his voice rough and low in my ear. "Come, Ry. Come for me."

That's it, I'm done. His commanding tone pushes me over the edge, and I come hard, a moan ripping through my throat. My hips are jerking as hot pulses spill across Logan's hand, and he follows seconds later with a broken moan before I feel his release coat my hand.

That's so hot.

For a moment, we just lay there with our hands still wrapped around each other, covered in each other's release.

At some point, we shifted further onto our sides so we could face each other fully, and I realize our foreheads are touching. I didn't even notice how close we'd gotten, but now all I can think about is how our mouths are just inches apart. *What would it feel like to reach out and capture his lips between mine?* My heart hammers in my chest, and I can feel his racing just as fast, but instead of leaning forward, he drops his forehead to my shoulder, and I feel his hot breath against my skin.

His fingers flex like he wants to reach for more, but he's holding himself back, and I don't know what this means for us.

My body's still buzzing, nerves lit up from the inside out in a way I've never experienced before.

"Jesus Christ," he murmurs. "That was...fuck."

I let out a little laugh over him breaking the tension, but all I can say is, "Yeah. Same."

I finally release his softening dick and hope that's not the last time I'll ever touch him as I reach for the tissues on the nightstand. I hand a couple to Logan and clean myself off, too. His fingers brush against mine, and that tiny touch sends a jolt straight through me. We've touched a thousand times and it's never had that effect on me—at least, not at this level of intensity.

He wipes himself off and tosses the tissue toward the small trash bin beside the bed, then lies on his back and hums quietly to himself like he's still processing what just happened. When he finally shifts, it's onto his side, propping his head up on one hand as he looks at me, really looks at me.

"You okay?" he whispers.

"Yeah," I say quickly, and I can't help but smile thinking about what we just did. "Yeah, I'm more than okay."

It's the bare minimum of how I feel. I want to tell him everything—how that didn't feel weird or wrong. How it felt perfect. Right. Natural in a way nothing else ever has. How I'm one hundred percent sure I'm bisexual after that experience. But I don't say anything because the second I open my mouth, I know I'll spill more than I'm ready to say, and I still don't know what this means for us yet.

11

LOGAN

When I first woke up this morning, I was half convinced last night was a dream. A hot-as-sin, absolutely-no-business-being-that-good dream where my *straight* best friend and I jerked each other off, moaning each other's names, and he came when I told him to.

He came when I told him to!

I know I technically instigated it, but he wanted to come. I just told him he could do it in my bed beside me, and couldn't resist joining in. Then, I unintentionally ran out of lube and offered a helpful hand. Literally.

And he *accepted!*

I'll never recover from that. Mark it down as the best thing that's ever happened to me.

I know it wasn't a dream, though, because the way he looked at me when I touched him is burned into my brain. And god, the *sounds* he made. The real thing is nothing like the way he sounds for the mic—it's so much better. I'd give anything to hear him moan like that again. *For* me. *Because* of me.

I've had sex before with both men and women, but nothing has ever felt like this. *Because none of them had been Ryder*, my mind whispers, and I know it's true.

He's still asleep next to me, and I want to shake him awake and ask him to do it again. It felt so natural, like a completely normal extension of our already *probably* co-dependent relationship. But, instead, I roll onto my side, prop my head on my hand, and watch him sleep for a moment. His face is relaxed and his lips are slightly parted, and god, I want to run my fingers through his wavy brown hair. I've always said Ryder is hot—not to him, of course—but I've thought it. And right now, he looks so peaceful and perfect. I'm thankful he's asleep because I don't know if I could bite my tongue if he weren't. All the feelings I have for him would probably come tumbling out.

I don't know what this means for us. We crossed *the* line, the one I drew in the sand nearly a decade ago. The one that always reminded me: he's your best friend. Your *straight* best friend. That reminder has always protected me from heart-break and false hope because when I didn't allow myself to think about any possibility of *more*, it wasn't a problem.

I'd only ever seen Ryder as my best friend. *Or tried to, and it usually worked.*

But now? After last night? That line didn't just blur.

It snapped.

Is Ryder questioning his sexuality? Or was he just horny from work?

In my experience, straight guys don't look at you the way he looked at me last night. But I *know* Ryder, and this doesn't make sense for him. He's never even expressed interest in wanting to experiment with guys, despite his career really selling it. He's probably been exposed to every sexual experience two guys can have together, and *still*, nothing.

I don't know what comes next, and I don't know where to go from here.

But I don't want to go back to never touching his dick again.

I swallow hard, trying to ignore the way my chest tightens at the thought. Because yeah, last night had been incredible, but if he wakes up and freaks out—if he looks at me like I'm a mistake and what we did was some 'oh shit' moment he wishes he could erase...

I couldn't handle that.

The last thing I want is to be the reason Ryder starts questioning everything about himself...only to end up resenting me for it. Even if that doesn't seem like the Ryder I know.

My mind is ping-ponging through every possible scenario, and I can't get it to shut off. I keep telling myself not to spiral —to wait, to see, to not assume the worst just because I've spent the last ten years preparing for rejection if I ever let my feelings surface. I need to do something to occupy my mind rather than staying trapped in this thought spiral.

Slowly, I sit up and get out of bed. My chest feels tight with everything I want to ask, but I let him sleep. I throw on a T-shirt and head for the kitchen, needing coffee and something to do with my hands while my brain eats itself alive with worst-case scenarios.

While I wait for the coffee to brew, I can't help but glance over my shoulder every thirty seconds, half expecting him to walk out of the bedroom fully dressed with his packed bag in hand, ready to bolt, but he doesn't. And when he finally makes his way into the kitchen, he's wearing nothing but his boxer briefs and *my* T-shirt as he reaches for a mug that says,

'*When life gives you curves, flaunt them.*' He chuckles to himself as he fills it, and I grip my mug a little tighter, awaiting what's going to happen.

He seems like his usual self, and when he finishes doctoring his coffee, he turns around and smiles at me like nothing's changed. He looks so good standing there with his bedhead and a crease from the pillow against his left cheek that I desperately want to smooth out.

"Morning," he says casually.

I stare at him for a second before speaking. "Morning, how're you feeling today?"

His eyes flick to mine, and something unreadable flashes across his face before he lets out a soft chuckle. "Good," he says.

Good? That's it? That's all he has to say? He's gotta be fucking with me. Usually, his laid-back attitude helps me relax, but right now it's like he's throwing a match on my already anxious thoughts just to watch them explode. My face must give away my internal thoughts because he laughs again before opening his mouth.

"If you're asking about last night," he says, tilting his mug toward me, "I've got a better question: why the hell haven't we done that before?"

My face immediately burns at that question, because of all the things I thought would come out of his mouth this morning, that one *never* crossed my mind.

But this has to mean he doesn't regret it, right? I can't help the slow, genuine smile that spreads across my face. "Guess we've been holding out on each other, huh?"

He grins back, and the tension in my chest loosens enough to let me breathe again. Maybe, just maybe, this means last night doesn't have to be a one-time thing. Maybe we're not standing on opposite sides of a divide we can't come back from.

"Seriously, though," Ryder starts, voice a little softer now. "That was—"

"Hot?" I interrupt, surprising even myself with how fast the word comes out.

He nods, without a second of hesitation. "Yeah, that." Now his grin matches mine, and we're just smiling at each other like fools.

He's not being weird about it, he doesn't seem to regret it, and he's acknowledging it. Maybe he is figuring things out and questioning his sexuality, even if he's not ready to say that out loud. And I get that. Talking about sex can be easier than talking about your sexuality, especially when it's so new. And that's a question I'm not going to ask. I don't want to make him feel pressured to label himself, especially if he's unsure. He knows if he wants to talk about it, I'm here.

Ryder tilts his head, still watching me over the rim of his mug. "You're thinking too hard," he calls me out. "You do that when you're trying not to say something."

The truth is sitting on the tip of my tongue—*I'm thinking about you, about last night, about how fucking good it felt, about wanting to do it again*—but I'm not ready to say that out loud yet, just in case. I don't want to tell him I want more —no, that I want everything—when I don't know how he feels about what we did, himself, or us. Realistically, he's probably still seeing how he feels about being with me, and I don't want to make him feel pressured to say more than he's ready for, especially since we're in such a high-stress situation.

Instead, I scoff, because of course he notices. "Yeah, well, maybe I'm still catching up," I admit, setting my mug down.

"This isn't exactly what I pictured waking up to this morning."

He smirks. "What, me standing here in your shirt?" He gestures vaguely to himself. "Or the part where we jerked each other off and I admitted I liked it?"

My breath catches. Because—*fuck*. Hearing him say that out loud so easily sends a rush of heat through me.

I swallow hard. "Both."

Ryder's smirk widens into a full grin, like he's enjoying watching me flounder. But my chest loosens at his admission, just enough to let hope seep in. I didn't realize how much I needed to hear him tell me he *did* enjoy it. That it wasn't the vulnerability of the situation we're in messing with his head or making him say or do something he didn't mean.

"You know, I'm just gonna throw this out there," he says, a teasing edge to his voice. "I'd love to do it again."

I nod, trying to commit every word of this conversation to memory because my *straight*-but-probably-questioning best friend said he wanted to jerk each other off again. *I can't believe this is real.*

"Me too, Ry. When I first woke up, I was half convinced it was a dream," I tell him. "I just wish the timing was different."

His brows furrow slightly, and I'm already kicking myself for saying that.

"What do you mean?" he asks when I don't immediately continue.

I exhale, running a hand through my hair. *Why did I have to open my mouth?* "I mean...I just wish we didn't have all this other shit hanging over our heads."

His jaw tenses, and it's like I pulled him out of his morning-after, post-first-time-with-a-guy bliss and dropped him right back into the reality we're facing.

"The emails."

I nod. "Yeah. I'm sorry for bringing it up, I just...there was this little voice in my head saying maybe you only went along with last night because you've been so stressed about everything."

Ryder doesn't hesitate. "No. That's not it at all." His voice is confident. "I wanted it, Logan. Not because of what's going on, because of *you*."

Did he just...?

A breath *wooshes* out of me in a big exhale, and I stare at him for a long second. He wanted it. He wanted *me*. I've spent years, every one since meeting him, trying to kill that desire for him. Telling myself repeatedly he's straight and we're *just* friends, because that's all we've ever been. And now, he's standing in front of me saying the words I've always dreamed of hearing.

I blink a few times, trying to make sure I'm not imagining it. "So...wait. You actually, like, you're into me?" I ask, stumbling over the words.

Ryder huffs out a soft laugh, but he looks a bit nervous as he responds. "Yeah. I don't know what that makes me. Bi, probably. I just know that I liked it a lot, and I'm serious about wanting to do it again."

My chest feels like it's going to explode with something that feels a lot like joy, and I know I'm not hiding how happy hearing that makes me. He said it. *Out loud.* And not in a moment of panic or confusion, but with honest certainty that makes me want to run over and kiss him.

He's telling me he's choosing *me*, and I need to let that matter more than the fear. I need to believe the words coming out of his mouth, not what my mind is saying to continue to protect me.

He's telling me he's probably bisexual, that *he likes me.*

I trained myself to avoid living in a world of what-ifs and convinced myself it was safer and smarter not to hope. And now he's just handing me everything I've always been too scared to imagine on a silver platter.

It's almost too much to take in.

"Thank you for telling me," I say, and his eyes meet mine. I close the distance between us to take his hand in mine. "Whatever label you do or don't want, it's yours. You don't owe anyone an explanation. Not even me, but I'm so glad you felt comfortable telling me."

He nods, and a smile spreads across his face that's so full of warmth and relief it overwhelms me. We stand like that for a few seconds, just holding each other's gaze, and it feels like something new is starting between us.

"Feels nice to talk about something exciting that isn't…all of that for a second," he says softly, eyes dropping to the floor.

"I know," I say, giving his hand a squeeze. "But, we still have to talk about it at some point. We can't pretend the last one didn't exist," I add gently.

"Yeah. I know," he sighs, dropping my hand, and I immediately miss the feeling.

"Do you want to talk about this now or wait until later?"

"Now. It'll be on my mind all day if we put it off," he says.

I nod, completely understanding. I haven't wanted to push him since the last email shook him so badly, and he hasn't been in the best headspace, but now that he's bringing it up, I think it's time.

"We should probably talk about who it could be. Get a list down. Aren't stalkers typically someone you know? Maybe we could narrow it down that way."

Ryder nods and sets his mug down. "Yeah. The last message made it pretty clear they think they know me. Like, really know me. But that's not exactly hard to say either, since I have public social media accounts and my voice is on a ton of audiobooks. They knew *exactly* when we left my house to come here, though, and that creeps me out. No way that email was a coincidence like I told myself the others were."

My stomach tightens. I hate that he has to deal with this at all. That just doing his job means someone out there can latch onto him like this and become obsessed enough to track him down.

"Anyone come to mind?" I ask. "An ex who's reached out lately? Someone you broke things off with or ghosted who might've taken it personally?"

The questions about his dating history leave my mouth before I can stop them. While they're meant to be helpful, I also can't help but wonder. The thought of Ryder dating anyone recently makes my stomach clench, especially since he just admitted he was into *me*. Still, I know I have no right to feel jealous over hypothetical dates, especially when those very things could be putting him in real danger.

Ryder huffs out a breath. "You know I don't date much. I've told you about every date or hookup I've ever had, and the last one was probably six months ago or so. All I do is work and spend time with you."

Fair point. He's never been the guy to chase relationships. He's had girlfriends here and there, but they were all mostly short, casual flings. Nothing that's truly stuck.

Now that I'm saying that, I realize he's *always* stayed with me. For a decade, he's been by my side. *That has to mean something.*

"No one else comes to mind either," he says, breaking through my thoughts. "It doesn't seem like someone who's given me weird looks about my career choice, since the person emailing seems to be a *big* fan of my work. I have a gut feeling it wouldn't be anyone from the industry, and my neighbors keep to themselves. Sure, there's that one kid always sneaking out, but I don't think I'm on that family's radar. It's not like I'm an accomplice or anything—he just occasionally creeps through my bushes."

I blink. "What?"

Ryder waves it off. "It's not important, just a neighbor kid probably going to parties. What about you?"

"There's one person," I say honestly. "Someone who's been popping up a lot lately. Everywhere we go, he seems to be there too."

Ryder's eyes meet mine, and he nods. "Ah, you're right. Kyle."

"Yeah," I nod. "Kyle. Something about him has felt off since the first time we met. He's seemed invested in *you* since the beginning, and he couldn't care less about me. Not that I'm complaining; I don't want his attention. But he acts like I'm in the way, which pretty much aligns with what the last email said." I shake my head, hoping I don't sound paranoid. "It just…it doesn't sit right with me. And he's here."

Ryder looks away for a second, and I can see the wheels turning in his head.

"You're right," he agrees. "Shit, Logan. I feel like it's gotta be him. But what do we even do with this speculation?"

"I don't know," I admit. "We need to figure out how to get proof it's him, I guess."

He runs a hand through his already messy hair, then nods slowly. "Alright. Should we maybe go to the bar Friday night, like usual? See if anything feels off? Or is that too risky?"

Maybe showing up will push him to do something we can use as evidence against him. We've locked ourselves in my apartment for days, and while the idea of walking into the bar where we know we'll likely come face to face with him doesn't sound like my idea of a good time, it still feels like our best option. Besides, it's *our* spot, not his. We'll be surrounded by people we trust, and that alone makes it feel less risky. "It's probably not the worst idea," I say.

Ryder seems to think it over for a moment before nodding. "Okay, let's do it," he says, sounding more determined now, even if I can tell he's still a little nervous, and I don't blame him. Kyle's a big guy, and he's pretty intimidating on his own. Add in that stare of his, and it's like he's sizing you up like prey. It's unnerving.

"In the meantime, though, there's gotta be more we can do," I add, almost to myself. My mind is already sifting through possibilities. We've got nothing but suspicion and a pile of anxiety, and the cops aren't going to do anything until it's too late. We could call them and give them Kyle's name, but again, there won't be anything they can do, especially because we don't even know his last name.

"Matt," I say, the name dropping out of my mouth like a light bulb flicking on. "Matt from work. He's our IT guy, and he loves this kind of stuff. He's always watching those murder documentaries and listening to true crime podcasts. He might be able to pull something from the emails like an IP address or a metadata tag or whatever."

Ryder raises a brow. "You think he'd help?"

"He owes me a favor. And honestly? He'd probably be

excited to dig into this. If there's anything in those emails we missed, he'll find it."

Ryder hesitates. "You sure we should pull someone else into this?"

"I trust him," I say simply. "And we need another set of eyes. This guy's targeting you—or us. If we want the police to take this seriously, we've gotta bring them proof and that means taking this into our own hands."

Ryder nods, slowly but surely. "If you trust him, I'm in."

It's not a fix by any means, but it feels like *something*.

"I'll call him," I say. "And in the meantime, we keep doing what we've been doing. Don't go anywhere alone. And promise me, if you get another email, I want to know the second it hits your inbox."

Ryder's lips curl into a smile. "I can't wait to continue to be stuck to you."

And fuck, that does something to me.

Because no matter how bad this gets—and I have a feeling we haven't seen the worst of it yet—there's no reality where I'm not by his side.

12

RYDER

Despite the small moment of relief when Logan told me his coworker was willing to help us this morning, it all vanishes with another goddamn email. This guy has some seriously fucked up timing.

Every time I hear my email notification go off, it feels like a trigger. I try to tell myself that it's anything but another message from the one person who's seemingly deriving pleasure from ruining my life, but as soon as I see the sender's name, my stomach drops.

Subject: *You're not listening.*

I didn't want to be upset with you, Ryder. I really didn't, but you keep ignoring me. Pretending I'm not here. Pretending he matters more. I've been nothing but patient. Why don't you realize he's holding you back? You know you're meant to be with me. So why won't you admit it?

Bile rises in my throat, and it feels like a punch straight to the gut. Whoever this is genuinely believes they're good for me. That Logan is the one standing in the way of our supposed happiness. How do they not see how deranged this is? How could they possibly believe this invasive approach would work? That threatening Logan would somehow make me want them?

If this is their idea of a romantic gesture, I don't even want to know what they think *disturbing* looks like. There's no universe where this is ever okay. No sane person would be interested in someone who stalks them, who invades their privacy, and then acts like they deserve a reward for it—and in this case, it feels like they think *I'm* the reward.

They've wedged themselves into my life and made me feel like I'm constantly being watched, and they think I should be grateful? That I'd respond to their email with a 'yes, come save me' plea and a trail of exclamation points?

It's fucking delusional.

Logan is everything to me, and somehow, this stalker is the only one who doesn't know it.

"Logan," I call out.

"Yeah?" he asks, coming over and sitting next to me on the couch.

I turn my laptop toward him, the email still open on the screen.

He grabs it, and his eyes narrow as he reads the email. "What the actual fuck?" he whispers, almost to himself. "They're trying to make it sound like *they* care about you? And I don't? What kind of twisted shit is this?"

I shake my head because I don't even know what to say. I don't understand their game here. "It feels like they really believe there's something between us, and you're somehow in the way of that. I don't know."

Logan clenches his jaw so tight I'm worried he's going to crack a tooth.

"That's fucking crazy," he hisses. "They're acting like I'm holding you fucking captive or something."

I don't respond yet, giving him time to process this and be angry. His rage is keeping him steady and giving him something to hold onto, while I feel like I'm barely staying afloat. I need him to be the one who holds it together.

"Fuck them, Ry," he says as his face burns a deeper shade of red. "How can you admit something when there's nothing to admit? I don't understand what the fuck they think is going on, but it's clearly a one-sided delusion on their end, and your lack of response should make them see that."

I nod, but it doesn't help because it feels like they won't stop. I crawl into Logan's lap and bury my head into his shoulder for comfort. His arms wrap around me immediately, and he rubs slow circles over my back.

"You don't have to be okay right now, Ry," I hear him whisper in my ear before he turns and kisses the side of my head.

"What if they don't stop?" I whisper, voicing my biggest fear, even if the words barely make it out. "What if it gets worse?"

"I don't know," he admits. "I wish I did, but I don't and fuck, do I hate this, Ry. I'm so fucking sorry you're going through this." He pulls back from me a little until I'm able to look him in the eye. He cups my face with trembling hands and rubs his thumbs over my cheeks. "I'd do anything to make this stop," he says with a broken look on his face, and I know it physically hurts him to see me like this.

"I know you would," I murmur. And I do know. I know he'd burn the whole world down if it meant keeping me safe.

If there was a way to erase every email, every invasion of our privacy, every fucked-up feeling crawling under my skin, and guarantee I'd never get another email from this person again, he'd do it in a heartbeat and I wouldn't even need to ask.

But this isn't a movie, and we don't have high-profile connections or a secret skillset we can tap into to take Kyle, or whoever this is, out. We're just two regular guys who are trying to navigate this terrifying situation to the best of our ability.

He leans forward and presses a kiss to my forehead before pulling me back into his arms. We stay like that for a long while until I finally roll off his lap to get some water.

Logan stands too. "I'm going to forward myself the email, and then I'm gonna call Matt. You okay for a minute while I do that?" he checks, and I nod.

As soon as he walks away, I'm hit with regret once again. I feel guilty for dragging him into this situation. He doesn't deserve to be treated like some obstacle instead of the one person who makes me feel safe. He shouldn't have to live looking over his shoulder because some anonymous asshole decided I belong to him when I don't. It's not fair to me, but it's definitely not fair to him. I should be the one protecting him right now, not the other way around.

My throat tightens as I think about everything Logan has done for me since this whole situation started. He's cared for me, distracted me, and let me fall apart when I couldn't hold it together anymore—and he's done all of it with so much compassion.

And last night…fuck.

I swallow hard, dragging a hand through my hair.

Last night wasn't a heat-of-the-moment 'I need to get off' experiment with him. It was *everything*. It confirmed every thought I've been having about him and my sexuality. Running out of lube was the push we needed—I don't know how we would've taken that step without that.

I feel like I'm turning into a character in one of the books I narrate—the guy who has a bi-awakening with his best friend. And honestly? I'm not mad about it at all. I want more.

Logan walks back into the room, his hair somehow even messier than before, but just as sexy. "Matt's looking into it," he says, dropping onto the couch beside me. "He's gonna see if he can track the IP address. Might take a couple of days."

I nod, trying to focus on his words, not the way his leg brushes against mine. "That's...good. Yeah, good. Thanks."

He looks at me suspiciously for a moment, and I feel like I'm giving myself away. "You okay? You're looking kinda flushed."

"Yep. Fine," I say a little too quickly.

He gives me a look like he doesn't buy it, but he also lets it go, and I appreciate that, because I still don't have the words to explain what's going through my mind. "Alright. Let me know if you need anything, yeah?"

How the hell am I supposed to explain what I'm feeling? That after a decade of friendship—and a lifetime of thinking I was straight—I suddenly can't stop thinking about him. About his hands on me. About how good it felt. I told him I'm likely bi this morning, but I didn't say the rest. Didn't tell him I've been thinking about him constantly.

I nod instead of opening my mouth, because what I really need is for him to touch my dick again. But I can't say that, and he doesn't touch me. Well, not in the way I want. Every time our arms graze or his thigh bumps mine, it sparks something low in my gut—something I don't want to stop. At this point, I'm half tempted to duct tape his hands to me.

I feel like I'm turning into a creeper myself because I can't stop admiring him. Can't stop looking at his stunning blue eyes and his even more ridiculous blonde hair that I now imagine tugging as I kiss him senseless.

He shifts slightly, leaning forward to toss his phone on the table, then leans back just enough that his shirt rides up to reveal a trail of hair that disappears into his waistband. And fuck, how have I never noticed how hot that is before?

"You wanna watch something? Or, I don't know, play a game?"

I blink, pulling myself out of whatever trance I was in, and stall for a second. "Uh, yeah. Sure. Whatever you want."

He raises an eyebrow. "That's not like you. Normally, you have opinions about everything."

I shrug, hyper-aware of how close we're sitting and still wanting him closer. "Guess I've got a lot on my mind."

"Alright," he says, his expression softening into something warmer. "You've been through a lot. Don't beat yourself up for feeling out of it. I'm happy to make the decisions for us if you want."

I nod, it's the exact thing I needed to hear. Well, almost. What I needed was for him to say, "Take out your cock and let me take care of you."

I know, I know. He touched my dick once and I've turned into the neediest, most desperate version of myself to ever exist, and I'm not even sorry. I can't find it in me to feel bad at all.

He lands on a sitcom rerun, the kind with horribly annoying canned laughter and bad jokes, and I try to let it pull me out of my head. Yet as the minutes tick by, my focus keeps slipping back to Logan. He's a magnet now, *my* magnet. I've always wanted to be around him, but this feels different. I've never felt this drawn to someone before. I didn't know this type of connection or level of desire was possible.

Even when I saw him jerking off in the shower, it was more so curiosity. But knowing what his hands felt like on me changed something in me. He must have some magic touch because it's all I can think about. It's all I *want* to think about.

I don't even realize I'm blatantly staring at him until he catches me. "What?" he asks, lips quirking into a grin.

"Nothing," I say too fast, looking away as my cheeks heat up.

"Sure," he says easily. Then he shifts closer, his tone softer. "Come here. Let me hold you, Ry."

About damn time.

I scoot closer without hesitation, turning to face him instead of the TV. His arms wrap around me, and I melt into him. I didn't even know how much I needed this until I had it.

"There," he murmurs against my ear. "That's better."

I exhale a shaky breath, my head tucked beneath his chin. His fingers start tracing slow, soothing circles on my lower back, and I feel myself finally letting go of all the weight I've been holding.

13

LOGAN

It's finally Friday, and even though it hasn't been a whole week since we last stepped outside the apartment, it feels like the walls are closing in. Not because of Ryder—being with him feels easy—but because I'm not built to sit still and wait. Especially not when we're being stalked by someone who isn't planning to stop.

We've already decided to go to Pine Bar tonight to see if Kyle shows and if our theory holds up, though I'd bet almost anything it will.

If he is the one behind the emails, I doubt he'll be able to resist showing up, hoping for some interaction with Ryder. Guys like him don't like to be ignored. They want a reaction.

Even the thought of him talking to Ryder makes my blood boil, but he still wants to do this, so we can only hope it'll give us something to prove it's him.

Matt's still working on it, and we sent the latest message to the cops too, like we've done with all the others, and got the same halfhearted response: "Thanks for keeping us updated. We'll have our cyber consultant look into it."

So helpful.

Either Kyle—or whoever this is—is a master at email encryptions, or the police aren't taking this seriously enough to dig into it.

The most I feel I can do, besides calling Matt and the police, is to stay close to Ryder and try to keep him grounded. But none of it's enough.

He hasn't complained about being in the apartment yet or how long anything is taking, but I know the cabin fever's getting to him, too. We've been living in artificial light with the blinds sealed shut and food delivery all week. We finally ordered groceries last night, though, and, as promised, lube. I'm grateful for the door peephole and the 'no contact' option to have your delivery driver leave the food at your door.

While we haven't jerked off together again—or jerked *each other* off—since the other night, I still want to be prepared, just in case. Ryder did seem eager to do it again, but I'm not going to pressure him, and he hasn't initiated. I want him to be the one to make a move because I never want him to feel like I'm taking advantage of the situation we're in or his emotional state. I also want to make sure it's what he wants after he's had more time to process.

But first, we need to go to the bar, and I really do need to talk to Mia. It's strange being close with people at their workplace, but still not having their phone number. I know I could've messaged her online, but I decided it'd be better to ask her in person about Kyle. See if he's ever asked about Ryder or said anything alarming. She's always been observant, so if anyone picks up on something, it'll be her.

We get in the car to drive to the bar, and we're there in no time. I pull up to the neon glow of Pine Bar's sign right by the door before turning to look at Ryder.

"You good?" I ask, grabbing his hand to give it a quick squeeze.

"Not even a little," he admits. "But I'm ready."

"Alright, remember, don't leave me," I say, cutting the engine. "Not even to go to the bathroom."

He laughs, low and suggestive. "Bathroom together from now on? I think I can get on board with that."

I laugh at that and let go of his hand to get out of the car. When we walk in, I scan the room but don't see Kyle yet. Although he's had a habit of coming in after us the last few weeks.

Mia lights up when she sees us. "Hey guys," she greets, starting to pour our beers.

I lean in a little closer, keeping my tone casual. "Hey, quick question. That new guy that's been coming here, leather jacket, big dude, name's Kyle. You know who I'm talking about?"

She raises a brow. "Kyle? Yeah. He gets a whiskey neat."

"Has he ever asked about Ryder?"

Her face shifts into something more cautious. "Uh, yeah, he did. He asked who he was the first time he saw him, and if the two of you were dating. Why?"

I shrug, trying to play it off. "Just wondering. Guy gives me weird vibes."

Mia leans in slightly closer. "You and me both."

That confirms that my gut hasn't been wrong. I nod my thanks and hand Ryder his beer that Mia set on the counter in front of me as we walk over to our usual table. We sit and wait to see if he shows up, and not even ten minutes later, he does.

"Logan," Ryder mutters with an edge to his tone, eyes locking on something behind me. "He just walked in."

I glance toward the door and see Kyle walk in and head straight to the bar. He waits a few minutes for Mia to pour his drink, exchanges a few words with her, and then, like I knew he would, he turns and scans the room, stopping dead when he sees us. He pauses briefly, then makes his way toward us.

"I can do all the talking again," I murmur to Ryder, and he gives a small nod.

Kyle walks over, wearing that same worn-in leather jacket, a pair of dark jeans, and black boots. He's got a smug grin on his face that's been rubbing me wrong since day one, and his eyes land on Ryder, as predicted. "Well, look who it is," he says conversationally. "Didn't think I'd run into you guys tonight."

"Why not? You've seen us here the last couple of Fridays." I state, once again, completely uncaring if I come off as rude.

Kyle chuckles, and the sound scrapes through my ears like nails on a chalkboard. But I don't let him get another word in. "Or is it because Ryder told you he's not interested in you, and yet, you keep showing up?"

That makes Kyle's smirk drop, and it's replaced with a death glare if I've ever seen one. Ryder lifts his beer to take a sip, and the movement catches Kyle's eye, and he shifts his attention to him now.

"Rough week?"

Before Ryder can answer, I step in once again, knowing how much it's pissing Kyle off to not get a chance to speak to Ryder himself. "No, we've been fine all week. Though it *has* been weird. Someone's been sending Ryder these strange emails. Supposedly a fan. But way too personal, you know?" I pause, then ask the question I've been sitting on. "You an audiobook guy, Kyle?"

As far as Kyle knows, Ryder isn't a narrator because we've never discussed our jobs—only that Kyle's here for construction. So, unless he *is* stalking him or interested enough to find his socials, he wouldn't know what Ry does for work.

"Sure, I've listened to a few," Kyle says, but I don't buy it. *Unless the few are Ryder's and Ryder's only.*

I raise an eyebrow. "Any favorites?"

He pauses, then says, "Nothing specific. Whatever pops up."

Don't buy that either.

"Interesting," I say slowly. "You ever recognize narrators by voice? Or gravitate to specific ones? Some people can't stand it if the voice is off. But when it's good, it sticks with you."

That gets me a look. Kyle shifts slightly, his smile tightening. "Doesn't mean I'm not a fan of a good voice."

His eyes land on Ryder and linger there long enough to make my skin crawl. He's got to realize we're on to him, but maybe he doesn't care. Maybe he wants us to know, especially since he made it known he was close enough to be watching in the first place. I hold the silence, waiting to see if he slips.

"Well," he says, gaze sliding back to Ryder like I'm invisible, "Good seeing you again. I hope we get a chance to talk more soon. Just the two of us. There's so much I'd love to say."

And like all the other conversations we've had with him, he walks away, and I can't help myself. "I'll be right back," I say to Ryder.

"What?"

"Just stay here."

I follow Kyle and grab his arm as he's walking away. He stops and spins to face me, yanking out of my grip.

"Listen, Kyle. Leave Ryder the fuck alone. I don't know what game you're playing, but he's not interested. He's made that perfectly clear," I seethe, keeping my voice low even as it trembles with barely-contained restraint.

He smirks, unbothered, then says something that makes my blood run cold.

"We'll see."

14

RYDER

All I want to do is shower off the night and bleach my memory of Kyle. His presence clings to me like a bad taste I can't spit out. Especially since I know we're right about it being Kyle. The more I replay everything in my head, the more unsettled I feel because it makes sense.

The first time I saw Kyle, he was sitting at the bar, already watching me. When our eyes met, he didn't even pretend to look away. He held my gaze like he wanted me to know he was looking. Then, every interaction we've had since then, he's been hyper-focused on *me*. And he's definitely not a fan of Logan. I don't believe he hasn't listened to the books I narrate, I just don't.

"I think I'm gonna shower," I tell Logan. "Try to clear my head."

He nods, and I make my way down the hall to the bathroom. While the water warms up, I undress and catch a quick look in the mirror—my beard's getting a little long, so I give it a quick trim before getting in the shower.

The second the hot water hits my skin, I feel the tiniest bit of relief. My body's been tense for hours. Kyle knew we'd be at the bar tonight, I'm sure of it. There's no way it was a coincidence. And the emails feel too personal, between the timing, the context, and the obsession disguised as affection. *It's got to be him.*

A shudder runs through me. I reach for the soap and lather up quickly, scrubbing harder than necessary, trying to wash off the sick feeling lodged in my chest. This whole thing is draining the life out of me. I'm exhausted from pretending I'm fine, even though Logan's never once asked me to be. If anything, he's given me complete permission to fall apart, and reassured me he'll be strong for both of us. He's been so fucking good through all of this. I don't know what I'd do without him. Hell, I should take him on a vacation when this is over. Somewhere warm. Mexico, probably, so we can lie on the beach and forget any of this ever happened.

By the time I step out of the shower and wrap a towel around my waist, I feel marginally better. I pull on some clean clothes, run a hand through my wet hair, and head back out to the living room, wanting to be close to Logan.

He's on the couch, watching me as I walk in. "Feel better?" he asks.

I nod. "Sort of."

"Good," he says, shifting to make room for me next to him on the couch, but I don't want space. I want to be on top of him, wrapped up in him. With everything that's going on, the dynamic between us has flipped. I'm needier than Logan ever was, but I don't care, and he's never once complained.

I don't take the space he made for me, and instead, I plop down on his lap. All I want are his hands on me, making everything else disappear. His touch seems to rewire my brain and leaves no room for fear, or noise, or doubt—only desire.

It's not just about escape, though. It's about him. The way I haven't been able to stop thinking about him. The way being near him isn't enough anymore because his touch feels essential. I need it as much as I need my next breath, and I need him to know how much.

"Logan," I whisper.

He turns to me instantly. "Yeah?"

I hesitate, unsure of what to say and how to bring this up, despite our conversation in the kitchen the other morning.

"The other night..." My voice catches as I trail off.

But Logan doesn't rush me. He simply waits for me to collect my thoughts, like he knows exactly where this is headed. As much as I appreciate what he's doing, I also want him to take the lead the way he's been doing with everything else lately.

Heat crawls up my neck and onto my face as I drag a hand through my damp hair, feeling like my whole body's vibrating with nerves. I don't think Logan would reject me, but still, I've never *asked* him to touch me before. This feels like a huge step. "Yeah. Uh...do you think..." I swallow, pulse hammering in my ears. "Do you think we could do that again? Like now."

He smiles at me with so much affection in his eyes, it's overwhelming.

"If you want to," he says. "Yeah. I want to."

I nod because my mouth won't work anymore.

He closes the distance between us and takes my hand. The gesture is so simple, but it makes my heart race. "Alright," he murmurs. "Come on. Let's go to bed."

I let him pull me down the hall toward his room with our fingers laced. The air is filled with so much tension, so many nerves. When we crawl into bed beside each other, it's like I suddenly forget how to exist. My limbs feel stiff, and I have no idea what to do. *Do I strip? Do I wait for him to make a move? Do I shove my hand down his pants?* The first time felt so natural, and now I feel like I'm a stumbling teenager trying to hook up with someone for the first time.

Logan turns to face me in bed and strokes my arm. "You sure you want this?"

My heart is racing as I respond. "Yeah," I whisper. "I do, I just…I don't know what to do." I let out a nervous laugh, hoping he doesn't take the semi-distraught look on my face for anything more than nerves about initiating. "I want this—want you," I clarify.

I'm not desperate the way I was last time, but the need for him is still there. I replay the way Logan sounded—the low groans, the way he said my name—and my cock starts to perk up. His moans were the sexiest thing I've ever heard, and I want to be the reason he makes those sounds again.

Logan grabs the new bottle of lube from the bedside table and pushes his pants down, kicking them off his feet. His semi-hard cock springs free and he squirts some lube in his palm and starts stroking himself slowly in front of me. My eyes are locked on the movement, watching every little twist of his wrist.

"Touch yourself," Logan's commanding, gravely voice instructs, and fuck, I obey.

Logan lets out a muffled groan that shoots straight through me, and some of my nerves begin to fade. Heat pools low in my stomach, and I mimic his earlier movements—stripping off my pants and slicking myself up with lube. I let out a shaky breath as I stroke myself.

"Ryder," Logan says, his voice low and rough.

"Yeah?"

"You're so quiet tonight. You sure you're good?"

"Yeah…need a little more to get into it tonight, that's all." I don't know how else to explain it—that I'm waiting for his moans to hit me like they did last time, so I can get lost in him.

Logan groans again, the sound quiet but deep, and his hand moves faster now. "Anything I can do?" he asks.

"I want to hear you moan," I say, completely shameless in my desires. "Then I want you to touch me."

Logan's whole body tenses, and he lets out a sharp, guttural sound. "Oh fuck," he groans. "Fuck, Ryder. That's the hottest thing I've ever heard."

I turn my head to look at him, owning what I just said. His lips are parted now, and his eyes meet mine. We're so close again. As close as last time, lying side by side with our heads on the pillows. God, he looks good. *Has he always looked this good? How the hell did he go from my best friend to this? To the only person I desire?*

"Keep going," Logan says, his voice low and commanding. "Keep touching your cock, Ry. Grab my wrist when you want me to touch you."

I want it now, so I grab his hand instantly and guide it to my cock, and the second his fingers wrap around me, he loses it. The moan he lets out at my cock in his hand makes me gasp and reach for him in return, my hand sliding around his cock like it belongs there. My strokes pick up, breath coming fast and shallow, my whole body trembling under the ever-building pressure.

"Oh, fuck." The words slip from my lips like I don't even have control of them.

"Feels good, doesn't it?" Logan asks, all breathy.

"Yes. Fuck, yes—it feels so good. I'm obsessed with your hands on me."

His groans mix with mine, low and needy, and for a second, it feels like the rest of the world disappears. It's just him and me and the sound of my name falling from his lips over and over—it's overwhelming in the best possible way.

"I want to try something," he says. "Can I?"

I don't even care what it is—I want it. *I want him.* So I pant out a desperate, "Yes."

He lets go of me, and I immediately whimper at the loss of contact.

"I got you, Ry. Sit up," he instructs, and I do.

I move, pressing my back against the headboard, my heart beating erratically with anticipation. He straddles my lap, facing me so closely, bare skin pressed against mine, our velvety straining cocks brushing together, and it sends a bolt of heat straight through me. He's heavy in a way that's impossible to ignore, and I'm really into it. His weight feels grounding. He's all muscle and warmth and hard edges, it's like being fully surrounded by him in a way I've never felt with any of my previous partners.

Before I can fully register what's happening, his hand wraps around both of us, and he starts stroking.

Oh fuck.

I've read about frotting before—hell, I've narrated scenes like this, described it in explicit detail. I thought I understood the pleasure, thought I'd read these moments enough to know exactly what it'd feel like. But nothing compares to the real thing. Nothing even touches it. This is so much better than anything I could've imagined.

This must be what Logan meant when he teased me about

missing out on essential research by never hooking up with a man before.

His silky cock drags against mine in the best way and his breath hitches when I rock my hips up to meet his rhythm. It's all so much, and yet, not close to enough. His grip on us is perfect; it's steady and firm, and I never want him to stop touching me.

Every time he groans, it drives me closer and closer to the edge. I want more. Need more. But I never want this to end.

He leans forward to press his forehead to mine. His breath ghosts my lips, and once again, I think about leaning forward and kissing him while his hand is wrapped around our leaking cocks.

"You're fucking beautiful like this, Ry," he praises. The words shoot through me, but not as much as when he leans in, lips brushing against my ear as he whispers, "Come for me, Ry. Cover our cocks in your cum." Before giving my ear a wet, teasing lick, I can't stop my mind from imagining what else his mouth can do.

He's so filthy when he's telling me exactly what he wants from me, and I break on his command. I groan as the tension snaps and I come all over his hand and cock, *just like he told me too.* He curses under his breath, still fucking up into his fist, chasing his own release. And fuck, he's loud as he follows me over the edge. *Just the way I like him.* His dick jerks against mine, his release coating my skin.

For a moment, neither of us moves. The only sound in the room is our ragged breathing trying to come back to normal as we stare into each other's eyes.

Logan is still straddling my thighs when he lets go of our cocks. Then, without a word, he lifts his hand to his mouth.

The one that had just been wrapped around us, stroking our cocks.

The one that's still coated in cum.

Our cum.

And without breaking eye contact, he licks the cum off his fingers—and my jaw drops.

It's another thing I've read a hundred times, but watching him do it? Seeing his tongue drag slowly over his knuckles with *my* cum on them?

Something inside me snaps, and the sound that leaves me doesn't even sound human.

"Jesus Christ," I choke out, my whole body tensing again. "Fuck, Logan. Fuccckkkk. That's so sexy. Why is that so hot?"

Logan's lips form a smug smile as he drags the pad of his thumb over his bottom lip, and he slowly licks it before pushing it in his mouth and letting his lips close around it. The whole time his icy blue eyes never leave mine and when he pulls his thumb out with a pop, I can't fucking breathe. All I can think about is how his mouth would feel sucking my cock like that.

How did I think I was straight before when that was so fucking hot?

The fantasies I've been having about him are *not* friendly. Not with how strong my desire is to crash my mouth to his, or how much I want to hear him moan, or how many times I've envisioned us coming together, or feeling his tongue on me. And watching him lick our cum off his fingers? That feels like the moment everything in my world finally shifted into place.

I thought I'd had plenty of what I previously thought of as 'great sex' in the past, but nothing, not a single experience, has ever made me feel the way I feel right now. Like my entire body is still aching for more, even after I came harder than I knew was possible *just from his hand*. I want to know what his mouth would feel like on my dick, my mouth, my hole. What it would be like to have him own me entirely, to hand over every bit of control and let him take me apart. What it would feel like to have him inside me, to be inside him.

I want him. Every single piece of him. I want it all.

These thoughts should probably send me into a full-blown identity crisis, but they don't. Because at the end of the day, I'm still me, and Logan has always been mine. Sure, maybe this changes a few things, but what doesn't change is how right being with him feels.

He's always been my favorite person, and now I want him in every way possible. I want to kiss him senseless and figure out what else we could be.

So, I'm not going to sit here and analyze the past ten years of my life, or wonder how I never realized I was attracted to men, or continue to question everything I know about myself, because the simple truth is I want this. And nothing has ever felt as much like *mine* as Logan does.

He climbs off my lap and goes to the bathroom to get a hand towel, and when he comes back, he raises an eyebrow like he's asking if I want him to clean me up. I nod because yeah, as hot as it was watching him lick my cum off his fingers, I'm not sure I'm ready to treat our cum like frosting just yet.

He doesn't say anything as he wipes me down, his touch surprisingly soft and gentle. And then, like wiping me clean wasn't the most intimate, boundary-blurring thing we've ever done in our friendship, he tosses the towel aside, turns toward me, and pulls the blanket up over both of us and snuggles in.

"Goodnight," he whispers before pressing a kiss to my forehead, and I swoon at the gesture.

15

RYDER

The drive to my house feels longer than usual. We haven't been here since the second email came, and we decided we should probably make sure everything's okay. My brain is in overdrive, cycling through every possible scenario, and none of them are good.

What if he broke in? What if it's not just words this time? What if he's waiting for us? What if my stuff's been stolen or trashed? What if, what if, what if...

I try to convince myself it'll be fine, but the knot in my stomach says otherwise. Because if his goal is to freak me out, he's done a damn good job, but there's no way I'm going to let him see that. I prefer to do all my spiraling in front of Logan and Logan only.

As much as I try to stay rational, I can't shake the tightness in my chest. I shouldn't feel this anxious pulling up to my own house, but I do, and that alone feels wrong.

When I park in the driveway, everything looks the same as when I left it. I don't know what I was expecting. Maybe windows shattered, my front door hanging open, a giant neon sign saying, 'he's been here,' but none of that was there. I'm sure that if something had been vandalized, one of my neighbors would have called me or the police.

Still, that does nothing to quiet the unease gripping my throat.

Logan glances over and takes my hand. "You ready?"

"Yeah," I mutter. "Let's get this over with."

"Truly the dream we're living," he deadpans.

We get out of the car and walk to the front door. As I turn the key, I hesitate for a second before pushing it open. To my relief, everything looks the same, but something still feels off, even though I'm sure it's probably in my head.

My eyes scan the living room like I've never seen it before, searching for anything that looks out of place or wrong. But everything looks to be exactly how I left it. Or close enough that I can't tell it's different.

Logan is standing beside me, doing his own sweep of the space. "Looks the same to me," he says after a beat. His voice is calm, but his shoulders are tense like he's waiting for something to jump out at us.

"Yeah," I say, though nothing about this feels particularly fine. It's almost worse that everything looks untouched, as if the danger is hiding just out of sight.

"I'm gonna check the office."

Logan nods and falls into step beside me as I head down the hallway. The floor creaks under our feet like it's warning someone we're here, which is insane because this is *my* house, though it doesn't feel like it right now.

The door to my office is ajar, which is probably how I left it. Slowly, I push it open and step inside. My desk is still a disaster of books, notes, and the coffee mug I left from the last morning I was here. It's all exactly how I remember it, and I keep reminding myself that's a good thing.

"Nothing looks out of place," I confirm to Logan.

He steps in behind me, his hand brushing my arm, and it settles something in my chest. "Let's check your desk anyway," he says, peering at the mess. "You know, just in case the stalker decided to alphabetize your sticky notes."

I snort. "Sorry, I didn't deep clean after being emotionally terrorized by my stalker."

"Oh, I'm not judging," he says, lips twitching, clearly judging.

"Insult my desk again and I'll make you organize it," I warn.

He leans in a little, voice dropping just enough to be flirty. "You know I'd do *anything* if you ask nicely."

I look at him, raising an eyebrow. "This feels like the strangest version of foreplay."

He huffs out a laugh at that. "Is it weird that I'm kind of into it?"

I shake my head, trying not to laugh as I turn back to the desk. "You're crazy."

"And yet, you still want me."

"I do, and that seems to be the real mystery here," I mutter, reaching for a stack of papers while he chuckles behind me.

He's probably not wrong to check my desk; it's a mess, and this person is obsessed with my work.

Wanting to get this over quickly, I start sifting through all my papers, and then my fingers freeze because there's no way I'm seeing what I'm seeing right now.

Tucked beneath my keyboard is a folded piece of paper with my name written on it in black ink.

"Logan, please tell me you put this here as some sort of fucked up prank," I beg.

But he didn't, I know he didn't. I've never seen this handwriting before, and it's not his. My pulse starts pounding so loudly it drowns out everything else.

The paper is in my hand, and I don't want to unfold it. I don't want to read the words on the inside, but I have to. Logan comes over and wraps his arm around my waist, steadying me.

I finally get the courage to open it, and it feels like someone knocked the wind out of me as I start to read.

"You sound so perfect when you read to me in here. But soon, you'll be able to read directly to me—no more mics or distractions. I have a special place just for us. We'll be together soon. Everything's falling into place."

The room tilts, and I'm convinced the floor is truly opening up below my feet, swallowing me whole. My knees go weak for a second, and Logan's grip on me tightens before I lose my balance entirely.

"Ryder?" His voice sounds panicked.

But I can't look away from the words—each one scrawled like a twisted promise. He's been here in my house. It's confirmed. We need to go. I need to get the fuck out of here. Every part of me is screaming to run.

I swallow hard. "Logan...please, let's go. Now."

He takes the paper from my death grip and puts it in his pocket. "Do you need anything before we leave?" he asks, and I barely hear him through my panic. "We're not coming back until this is all over."

But I can't get my mouth to open to respond. My feet feel rooted to the floor, even as my brain is yelling at me to move. All I can think about is how he got in. When he got in. How long he was here. How long he's been watching.

Shit...is he watching now? Is he in the house now? *We need to go.*

I finally shake my head in response to Logan's question because I still can't get words out. He slides his fingers through mine and pulls me toward the front door. Outside, he reaches into my pocket for my keys and locks the door behind us, even though it feels pointless. He already knows how to get in. What good is a lock now?

He doesn't say anything else as he guides me to the car and opens the passenger door. I climb in without a word. When he gets behind the wheel, I see his eyes flick obsessively to the rearview mirror as we pull away to see if anyone is following us.

"I think we should go straight to the police station," he says.

I turn my head, raising an eyebrow, but the words still won't come.

"They probably won't do much," he mutters, his jaw tight with frustration. "But they can at least look at the handwriting. This one feels more threatening. Don't cops have someone who analyzes stuff like that? Maybe they'll take it more seriously this time with physical proof."

I stare out the windshield as Logan takes a turn away from his apartment and toward the station. I'm not sure what the police can do, but I don't know what else we can do. His coworker still hasn't been able to find anything yet.

"Yeah, okay. Let's try," I say, giving in.

After a few moments of tense silence, his right hand drops from the wheel, reaching across the center console to rest on my thigh. The warmth of his palm seeps through my jeans, and without thinking, I reach down and place my hand over his, holding it there. His grip tightens slightly, just enough to let me know he notices.

We ride in silence until we arrive at the police station, and the nerves that never entirely dissipated come rushing back in full force. I don't want to be here. At all. It feels like they haven't taken any of this seriously the last few times Logan updated them. I'm not sure if it's because I'm a man or because there hasn't been anything explicitly threatening in the emails, but either way, I always hate how I feel when we talk to the police.

Logan lets out a deep breath, his hand slipping away from my thigh as he parks, and I want to grab it and put it back where it belongs.

"You ready?" he asks, turning to face me.

I nod because I know we have to do this whether I want to or not.

We step out of the car and head toward the station's entrance. Logan's hand brushes against my lower back as we walk in, and he leans in to whisper in my ear, "I got you, Ry. Promise."

Those few words are exactly what I need to hear before we walk in. The officer at the front desk barely looks up as we approach. "Can I help you?"

Logan clears his throat. "We need to report a case of harassment, stalking, and breaking and entering. My friend here has been receiving threatening messages, and we just found a note inside his house. Someone had to have broken in to leave it there. We've reported multiple other incidents already for this case."

The officer straightens slightly, his eyes flicking between us. "Alright. Let's get some more details. Come on back."

He buzzes us through the metal door, and we walk into the back of the department. The officer leads us into a small meeting room with an old metal table, and it feels like we're the ones about to be interrogated.

He gestures for us to sit. "You mentioned you've already got a case started. Who have you been working with?"

We go over some of the standard details—our names, the officer's name—who is, of course, not working today—the case number, a brief overview of the past emails, and the note.

"Alright, thanks for getting me up to speed. Since Office Donnelly is off today, I want to introduce you to someone who I think can help. According to your case file, he's been the one looking into the emails for your case. Give me a moment to get him back here."

Then he radios for someone named Pearson to come to room three.

A few moments later, the door swings open, and I swear the world stops turning because there's no fucking way this is happening right now.

There's no way *Kyle* is standing in the doorway holding a laptop in one hand and a coffee in the other.

What the fuck?

"Gentlemen," the officer says, utterly oblivious to the way my entire body locks up. "This is Kyle Pearson. He's in town consulting for us. He's our security and cyber guy, so he'd be the best one to look at those emails with you. As I mentioned, he's been looking into the other ones you've reported."

I see his mouth move and I hear the words, but they don't make sense. There's no way.

Kyle? A consultant? For the police?

But then his lips curl into a smirk, and he looks a little too pleased. "Funny running into you guys again. Seems we can't stay away from each other, huh?"

I clench my jaw so hard it hurts. Funny isn't the fucking word for it.

There's no way *Kyle* is here to *help us* with this case. The case where we're ninety-nine percent sure *he's* the one behind the emails. Not the one fucking helping us.

The more I think about it, the sicker I feel.

Kyle has shown up every single time we've left the house since he first talked to us—at the bar, the farmer's market, and now here. Not to mention, we've *barely* left the house, and instead of looking nervous or surprised, he seems thrilled that we're here asking for *his* help.

And he's wearing that fucking leather jacket.

But my thoughts snag on something he told us the night we met—he said he was in town for construction.

I'm kicking myself right now because we should've called the police to come to my house. Instead, I was so anxious to get out of there. We should've had them sweep for fingerprints, but I'm sure Kyle would've blamed it on him being there if they had found any of his DNA.

This whole thing is so fucked.

I glance at Logan, and if looks could kill, Kyle would already be a dead man. Logan is glaring at him with the most hateful look I've ever seen on his face.

I swallow hard, trying to keep my voice level as I speak. "You...work here?"

Kyle lets out a chuckle at my disbelief. "Sort of. I'm

helping upgrade their systems, making sure they're up to date with tracking and cybersecurity. Pretty much all the station's online systems. You'd be surprised how outdated some of these police systems are. Your case came in *right* on time for me to be able to take it over," he smiles, and I want to puke because it all clicks.

It's why we've had no luck tracing the emails. The police have been handing them straight to Kyle, the same person who is sending them. Matt's been chasing a dead end this whole time because Kyle's already two steps ahead, orchestrating the entire thing. He sent those cryptic emails *knowing* we wouldn't be able to trace them. Knowing that he'd be the one the officers would turn to since he's their 'cyber guy.'

"I thought you were here for construction?" Logan asks, his voice cold, every word laced with suspicion.

"Huh. Did I say that?" he taunts.

Logan's jaw tightens. "Yeah. You did."

Kyle lets out a small chuckle once again, and it makes my skin crawl. "Must've been a misunderstanding," he says easily. "I do plenty of consulting gigs. Last one was construction. Plus, I'm working on a construction project of my own right now for something special."

Logan shifts slightly next to me, but I don't take my eyes off Kyle. He's too smooth and far too comfortable lying through his teeth. He should *never* be in this room.

He must not want Logan asking questions, though, especially in front of his temporary co-worker, because he leans forward across the table just enough to invade Logan's space. "What's with all the hostility, man? Thought we were getting along just fine, no?"

To his credit, Logan stays eerily calm, despite the tension rolling off him in waves. "Hostility?" he repeats, tilting his head. "That's an interesting word choice. Considering all the hostile shit Ryder's been dealing with lately."

Kyle's expression doesn't change.

Does he know we're onto him? If he does, he doesn't seem worried about it. But why would he be when he's the one standing here with a temporary badge? The truth is, unless we can catch him red-handed, his word will always and forever outweigh ours.

I don't know what the hell we're supposed to do next. But Logan's not backing down.

"You know all about that, right, Kyle?" Logan taunts. "Some creep's been emailing Ryder and got this delusional crush on him. Thinks I'm the problem. I'm sure you read all about it in those emails you've been sending. I mean, reading."

Kyle blinks, but gives nothing away, and my heart is in my throat at Logan's jab.

"Sounds pretty messed up," he says evenly.

That piece of shit.

I force myself to open my mouth and speak this time. "Yeah. Someone's been sending me emails for a couple of weeks, and now they've left a note *inside* my house." I let that last part sink in, watching his face for any reaction. "They think we'll end up together which is fucking laughable," I add, lacing the words with as much disgust as I can manage.

Kyle's jaw ticks slightly—and I know I've hit a nerve.

Good.

I lean in a little, just enough to twist the knife. "They think they know me. Think I'd want someone who hides behind anonymous messages, breaks into my home, plays these mind games instead of acting like a decent human being." My gaze stays locked on his. "They don't get it. I'd never want someone like that. Not in this lifetime. Not in any lifetime. That's a small, pathetic man I'd never respect—let alone desire."

Logan picks up on my cue, his tone sharp and cold. "It's sad, really. Thinking that if they invade someone's life enough, or scare and isolate them, they'll get what they want. Like that's love." He lets out a humorless laugh. "It's not. It's pathetic."

The smirk on Kyle's face slips for a second before he pastes it back on. That small crack is all I need to know we're getting to him.

The officer who introduced us to Kyle clears his throat. "We're going to keep looking into it," he says, clearly trying to redirect before things explode. "Kyle's been working hard online for you both, but if there's anything relevant—"

Logan cuts him off. "And why exactly did you hire him?"

The officer looks at Logan for a moment before answering. "Kyle's consulted for us before. He came with a strong recommendation. Does good work."

Kyle turns that punchable smirk toward us, and I want to knock it off his face. "I'd be happy to work more closely with you, Ryder," he says smoothly. "Tech is my specialty, but maybe I can come see your place, check if there's anything else you might have missed."

A chill runs down my spine. He's toying with us.

Logan stands suddenly, and he leans over the table, a dangerous smirk of his own spreading across his face. "That won't be necessary," he says. "We've got it covered."

Kyle glowers at Logan, and I can't tell what he dislikes more, him or his answer. He wants control—to know every move we make, and he knows we're refusing to give that to him.

The other officer breaks the tension. "We'll take that note you found so we can make copies of it, and we'll keep the original in your file."

Logan pulls it from his pocket and hands it over. "It was tucked under his keyboard," he says, glaring at Kyle the entire time. "We're positive it wasn't there before the stalking started."

The officer reads it, his mouth tightening into a thin line. "Alright. We'll send it to forensics to analyze the handwriting, but I'll be honest—these cases are tough. Without a clear suspect, there's not much to go on."

I almost laugh at the irony of this situation.

"Actually," the officer continues, turning to me, "I'm sure you've been asked before, but is there anyone you think who might've left this?"

Sure, officer. He's sitting right next to you—your trusted consultant. I want to say it so badly, but I can't. Not yet. Not without proof.

"No," I lie, my voice even. "No one comes to mind."

Logan shifts beside me, and I know he wants to speak up badly, but we're not stupid. We have to play this right. If Kyle is working with the people who are helping us and they view him as a co-worker, are any of them really on our side? Or would they dismiss us and take his side? Saying it too soon could ruin our chances of turning Kyle in with proof.

Kyle, on the other hand, is the picture of ease. Smiling away over the fact that we didn't say his name.

The officer closes the file and stands. "Alright. We'll get moving with this new evidence. If anything else happens, call us immediately. In the meantime, I recommend setting up some security cameras in and around your house, Ryder."

I nod, my stomach sinking because, of course, that's their

solution—more waiting. More hoping whoever this is—Kyle, probably—slips up and hands them the perfect evidence so they can close the case without actually doing anything.

We stand, and Logan nudges me toward the door with a steady hand at my lower back. Every instinct in my body screams to get the hell out of here fast, but Kyle must see it as his last chance to rattle me.

As we're about to step out of the room, he leans in, voice low and sharp as a blade. "Don't worry, Ryder. I'll keep an eye on you—closer than ever."

Those few words hit like a shock to the system—everything in me goes still, and my lungs forget how to work. The edges of my vision blur, and my brain's screaming at me to move, but, once again, my feet won't budge.

Logan catches it immediately and lunges between Kyle and me, shielding me like a wall.

"Leave us the fuck alone," Logan growls, his voice lethal. "There's no world—none—where he'd ever fucking choose you. Take the fucking hint. He doesn't want you!"

Kyle's smirk only deepens, like he thinks Logan's bluffing. Then, with a voice that makes panic claw up my throat, he mutters, "We'll see," before shoving past us and leaving the room.

My breath starts to come out in short, shaky bursts. I've never had a reaction like this, not one that's so physical and all-consuming to the point I can't control my body. I'm trying to breathe, trying not to cry, and the next thing I feel is Logan's hands cradling my face. He gently tilts my face to meet his eyes and runs a thumb over my cheek, bringing attention to the tears that are falling.

"Baby," he coos. "Are you okay?"

Baby?

Baby.

The word hits me like a lifeline and drags me back to him, to safety.

I meet his gaze—concern etched in every inch of his face —and I hate that I've scared him. But I need him. Throwing my arms around him, I grip him to me as tightly as possible, pressing myself into his chest to breathe him in. "No, take me home."

16

LOGAN

I've never hated anyone as much as I hate Kyle.

He's somehow conned his way into a position of trust and power, and the second those smug words left his mouth—'we'll see'—I wanted to put him through the fucking wall, but Ryder needed me more.

The look on his face after Kyle whispered in Ryder's ear made my vision go red, especially because Ryder's been right all along. The law isn't here to protect us—at least, not with this. Not when your stalker is the one 'investigating' your case. He'll always be believed over us; it's just the reality of our situation.

We'd need irrefutable evidence—something they can't ignore, spin, or excuse.

But right now, I need to focus on getting him in the car. He's gripping my hand like it's the only tether keeping him from completely falling apart.

We don't speak on the drive back to my apartment, but once we get inside, he collapses on the couch and clutches a throw pillow to his chest. The sight destroys me. The fact that

Kyle has managed to make Ry feel unsafe in his own home and in every area of his life makes me furious. I want to fix it for him and take all the weight off his shoulders, but I know there's nothing I can do to erase what's already been done other than be there for him.

I miss the carefree, messy, slightly chaotic, always-late version of my best friend whose smile lit up everything around him. But even like this, I love him just as much. Maybe even more because I love how comfortable he is being so vulnerable with me.

Grabbing a bottle of water and making him a plate of food, I head back into the living room.

"Here," I say, holding the bottle out.

He blinks like I've pulled him from a nightmare. Slowly, he reaches out and takes it, murmuring a soft, "Thanks."

I sit next to him, close enough that our thighs brush. Hoping he can feel me there and that it's grounding.

"You know," I start, keeping my voice light and going for a hint of humor since that's our best form of communication. "If this guy thinks he knows you better than I do, he's seriously delusional."

"Yeah? And why's that?"

"Because I know your coffee order. Your favorite takeout. What you'll get at pretty much every restaurant in town. I know your go-to drink, the exact way you fold your towels, and how to get you to stop snoring. I've survived years of your relentless teasing and chronic lateness, and even accepted your completely unhinged opinion that beans are not a crime against humanity."

The corner of his mouth twitches.

"They're gross, Ry. Refried beans, especially. They're like a plate of brown mush. You have to admit that."

And then finally, a genuine smile takes over his face, and he laughs at my extreme distaste for beans. It's the best thing I've seen in days. Even if it's quick, it feels like a goddamn victory.

"Guess that does make you an expert," he says. "And beans are good."

"Damn right it does," I say, nudging his knee with mine. "And since we're having a bad day, I'll ignore the second part. But me knowing you so well is how I know we'll figure this out, because no one, and I mean no one, knows you better than me."

His eyes lift to mine, and something flickers there. Guilt, maybe. I don't know.

"I hate that you're caught up in this because of me," he says quietly.

"Don't do that," I say, cutting him off before he can spiral. "We're in this together. End of story. I love you and there's nothing else I'd rather do than be here by your side, no matter what happens."

Oh, fuck.

I just…

Did I make this weird by saying I love you?

We've said 'I love you' before, so many times over the years. But not since we started…whatever this is. Not since I touched his dick. Or introduced him to frotting. Or licked his cum off my fingers like it was frosting.

I still can't believe I did that.

All of my chill has left me, apparently.

And I called him *baby* earlier. Why do I keep pushing him when he's already dealing with so much?

Before I continue this spiral, his voice cuts through the noise in my head.

"I love you, too, Logan."

Those five words make all the air rush back into my lungs, and I feel like I can finally breathe again. It's not an I'm *in* love with you admission, but I think it carries far more weight than all the ones that've come before, even though I'm falling harder and faster than I ever have in my entire life.

"Good," I say, nudging him with a small grin. "Because I was gonna be real embarrassed if things got weird by saying that after we've touched each other's dicks."

He lets out a real laugh. "We're way past weird, Logan."

"Fair point," I admit.

Then Ryder shifts, turning to face me on the couch.

"You're my person, Logan," he says softly.

I move to mirror him, and take his face in my palm. His breath comes out in uneven pants, but he doesn't move. He looks at me, and god, I could drown in those big caramel brown eyes with golden flecks.

With his face still in my hand, I whisper, inches from his mouth, "You really mean that?"

Ryder's lips part slightly, and he nods once. "Yeah," he says, like there's not even a shadow of a doubt. "I do."

My hand slips from his cheek, trailing down to rest at the base of his neck, and I can't deny how intimate it feels.

"You're my person too, Ry," I whisper.

We're so close, both of us shifting forward just a smidge, and I feel his breath fan over my lips. For a moment, everything stills. I want to stay here forever, even if we never go further than this—just him and me, pressed close, breathing in sync—I want it.

Then, barely above a whisper, as if he can read my thoughts, his voice cracks through the silence, and he asks the question I've been dying to hear. "Can I kiss you?"

Every thought I had before his question is erased and replaced by the thought of him kissing me.

Him. Kissing me.

My pulse hammers as I pull back enough to meet his eyes —and fuck, the way he's looking at me...something opens in my chest and I don't fight it. Not one ounce of me even wants to try. All I do is nod, and that one gesture changes everything.

He leans in, his lips meeting mine, and I'm kissing him back in an instant. The second I do, the world tilts on its axis.

His lips are soft and warm. It's new, yet somehow familiar, and it's the most magical thing I've ever felt in my life. I'm completely unsure how I've survived this long without ever feeling his lips on mine.

Ryder makes a quiet sound in the back of his throat, something between a sigh and a moan, and it sends a jolt of desire straight to my chest. Then he moves to deepen the kiss, and I meet him halfway, swiping my tongue across his bottom lip, and he lets me in.

Heat rolls through me like I'm burning from the inside out as his fingers slide up my chest and curl around the back of my neck. I groan, tugging him closer until he's in my lap, his weight settling against me like he belongs there—and I'm certain he does. He's heavy, but it feels exactly right as every one of my senses is engulfed in him.

His fingers thread into my hair, and he gives a slight tug that makes my breath hitch, and I tilt my head, deepening the kiss.

I can't get enough, and from the quiet, needy sounds he's making, he feels the same way.

He pulls back enough to whisper my name; his voice is so

needy, I can't help but kiss him again because I can't not kiss him. Especially not when he sounds like that.

When we break apart again, his eyes drop to my hard cock that looks like it's ready to bust through the seams of my pants.

"Can I...?" Ryder asks, as he hooks his finger into one of my belt loops.

He doesn't finish the sentence, but I know exactly what he's asking—and I want it. I want anything he's willing to give me. *Anything.*

"You can do whatever you want," I rasp. "Anything."

He unbuttons my pants and tugs them down my thighs, and I lift my hips to help as he climbs off my lap. His fingers brush against my skin, and it feels like I'm being electrocuted by a thousand tiny jellyfish in the best way. My cock springs free, stiff and already leaking, and I don't miss the way his breath hitches when he sees it.

"Ryder," I murmur.

"Yeah?"

"You're perfect." I reach for him, pulling him back down next to me, and cover his hand with mine. "Anything you do, I'll like."

He kisses me quickly, then pulls back, and I watch as his hand wraps around me, and his first stroke feels so perfect I can't stop the grunt that slips out. His eyes widen slightly at that, his lips twitching into a smirk. He loves it when I'm vocal, and I don't want to deprive him of anything he desires.

"You like that?" he checks.

"Yeah," I confirm, breath shaky. "Told you—anything. It's so fucking good having your hands on me, Ry."

He licks his palm and goes back to stroking me, his grip firmer now as he finds a rhythm. His thumb occasionally swipes over my slit through my precum, slicking me up like he already knows what I need.

"Ryder," I groan, voice laced with want. "You're driving me insane right now. It feels so good, baby. I love the way you touch me."

His eyes find mine as I once again let the word *baby* fall from my lips, but all I see in his gaze is hunger. I need to get my hands on him before I lose it.

"Take your pants off," I choke out.

He doesn't hesitate. Just shoves them down in one hurried motion, revealing his hard, leaking cock, and I can't stop the low groan that rumbles in my chest seeing him like this. He's gorgeous—long and thick, flushed deep red, with precum already pearling at the tip and trimmed hairs at the base that I want to bury my face in. The curve of him is enough to make my mouth water, and I notice the way he twitches under my stare, like he's both nervous and fully turned on.

I want to fall to my knees and praise him. Relish in how incredible it is that I get to have him like this.

"Guess I'm not the only one losing it," he teases.

"It's all your fault, baby," I groan. "Seeing you like this feels like...fuck, I don't even know, I can't think straight."

"Good," he rasps. "Because I haven't been thinking straight since the first time you touched me like this. In any sense of the word."

I grin and reach for him, wrapping my hand around his shaft, and he sucks in a sharp breath at the contact.

"Can you stroke us together again? Please," he begs, and I don't hesitate.

"Fuck yes, but I don't want to go to the bedroom to get the lube. I'm going to suck your cock for a minute, get you nice and wet. Okay, baby?"

Ryder's eyes widen, and his mouth parts on a gasp, and I worry I just broke his brain. He stares at me for a moment before he finally manages a nod. Licking my lips, I grin at him and pull him into a kiss before dropping to my knees in front of him. I slide in between his thighs and lick the salty precum that's waiting for me. He twitches against my tongue as I do, and it sends a surge of heat to my dick. I can't help but reach down to stroke myself slowly, just the way I like, as I take him deeper into my mouth.

"Ohhh, Loge, that feels so good," Ryder groans, as his fingers find my hair.

This is the first time I'm sucking his cock, and selfishly, I want to ruin him for anyone else. I want to be the best he's ever had. I want every girl who's had his dick in their mouth before me to pale in comparison. I want to be the *only* one he ever thinks about again.

I swirl my tongue around the head of Ry's cock before sucking him into the back of my throat and swallowing around him. His hips buck slightly, pushing his dick even deeper into my throat and all I can think about is him fucking my face. The thought nearly pushes me over the edge, so I ease up on stroking myself, wanting to focus my full attention on him. Moving my hand to his balls instead, I cradle them before giving them a gentle tug, and he lets out a shuddering grunt, the sound only spurring me on. My lips wrap around him as I hollow my cheeks, letting my tongue glide along the inside of his velvety cock. I work him slowly, licking and sucking, letting him feel every movement until he's slick and dripping wet with spit.

When I finally pull back, I wipe my mouth with the back of my hand, a small smirk tugging at my lips over how completely and beautifully wrecked he looks in his moment, panting like he ran a marathon.

"How was that, baby?" I ask, my voice rough from taking him so deep.

Ryder lets out a shaky laugh, his head falling back against the couch. "Holy fuck, you could've been sucking my dick this entire time! You've been holding out on me!" he practically shouts. "But, yeah…that was more than good. Fuck, Loge. You're so good at that. Best blow job I've ever had and I didn't even come."

I smirk, feeling pretty fucking pleased with myself for accomplishing exactly what I wanted to. If he's praising me this much after only a couple of minutes with his cock in my mouth, I can't wait to show him what else I can do. But first, I want to give him what he asked for.

I crawl onto his lap and line our dicks up, using the wetness from him to stroke us both at once. I make a mental note that we need a bottle of lube in the living room. Actually, every room. A minimum of one bottle per room to start.

"Fuck," he breathes, his head tipping back immediately upon the contact. "Logan, that's—oh, fuck."

"Good?" I ask, leaning forward to grin against his neck.

"Yeah," he rasps, his hips moving instinctively to match the rhythm I start. "Better than good. Jesus."

The slick glide of our cocks together is almost too much mixed with the way Ryder is fucking my fist. I feel the way his body trembles against mine as a string of curses spills out of him, and it sets my pulse on fire.

I swipe my thumb over the leaking heads of our cocks, gathering the precum mixing between us and instead of using it as lube, I bring my thumb to my mouth and suck it slowly while his eyes are locked on mine. The taste of us together is intoxicating, and I can't help but let out a moan.

Ryder's eyes darken, and his breath hitches at the sight. His chest rises and falls like he can't get enough air. "You're —" he starts, but the words disappear into a groan.

I let my thumb slide free with a soft pop, licking my lips with a smirk. "You like that?" I rasp. "You look like you're about to lose it."

He lets out a strangled sound that I love hearing. "Logan," he pants, his voice fraying at the edges. "I—fuck—I can't—"

"Come," I growl, my strokes growing firmer, faster. I lean in, letting my breath ghost over his parted lips. "Don't hold back. I want to see you fall apart, Ryder. Come, baby."

His head falls back against the couch. "Fuck, so...close," he gasps.

"Do it," I demand. "Come for me. Show me how good it feels. How much you like watching me suck our cum from my fingers."

That does it. He falls apart with a broken moan, his release spilling between us, and I don't let up. I stroke him through it, watching his expression transform from tension to bliss. It's the hottest thing I've ever seen, and my own orgasm crashes into me. I bury my face in the crook of his neck and breathe him in. It's all sweat, and sex, and Ryder.

For a long moment, there's nothing but the sound of us catching our breath until Ryder lets out a soft laugh, wrapping his arms around me. He holds me close as he shifts us so his forehead rests against mine. "God, you're so hot. How did I never notice before?"

I can't help but smile, letting the moment settle between us as I brush my nose against his. "I can't wait to show you what else we can do now that you've finally caught up." Then I lean forward and press my lips to his.

When we finally break apart, I press a lingering kiss to his forehead. "We should probably clean up," I murmur, feeling the cum cooling on our skin, though I make no effort to move. "But I kind of like us like this—sticky, spent, and completely wrecked on my couch."

Ryder laughs again, and hearing that sound feels so right, especially after everything we've been carrying. "Ugh," he groans dramatically. "Fine. Shower?"

I grin. "Together?"

He shoots me a look, a smirk tugging at the corner of his mouth. "You know it, *baby*. Those are the rules, remember?"

My stomach flips. Goddamn. I know he's emphasizing the word because I let it slip a time or five, but I need to check in with him.

"You like it when I call you that?"

"Yeah. I do, Lo," he confirms and fuck, I really like *that*. I can't help but lean forward to kiss him again, low and lingering, just because I *finally* can.

"Good," I murmur, letting my lips brush against his jaw before nudging him toward the edge of the couch. "Now, come on. Before we end up doing this all over again."

Ryder smirks. "And that would be a bad thing?"

I already know I'm never going to get enough of him.

17

RYDER

After a quick breakfast and a lingering kiss from Logan that left me flushed and grinning like an idiot, I'm in a great mood to work. I settle into the closet that doubles as my recording studio and skim through the chapter I'm about to record.

I'm onto a slow-burn romance now, one of my favorite tropes to narrate. I've always loved the tension that builds between characters on the edge of something more. This book's about two best friends who've spent years tiptoeing around their feelings for each other—until one of them gets dared to kiss the other. That's the moment everything cracks wide open, and they realize their attraction for each other.

While no one dared Logan and me to do anything, it does feel like we've had an outside force pushing us together. Which is ironic, considering that same force wants me for himself, which is *never* going to happen.

I read the book out loud to myself first to warm up and get into the right mindset.

"You've always been more than a friend to me," Bry admits, his voice trembling. "I just didn't let myself see it until now."

"And now?" Zach asks. "What do you see now?"

"Damn," I laugh to myself. "Could this be any more on the nose?"

I've narrated dozens of bi-awakenings before, but this one hits differently. The words in this novel feel like they were written for Logan and me. I mean, how many times have I fallen in love with fictional best friends who find their happily ever after together, all while completely ignoring the fact that I'm living the same story?

I lean back in my chair, rubbing a hand over my scruff as a smile tugs at my lips. "I'm a goddamn cliché and I'm not even mad about it." If someone had written this book about us and my bi-awakening, I'd roll my eyes at how obvious it all is. But living it is something else entirely.

I continue reading out loud, getting lost in the story and slipping into the right headspace to start recording.

"I see it so clearly now," Bry whispers. "And it's you. It's always been you, Zach. No one gets me like you. No one has ever made me feel like you do. Even when we were 'just friends,' you were the one I always wanted. No one else has ever come close."

"We should've known, Bry," I mutter to myself. "The universe has been hinting at it for years, and I didn't get it, either. Not until now, and I'm so glad I got the hint."

A knock on the doorframe pulls me from my rambling. I turn to find Logan leaning against it, arms crossed, smirking at me.

"Talking to yourself again?" he teases.

"Can't deny it when you're caught red-handed," I laugh. "What's up?"

"Wanted to check in." His gaze flicks between me and my mic setup. "Good story?"

I just shake my head, waving a hand at my tablet. "Yeah, turns out I've been narrating my own life story for years through different novels. Had a big realization."

Logan raises an eyebrow, curiosity sparking in his eyes. "Oh?"

"Best friends, years of unspoken feelings, one moment that makes it all click—it's basically us. Except, you know, minus the stalker. And they all get my sexy voice to bring it all to life."

He chuckles and steps closer. "So," he says, tilting his head, "what's the big realization?"

"That the narrator should've seen it coming a mile away." I meet his eyes. "Because while I've been reading bi-awakenings and best-friends-to-lovers stories for years, I didn't realize that'd be us some day. My own story."

Something flickers across Logan's face, and he reaches out, brushing his fingers against mine where they rest on the desk.

"Guess it's a good thing you finally caught up," he murmurs.

I push up from my chair and press my lips to his. "Guess so, babe."

"You're completely okay with this? With us? No freak outs? I know we've talked about us a little, but I want to make sure you're good with this," Logan checks.

I'm glad we're finally having this conversation so we can lay it all out there because the truth is, I'm not panicking. At all. Because it's him, and Logan has always felt like mine. The pieces were always there, scattered across the years we've spent side by side—I just hadn't put them together until now.

I think back to how everyone we've ever dated always seemed like they were getting in the way of our time together. It's not like I didn't care about them or didn't want to spend time with them, but they weren't Logan. Logan always came first because none of them understood me like he does. They didn't challenge me or make me laugh the way he does. They didn't show up for me the way he always has.

"Yeah, Logan. I'm completely okay with this. More than okay, actually. It's always been you. I just didn't see it clearly until now. Until he pushed me straight to you."

I shake my head, overwhelmed by how surreal it all feels. It's wild that something so dark and fucked up is what cracked everything open. I hate what we've gone through. I hate that someone's obsession forced us into survival mode and stole our freedom and safety, but I also can't ignore the clarity it brought.

"It's crazy, right?" I continue, "I've probably narrated a hundred scenes where the best friends fall for each other, and read a hundred more. You'd think I would've figured it out sooner, but I somehow didn't see it before."

"I did have platonic feelings for you all these years, except maybe right when we met. But the second you said you were straight, I buried those feelings so deep I almost forgot they were there. Then, when *he* showed up that first night and you kept looking at him before I knew what was happening, I hated it. I felt so fucking jealous you were looking at a man who wasn't me. Then you walked in on me in the shower and didn't immediately bolt…and yeah, all those boundaries I set? They started to blur real fast."

My entire body burns hotter than the sun. "Seeing you in the shower was my moment, too. Good thing I was on time for once, huh?" I mutter, burying my face in my hands as I laugh.

He chuckles, prying my hands away, forcing me to look at him. His fingers slide between mine, and his voice drops to something softer. "Best timing you've ever had," I agree.

"I just can't believe that after narrating all these stories, it took you jerking off in the shower to make me realize I wasn't as straight as I thought. Then laying next to you, horny out of my mind from feeling you on top of me, to the point of telling you I needed to jerk off—that sealed the deal on my bi-awakening. Actually, no," I laugh. "It was you running out of lube and offering to *share*. That finally sent the message loud and clear."

He laughs at the memory. "You looked like you were about to combust. I had to offer a helping hand. What kind of friend would I be if I didn't?"

"Yeah, well, can you blame me?" I shoot back, glancing at him over my shoulder. "You were lying there, all smug and calm, acting like it was normal for grown best friends to jerk off next to each other in bed. We're not in college anymore."

"It *is* normal," he says with a shrug. "But usually it ends up right where we did. And don't think I didn't notice you running mental laps trying to convince yourself it didn't mean anything before you touched me."

I groan, covering my face again. "I didn't know what to do. I wanted to do it but had, like, eight conflicting emotions happening at once. How was that only a couple of weeks ago? And how was it just last night that I finally got to kiss you?"

"You were figuring things out," he validates. "It's not supposed to be neat and tidy." Then he leans forward over me, his smile teasing, his tone soft. "And now you get to kiss me anytime you want."

I don't hesitate. I pull him into me and kiss him with everything I've got, and when we break apart, I whisper, "This still feels surreal. I should've known it was always you."

"Just because it took us a little longer to get here doesn't mean what we have is any less real," he says, and I kiss him again because I can't help myself.

"Hey," Logan says, nudging my shoulder with his. "At least we know the story has a happy ending. And that means we'll get ours too, baby. I know it."

I glance up at him, and the look in his eyes makes my breath catch.

"Yeah," I say softly, my chest tightening in the best way. "I can't wait until we can just be. Go out into the world without looking over our shoulders. Just exist."

"That day's coming," he sighs. "We'll get there. And when we do, I'm taking you on the cheesiest date you've ever been on. Think candles, roses, some overpriced restaurant where the portions are tiny but they charge you double for 'ambiance'."

I laugh, and it feels so good. "That sounds ridiculous, and I'm so in."

"Yeah, well," Logan says, grinning as he leans in until his forehead bumps gently against mine. "You deserve ridiculous. All the good, ridiculous things, and I can't wait to be the one to give them to you." He looks at me and swallows hard. "So...are we doing this? Like, for real? Because I'd like to call you my boyfriend. If that's something you want, too."

My heart stutters, and I grin so hard it hurts. "Yeah, Logan. I want that. I want you, *boyfriend*."

His grin is immediate, and when he pulls me into a hug, I sink into it without hesitation. "You're such a sap," I murmur, as I tuck my face into his neck, still smiling.

"You like it," he says, and I nod against him, because I really, really do.

18

LOGAN

It's been quiet since we left the police station, and I'm not sure if that's a good thing or the calm before the storm. Maybe Kyle finally decided to back off because he realized we're on to him. Or maybe he's being more calculated. The not knowing is what gets me, and I have a bad feeling it's the latter. It seems far more likely.

Ryder and I have been living in our own little bubble lately. He wants me, and I want him, and for the first time in weeks, we've been happy. It's easy—easier than I ever could've imagined. It's like everything slotted into place the second we realized we both wanted each other.

I walk into the living room with two bottles of beer to find Ryder already on the couch, scrolling on his phone, looking suspiciously pleased with himself.

"You're grinning like an idiot," I tease, handing him a bottle before dropping down beside him.

"Maybe I'm just happy," he fires back, and my smile only grows.

I raise an eyebrow, settling in closer, our knees brushing. "Yeah? What's got you so happy then?"

He shrugs, taking a sip of his beer before leaning back against the cushions. "Dunno. Today feels like a good day, I guess."

Seeing him like this makes me the happiest man in the world, and I'd do anything to keep this smile on his face.

"You know," I muse, setting my beer on the table. "I like happy Ryder. A lot."

"Yeah?" he smirks.

"Yeah, baby," I say, reaching out to tuck a piece of hair behind his ear, letting my fingers linger against his skin. "Almost as much as I like desperate Ryder."

The blush creeping up his cheeks is immediate. "You're the worst."

"Hmm," I hum, dragging my fingers down his arm. "I don't think so. If I recall correctly, you like me. A lot, even. Don't ya, boyfriend?"

He scoffs, but he doesn't move away. If anything, he leans in a little closer. "That's debatable."

I smirk, tilting his chin up with my fingers. "Oh, Ry, we both know it's not. But don't worry, I like you back just as much. Probably even more."

"It's not my fault I'm so irresistible," he winks.

"Oh, believe me, I'm painfully aware."

"You saying I've been your biggest weakness all along?" Ryder beams at me.

I roll my eyes. "Says the one who begged me to touch you while you came all over both of us like you've been waiting your whole life for it."

"What can I say? You're irresistible, too," he says, laughing as his cheeks turn red.

"You've set the bar real high for how much you like me," I smirk before continuing. "And my dick."

He laughs for a moment, then grows serious, his mouth parts slightly. "I do. I really do," he breathes.

I close the distance between us, my lips finding his in a kiss that's soft but insistent. Ryder gasps against my mouth, his hands sliding up to tangle in my hair. He mauls my mouth like it's the oxygen he needs to breathe, and god, I want it all.

Ryder is objectively hot, with his wavy brown hair that always has that perfectly tousled, I-don't-even-try look, and that tiny scar from his childhood above his left eyebrow only makes him more unfairly captivating. Ryder is a perfect contradiction—rugged charm wrapped in soft vulnerability—and I know I'll never get enough of him. I want him every day for the rest of our lives, and even though I've barely had him, I know forever won't be long enough with him.

There's no going back. Not now. Not ever.

I break the kiss momentarily to tug my shirt over my head while he does the same. My fingers find the button of his jeans and push the fabric down his legs. "Hips up," I say as I move to slide off his jeans and boxer briefs. Once they're off, I waste no time, leaning forward to press a kiss to the tip of his cock before licking up and down his erection.

"You are so fucking sexy," I say, my voice rough with want. And that—that is what he needs. I've learned Ryder loves praise during sex, and I want to constantly praise him, to give him everything he desires. His eyes darken, and his lips part as my words seem to light something inside him. He surges forward, his hands fumbling to get my pants off with absolutely no finesse until we're both completely naked.

"You want to get out of your head? You want to just feel? You want me to take care of you?" I ask.

"Yes," he breathes. "Yes, please."

My cock twitches at the way the word please falls from his pink, fuckable lips.

"I'll take care of you, baby."

He nods, and I know he's done talking—at least for now. He's ready to feel. Wants to ride the high of the last few days while everything still feels good. I slide off his lap and drop down onto my knees between his legs, letting my mouth trail down his body. Licking and sucking each of his nipples before moving to his cock. His hips jerk beneath me, and he lets out a low groan.

"Oh, fuck—Loge," he gasps, his voice raw with pleasure.

The sound of my name falling from his lips makes me lust-drunk for him, and I take him to the back of my throat, humming around him before giving him a hard suck. He lets out a low groan, and I can't stop the grin tugging at the corners of my mouth even as I keep my rhythm steady, bobbing up and down.

"Shit—Loge—fuck, that's…so good. So fucking good." His voice is already breathy, and his thighs are tense under my palms.

I pull off him slowly, letting my lips drag up his cock until he slips free with a soft, wet pop. His cock is glistening, and I can't resist licking him from base to tip. He's just so damn irresistible.

"You taste so fucking good, Ry," I murmur, my voice low and rough. "I could stay here all night, just like this, with your cock in my mouth. Hmm, we should try that sometime."

"I don't think I'd survive that," he says on a breathless laugh.

I smirk, pressing a kiss to the inside of his thigh. "You'd be surprised what you can handle. Wanna find out?"

"Jesus," he mutters, his cheeks flushing a deeper red. "You're going to kill me."

"Not a chance," I say, grinning as I wrap my hand around him. "I'm going to make you feel alive. Give you the best orgasm you've ever had."

He gasps at the friction before I lean down to tease his tip with my tongue until he's begging for my mouth again.

"Please," he whines, and I give him what he needs. He gasps as I suck him to the back of my throat, and I love his reactions. Love how desperate he becomes, how needy he sounds, and I'm not ready for this to end anytime soon.

"Lo—oh, fuck—I'm not gonna last," he pants. His whole body tenses, his thighs trembling under my hands as I slow the motion of my strokes.

"Don't come until I tell you," I say, pulling my mouth off him.

"Logan," he gasps, his voice cracking. "I don't think I can—"

"You can," I say firmly, my hand sliding up and down his hard-on. My thumb teases over the slick head, circling the sensitive ridge before easing back down, using my saliva as lube. "You're gonna hold it for me," I say before taking him back in my mouth.

Ryder nods frantically, his breaths coming fast and uneven. "Oh, fuck—" His hips thrust up again, and I press my a hand to his stomach to hold him in place. "Oh my god, Loge."

I pull off, pressing a kiss to the tip of his cock, letting my tongue flick over the slit, and he shudders. "I want you right here, hanging on for me."

"Please," he whimpers, his hands gripping the back of the couch. "I can't—"

"You can," I murmur, letting my lips drag along the length of him, kissing and licking but avoiding giving him the friction he craves. "You're doing so good for me, Ryder. I love seeing you like this."

He whines, hips lifting off the couch again, his entire body begging for release even as he tries to hold back. "I'm trying —so hard, but I can't—Loge, I'm so fucking close. Pleaseee."

I wrap my hand around him again and stroke, keeping him on the edge without letting him fall. "I love hearing you beg," I say, kissing the inside of his thigh. I tease him even more, leaning forward to suck his right ball into my mouth before moving to the left.

"I hate you," he mutters weakly, but the broken moan that follows gives him away.

"No, you don't," I say, releasing him and sucking his shaft back into my mouth. I suck him slow and deep, my hand twisting at the base in a rhythm that's driving him crazy. His cock twitches against my tongue, and his whole body is trembling as he tries to hold back. I want him to experience pure, euphoric bliss—to think of nothing else except how he feels right now.

I pull off, stroking him faster now, giving him what he needs. "Come for me, baby."

And before I can even finish the sentence, his release starts spilling over my hand. I take him back into my mouth as fast as I can, and suck down every last drop, watching as his body shudders through his orgasm.

When he has nothing left to give, I pull off his cock, swallowing everything, then lick the stray cum off my hand as he watches. His chest is still heaving, his pupils blown wide as he stares at me like I'm something unreal.

"Fuck, Lo," he rasps. "I've never—never come like that

in my entire life." He lets out a shaky breath, running a hand through his sweat-damp hair. "That was—fuck—that was the best orgasm I've ever had. I don't even have the words."

I smirk at his reaction, wiping my mouth with the back of my hand before leaning in and letting my lips graze his jaw.

"Good," I murmur. "You were so perfect for me, baby. You don't need to have words."

His breathing begins to steady, and then his gaze drifts lower—settling on my still hard cock. His lips part slightly, tongue flicking out to wet them, and fuck if that doesn't send a fresh wave of heat through me.

He hasn't taken me in his mouth yet, but the thought is there. I can see it in the way his blush deepens, spreading across his cheeks and down his neck. When his eyes finally flick back up to mine, there's a mix of nerves and curiosity swimming in them.

"What about you?" he asks softly.

"Do you want to try, baby? It won't take me long—getting you there set me right on the edge."

His throat bobs as he swallows, his fingers twitching like he's still debating it. Then, slowly, he nods. "Yeah," he murmurs, voice rough with something between nerves and anticipation. "I—I want to try."

Fuck me.

My cock twitches at the thought of his lips around me, and I reach up to cup his cheek, running my thumb over the heat of his flushed skin. "You sure?" I ask, even though I already know the answer.

He nods again, more confident this time. "I want to. I just…" He exhales, his gaze dropping again. "I don't know if I'll be any good."

I tilt his chin up so he has to look at me. "Baby, you could just breathe on me, and I'd probably come."

That earns me a soft laugh, but it seems to be all the encouragement he needs.

"Switch spots with me," he says, and I do.

I sit on the couch while he crawls between my legs and places his hands on my thighs. His palms are warm, and my breath catches as he leans in and presses a kiss to my hard tip, like I'd done for him. Then, he parts his lips and drags his tongue over the head of my cock, a slow, teasing swipe— testing it out. He's understandably hesitant at first as his lips stretch around me, taking the head of my dick into his mouth, tongue flicking curiously along the underside of my cock.

I groan, my head falling back. "Jesus, Ryder…"

He hums in acknowledgement of my praise, the sound vibrating against me. He keeps me there for a moment, adjusting to the feel, before popping off. But then he looks up at me, wide-eyed, with spit trailing from his mouth to my cock, and fucking hell, I'm done for. I let out a little gasp at the sight. He smiles at that, lets out a breath, and takes me into his mouth—a little deeper this time—and sucks.

"Shit—Ryder—" My voice is shaky, and my hand flies to his hair, not to push or guide, just to hold on.

He pulls off enough to speak, his breath hot against my cooling skin. "Is that good?" he asks, his voice so soft, so fucking sweet, like he's not currently destroying me with his mouth.

I let out a shuddering breath at the effect he has on me. "Yeah, baby. Too good. I'm not gonna last long."

His blush deepens, but his lips curl into a small, almost proud smirk. And then he goes back down, hollowing his cheeks and taking me a little deeper. His tongue moves in slow, experimental strokes, each one making my stomach clench tighter. The tension builds fast—hot, desperate, and fucking impossible to stop because his mouth on my cock is my fantasy come true. I'm gonna come. Fuck, I'm already right there.

"Ryder—I'm gonna come, pull off. I—fuck—" I barely have time to warn him before the pleasure snaps through me, white-hot and all-consuming.

But he doesn't pull off.

He lets out a muffled sound as I spill into his mouth, his hands bracing against my thighs, but he takes it. All of it. Swallows every drop he can as I shake beneath him.

Finally, I collapse back against the couch, boneless and breathless. Completely done for.

Ryder pulls off with a soft, unsteady gasp, wiping his mouth with the back of his hand as his eyes find mine. His cheeks are flushed, his lips red and swollen, and something about that look sends a fresh throb of heat through me, even though I just came harder than I ever have in my life.

I reach for him, pulling him up and cradling his face in both hands. "Jesus Christ, baby," I rasp, pressing my forehead to his. "That mouth."

"I take it that means I did okay?" He asks nervously.

I groan and kiss him—hard—tasting the mix of our releases between us. "You were perfect," I murmur against his lips. "So fucking perfect."

He melts into me, and I can't stop myself from brushing his hair back, fingers combing through the soft strands as I tilt his chin. "How was your first experience?"

Ryder groans dramatically and drops his head onto my shoulder. "Logan, you can't ask me for blowjob feedback like it's a customer service survey."

I huff out a laugh, dragging my hand down his back. "Fine, fine. But, I'm just saying, if I was filling one out? Five stars. Would recommend. Will absolutely be returning."

"God, you're so annoying," he says, but he's laughing, and it's the best sound in the world. "But yeah, I liked it too. Would also return."

I kiss him again, savoring this moment, and when we break apart, I hear him whisper, "I can't believe this is real."

19

LOGAN

I 've never felt rage like this before.

For the first time in my life, I understand the urge to punch a hole through drywall, throw a glass at the wall, or to strangle the life out of someone.

I am fucking *fuming*.

This is the most manipulative, disgusting, twisted thing you can do to another human. It's a deliberate invasion of our privacy to take something so intimate and personal and use it against us. It takes a truly depraved person to do something like this.

The mixture of rage and nausea isn't going away. My hands are shaking, my vision is hazy at the edges, and I can't get the images out of my mind. Kyle turned something beautiful between Ryder and me into something tainted with his sick obsession. He twisted what was ours into a way to try to take back the upper hand and exert control over us.

And what it's doing to Ryder is fucking gutting me.

Nothing he's done to this point compares.

Ryder's gone completely still beside me, except for his

silent tears and shaky hands. He looks utterly and completely defeated because Kyle tried to strip him down to nothing, and make him feel exposed in a way I can't fix.

And that's what makes me so angry. I will never, ever be able to erase the fact that his first blowjob was watched and recorded without his knowledge or consent.

The words from the email play on a loop in my head, each repetition fanning the flames of my anger.

I know you're confused right now. He's been filling your head with lies and pulling you away from who you really are. But this? This isn't you, Ryder. I'm disappointed in you. But let me be clear, if I see him with you again, I won't be so understanding. And trust me, neither of you wants to find out what happens then. I'd hate for either of you to get hurt because you didn't listen. This is your last warning.

Ryder saw the email come through first. Kyle took it to an entirely new level that was not okay. *None* of this is okay, but this is fucked up even for him. I could tell as soon as I watched Ryder's face pale that something was wrong.

When I asked what happened, he didn't answer. Just turned the laptop in my direction, and I could see a video clip pulled up. I knew before he even pressed play what it was. He did too.

I read the message, and my stomach dropped; the words not fully registering until he clicked play. Then a cold, violent fury spread through my chest as I watched the screen.

It was us. Last night. Ryder was on his knees between my legs, looking up at me with my cock in his mouth. That sick fuck must have watched the whole thing because I only lasted a couple minutes at most. The way he violated us for his sick agenda makes me nauseous. He has turned one of the most intense, raw, and incredible moments of my life into something tainted.

I hadn't even considered being watched last night. Not once. Because why the fuck would I? We were in my apartment, in our goddamn space, living in artificial light because the curtains are always closed, but there was a crack in the curtain. He was so invested that he filmed through that sliver of an opening. It's deranged.

A stuttered breath draws my attention back to Ryder, and he looks like he's on the verge of tears. I can be furious later because right now, I need to be there for him. I reach for his hands, lacing our fingers together. I can feel his pulse hammering, and I need to pull him back to me.

"Ryder," I say, my voice steady. "Hey. Look at me."

He does, and fuck—the devastation in his eyes guts me.

"This doesn't change anything," I soothe, squeezing his wrists. "He doesn't get to take this from us. He doesn't get to make you feel ashamed for something that was ours."

Ryder sucks in a shaky breath, his expression cracked wide open. "But he saw it, Logan," he whispers. "He watched us, and now he's holding it over our heads. What the fuck is he even going to do with this video? What about his threat?"

I don't know. I honestly don't, and that kills me.

My gaze flicks back to the screen, and there it is. The fucking edge of the curtain in the corner of the frame. They've been closed for days. I didn't even think to double-check before we did anything in the living room. I only wanted to make him feel good.

"Fuck!" I roar, raking my hands through my hair. "I'm sorry. I'm so fucking sorry, Ryder. This is all my fault. The curtain—I should've checked."

"No," Ryder says sharply.

He stands, stepping in front of me, and grabs my face with trembling hands, forcing my gaze to his.

"Don't do this," he says. "Don't put this on yourself. This isn't your fault."

But it is. I should have been more careful. I should have checked. I should have known—

"He did this, Logan," Ryder says, cutting through my thoughts. "This is what he does. He wants us to feel like this. Exposed. Humiliated. He wants us to be scared, and he wants us to be obedient, to stop being together. And now he's got the blackmail he's been waiting for. But I don't want that, Lo. I don't. I don't care what he says, I want to be with you, so I'm going to be."

I nod in agreement. "All I want to do right now is find him and make him regret ever fucking breathing near you," I snarl, attempting to point my anger at Kyle instead of myself.

"Get in fucking line," Ryder bites out, but it's not at me—it's at the sick bastard who did this. "I want to find him and end this myself. Fuck him for thinking he can do this."

I grab him and pull him into me, holding him so tight against my chest I can feel every furious breath he takes. "I know, baby," I whisper into his hair. "I know."

For a moment, he lets himself cry, grabbing my hoodie and burying his face into my shoulder. All I want is to take his pain and hurt away. I'd carry every goddamn ounce of it if it meant he didn't have to.

He pulls back and looks at me, his cheeks blotchy from tears and anger. "I'm not ashamed," he says, sounding so sure of himself. "Not of what I did. Not of you. Not of anything in that video. Fuck him for trying to make me feel like I should be."

My throat tightens at that, and I swallow down the emotion clawing its way out. Cupping the back of his neck, I press a kiss to his forehead. "Me neither, baby. Now, grab your shoes. I'm not wasting another second without cameras surrounding every inch of this place."

Ryder stares at me for a second, then nods. "Guess it's time, huh?"

"Yes." My voice is firm. "If he's still out there watching us, I want to catch him. I want fucking concrete proof so we can end this and send his ass to jail."

"Alright," he agrees. "Let's go. Fuck this guy."

HUNDREDS OF DOLLARS LATER, WE HAVE EVERYTHING WE think we'll need—or at least everything we can reasonably set up in my apartment. A doorbell camera for the front door, one to cover the balcony area, and a couple of indoor cameras to monitor the living room and the hallway leading to the bedrooms.

We also grabbed four additional cameras for Ryder's house. Two motion-activated cameras with floodlights for the front and backyard, plus two indoor cameras to cover the entryway and the back door. I want every angle covered. If Kyle even thinks about lurking or breaking in again, we'll catch him.

I felt a little better as we loaded up the cart, until we reached the checkout counter and the guy opened his mouth. He made some stupid jokes about us trying to set the world record for most paranoid couple, laughing like this was an over-the-top precaution instead of a desperate attempt to feel safe again.

I hate when strangers try to crack jokes, especially when they don't realize they're hitting a nerve. I'm sure he wasn't trying to be an asshole, but the comments still made me irrationally angry all over again—and then I felt like I was the asshole. I must've shot him a look that screamed shut up, because after that, he cleared his throat, continued scanning, and told us to have a nice day.

All I've been today is angry, even now, as we're unboxing the cameras, I'm furious at the situation. At Kyle. But mostly, at myself for not making sure the blinds were fully drawn.

Last night, I couldn't think. It's like naked Ryder makes it impossible to focus on anything but him. But knowing what I know now, I'd give anything to go back and rewind and make sure the night stayed ours.

I can't even absorb the instructions I'm staring at, as I feel the weight of Ryder's gaze on me. I don't look up until I feel his hand on my chin, tilting my face to meet his.

"Logan, you're blaming yourself, and I need you to stop." His eyes search mine, and I swear he sees everything I'm feeling. "You think this is your fault, but it's not. I promise you, it's not."

I swallow hard, my chest tightening, and I shake my head. "Ryder, I—"

"No, babe. No." His thumb brushes against my lips. "You're carrying this weight, and you don't have to. It's not yours to carry. You did nothing wrong."

"But—" I start, my voice breaking, but Ryder cuts me off again.

"You didn't do this," he says, more firmly now. "And yeah, maybe we should've checked the blinds, but we didn't because we were in the moment, Lo. We wanted each other that badly, and I refuse to feel guilty about that. I won't apologize for that. No part of me blames you, please believe that."

I stare at him, wanting to believe him, and before I can say anything else, his lips are on mine. The kiss is soft, but it's like he's trying to help me understand how serious he is.

When we break apart, his beautiful brown eyes land on mine. "We're going to get through this," he promises. "But not if you keep tearing yourself apart over something you couldn't control."

I nod, the lump in my throat is making it impossible to speak.

20

RYDER

"What? For how long?" I try to keep the panic out of my voice.

Logan just got an email reminder for their company's mandatory HR meeting tomorrow, and I somehow hate email even more now. It's not a surprise—they do this every quarter—but with everything going on, we completely forgot it was coming up until the reminder hit his inbox.

We've been grateful they've let him work from home this whole time without complaint, but what meeting needs to happen in person at this point? They're a creative agency for fucks sake, they all know how to do virtual meetings. There's no reason Logan needs to sit in a meeting room and leave me here all alone.

This is the first time I'll be alone since this whole nightmare with Kyle started, and I'm trying not to show how much that's affecting me. As promised, Logan hasn't left my side at all, and the thought of being separated from him makes my stomach churn, especially after the last email. It left me feeling so powerless, exposed, and utterly violated. That was

one of the most intimate moments of my life, and the fact that
Kyle saw it makes my skin crawl.

That video was proof that no matter how safe we thought
we were by locking ourselves in the apartment, he's still steps
ahead, and he's not giving up. And his idea that I need saving
from Logan, of all people, is laughable. All I need is for him
to excuse himself from our lives forever.

But if there's one thing I'm sure of, it's that he's *never*
going to come between Logan and me. Ever. All he's
managed to do is push us closer, and I don't think he even
realizes it. After everything that's happened lately, I'm positive Logan is my future. There's no world where we don't end
up together.

"Usually, they're about two or so hours, so I'll probably
be gone three-ish hours," Logan says, breaking through my
thoughts. "I won't stick around any longer than I need to. I'll
do what I need to do and come back home to you as fast as I
can, I promise."

Being apart from Logan was something I knew I'd have to
face eventually, but now that it's happening, I'm not ready for
it. It's probably irrational and unhealthy to need him this
much, but the moment he said he had to leave, I felt panic
start to set in. I'm not ready to be without him.

"I don't like leaving you here alone," he adds, like he can
sense what's going through my head.

So don't.

I want to say it, but instead I force myself to nod, even
though every part of me is screaming to ask him to skip it.
"It'll be daytime. I'm sure it'll be fine. Kyle will probably be
at work, and we've got the cameras now," I say instead.

Besides, it's only three hours. I used to go days without
seeing him, but I'm no longer the same person I was before

this all started. Not after I learned what it's like to be his sole focus, to get all his kisses, to feel so completely and utterly loved—even if neither of us has said we're *in* love with each other yet.

I feel it.

It's not a new feeling, either. It's more like...all these years of knowing him are suddenly coming into focus in a new way. The signs have been there for years, I just didn't let myself see them, and I wonder if he convinced himself it was all platonic, too.

There was the time I had the flu, and I told him to stay out of my room so I wouldn't get him sick. While I was sleeping, he ran to the store to buy ingredients to make me homemade soup. Then, despite my protests, he sat on the floor next to my bed with his pillow and blankets, in case I needed anything, and so I didn't have to be alone.

Or the bookshelf I'd bought and let sit unassembled for far too long. One Saturday, I came home to find it fully assembled and lined with all my favorite books. When I asked him about it, all he said was, "You weren't going to do it, and I got bored." All of my books are still organized by color, and I never want to change that because it's so Logan, and every time I look at them, it reminds me of him.

Whenever we take road trips to visit my mom, he always puts on my playlists. I know he's grown to like my music over the years, but he does it because he knows it makes me happy. And he almost always comes with me, like we've been boyfriends all along.

Any time I've gone without him, it's felt like something was missing, and even though I love my mom, I didn't enjoy the visits as much. It felt like I was always counting down the hours until I could be back with him.

And then, the Monday a few weeks ago, when I called him to tell him about the email while he was at work, he didn't hesitate to tell his boss he needed a half day, and he showed up at my door. Told me to pack a bag and told his boss he needed to work from home indefinitely.

I used to think that was just Logan being Logan. That he's a good friend who cares about me, but now I see it so much more clearly. You don't make soup from scratch when someone is sick and sleep on the floor beside their bed unless you love them. You don't drop everything or take half days to make sure someone isn't alone through something scary unless they matter more than anyone else.

He's been loving me in a thousand quiet ways over the years, and I've been loving him back just as long.

If this is what it feels like to fall in love with your best friend—this slow, steady, undeniable realization that everything you've ever wanted has been standing beside you the whole time—then I'm the luckiest man alive.

I'm more dependent on him now than I've ever been in the ten years we've known each other, and I'm not ashamed of that. Not after everything we've been through. Not after the fear, the violation, the way he's shown up for me without hesitation every single time.

That kind of love—the quiet, constant, show-up-every-day kind—doesn't scare me.

Losing it does.

And the idea of being without him, even for three hours, feels terrifying.

Logan nudges my knee with his. "Hey."

I look up and he's watching me carefully. "I'm coming back. You know that, right?"

I nod, my throat tight.

"I won't be gone long. I'll text you the second I get there and when I'm coming home. It should be right around lunch," he reassures.

"Okay," I croak out as I reach for his hand and thread my fingers through his. I love being able to touch him so freely. "I just hate how hard this feels," I whisper.

"I know, baby." He nods. "But it won't be like this forever. We'll figure out how to prove it's him. Just a little longer," he soothes, leaning forward to press a soft kiss to my temple.

"Now come on, let's go lay down. I need to wrap myself around you, okay?"

21

LOGAN

I wake up before my alarm because my anxiety over going into the office won't let me sleep. I've been tossing and turning for what feels like all night—it's a miracle Ryder is still snoring lightly beside me. He's always been a heavy sleeper, though, so I lean over and brush my lips against his forehead before dragging myself out of bed.

He's so cute like this, peacefully curled up in the sheets, completely unaware that my brain is spiraling over leaving him. I want to crawl back in and pull him into me, pretend the rest of the world doesn't exist.

The realization hit me hard last night that the only thing in the world I care about now is him. We curled up together, kissed slowly, held each other through every lingering and unspoken fear, and it ended up being one of the best nights of my life. That makes leaving him alone for hours on end today feel even more unbearable. I don't want him out of my sight for a second.

I sigh and force myself into the morning routine I haven't missed at all, starting by turning on the shower. When I step in, the water is scalding against my skin, but I don't care. I hope the burn will settle my thoughts, or at least distract me from them, but they keep playing on repeat.

What if something happens while I'm gone? What if Kyle takes my absence as an opportunity? What if I'm not there when Ryder needs me?

By the time I step out of the shower, I'm already exhausted. I head back into the bedroom, and Ryder's still sleeping, his arm draped over the spot I left. The sight makes my heart clench, and I want nothing more than to stay here.

But I know I can't.

Work has already been more than reasonable, letting me work from home because of the stalking and harassment. I know I need to go in today if I want to stay employed, but this situation is pushing me closer and closer to saying 'fuck it,' and finally quitting my job to explore freelancing.

Dragging my eyes off Ryder, I walk to the closet to get dressed before making my way to the kitchen. I start the coffee and take two mugs out, one of which is Ryder's favorite. Well, he says he hates it, but he grabs it more than any other mug, so that's Ryder for 'this is my favorite.'

It says, *'I've got a dig bick,'* followed by *'you read that wrong,'* in a small font below it. He's complained since the first mug he got at a white elephant exchange, but I know he secretly thinks they're funny, so I keep collecting them. Every time I bring home a new one or gift him one, he sighs dramatically and mutters something about how I should stop wasting my money on these 'stupid mugs,' but sure enough, he still always uses them.

When the coffee is ready, I fill our mugs, doctoring his the way he likes it. He still hasn't come out of here yet, but there's no way I'm walking out the door without saying goodbye, so I grab both mugs and head back toward the bedroom. If I only have a few more minutes before I have to leave, I'm going to spend them with him.

Setting his coffee on the bedside table, I slide back into bed and settle close. The warmth of his touch immediately starts to ease my nerves, even as I count down the minutes until I need to leave.

He stirs slightly, and I reach out to brush my fingers through his brown hair. "Morning, baby," I murmur, leaning down to press a gentle kiss to his head.

His eyes flutter open, and a slow smile stretches across his lips. "Mmm…coffee?" he asks, voice rough with sleep like it always is when he first wakes up.

"On your nightstand, sleepy."

He grunts in approval but makes no effort to sit up and grab it. Instead, he buries his face against my chest and slings his arm across my stomach. "Too early, don't go," he mumbles.

I let out a small laugh, running my fingers up and down his back. "I agree. I wish I could stay." *More than you know.*

Ryder lifts his head enough to peek at me through barely open eyes. "So don't go."

God, I want to listen to him so badly, but I know I don't have a choice. I lean in and press a kiss to his temple this time. "You know I would if I could. I don't want to leave you, but I have to go, baby. It's mandatory."

He groans, then finally pushes himself upright to reach for his coffee. He takes a slow sip. "I hate this," he admits, and I nod.

I cup his face in my hands, grazing my thumbs over his cheekbones. "Me too. You remember what I said, right?"

He nods.

"I mean it, Ry," I continue. "If anything feels off, call me. I don't care what it is. I'll sprint out of that meeting and get here as soon as I can."

"I know," he says softly. "I will."

"I've gotta go," I groan. "Fuck, I already miss you."

We both stand, and he walks with me to the door. I kiss him slowly and deeply, letting myself get lost in him for a second longer. Then I force myself to pull away, resting my forehead against his.

"I'll be back before you know it, and I'll call you when I'm on my way home," I promise.

He swallows hard, pulls me into a hug, and whispers, "Okay. I miss you already, too."

I squeeze him tighter, take a deep breath, and finally step back. Before I can change my mind or do something like tell him I'm in love with him, I grab my keys and walk out the door.

I curse everything as I drive away from the apartment, and I don't feel any better when I park in the office parking garage. Everything feels wrong, and I can't pinpoint why, maybe because I feel like I don't belong here anymore.

When I walk through the parking garage and into the office, I'm met with the familiar fluorescent lights that buzz overhead. The office smells like burnt coffee and cleaning products, and it feels hollow and cold despite the fake plants and wall art. It never used to bother me before, but after being away for so long, I can't stand it. All I want is to go home to Ryder and wrap my arms around him.

"Logan! There you are. We've missed you around here."

I flinch at the sound of my manager's voice, pasting on a polite smile as she approaches.

"Conference room B in five!" she says, overly chipper.

"Heading there now," I answer as enthusiastically as I can manage.

She gives me a thumbs-up and walks away, her heels clicking against the tile. I stand there for a second, trying to mentally hype myself up for something I don't want to do.

There are a few people in the room when I get there, so I pour myself a cup of the coffee waiting on the counter and pull out my phone.

LOGAN:

Miss you already. Everything okay?

His reply comes almost immediately.

RYDER:

I'm good, just working. Cameras are quiet.
Don't stress, okay?

I exhale and type back a quick response.

LOGAN:

I can't help it when you're involved. You
mean too much to me, baby.

I make my way to a chair near the back of the room, nodding at a few coworkers as they chat about projects and after-work plans. Everything around me feels completely normal, so why can't I shake the feeling that everything's about to come crashing down?

The meeting starts, and I try my best to focus—the HR rep drones on and on about updated policies and workplace initiatives. I scribble a few notes to look engaged, but the only thing on my mind is Ryder.

I pull out my phone to check the cameras in hopes of

easing my nerves. Like he said earlier, nothing is showing up, but I do see a new text from him.

RYDER:

Miss you too. Do what you need to and come home to me soon.

I smile to myself before being yanked back to reality.

"Something interesting, Logan?"

I jerk my head up, meeting the HR rep's pointed stare.

"No, sorry," I say quickly, shoving my phone back into my pocket, even more annoyed about the interruption.

The meeting drags, each minute stretching painfully long. By the time it ends, I'm out of my seat before anyone else. I have no idea why I even needed to be here in the first place. I get that it's a required quarterly meeting, but it feels like a complete waste of time. I showed up and did my part though, so now I'm getting the fuck out of there.

Any overachieving I used to do? Dead and gone.

I wave a few half-hearted goodbyes, pack up my bag, and head for the parking garage. I'll call Ryder once I'm on the road, like I promised—he'll want to know I'm on my way.

My footsteps echo across the silent parking garage in a way that sets my nerves on edge. I keep glancing over my shoulder, but there's nothing there.

When I near my car, I let out a sigh of relief and hit the unlock button. The chirp echoes louder than it seems necessary, and suddenly, I feel like a target has been placed on my back.

I should have unlocked it with the key, damn it.

I reach for the door, fingers barely grazing the handle, when a voice I never wanted to hear again stops me cold.

"Logan."

My breath locks in my throat as my hand stills. A sickening wave of unease curls through my gut, forcing me to turn around slowly as my heart hammers in my chest.

Kyle stands a few feet away, hands buried in the pockets of a dark zip-up sweatshirt. Guess he decided to leave the leather one at home today. He's wearing jeans and boots, and it feels like everything he put on was intentionally chosen to blend in.

And, of course, he knew I'd be here. He probably followed me here or hacked into my fucking email, but none of that matters right now because he *is* here, stepping closer to me.

"You fucked up, Logan. I told you that you shouldn't have touched him, but you didn't listen. It's your loss because he's mine now."

The rage I felt the other day somehow pales in comparison to this because Ryder is *mine*. "He doesn't want you," I spit. "He'll never want you. This obsession has gone too far, you need to let him go."

An amused look takes over his face, and I'm seconds from punching it off of him.

"Obsession?" He laughs bitterly. "No, you've got it wrong, Logan. You're the one who's obsessed—clinging to him and sticking by his side like a parasite. He doesn't want you, and I promise you he won't miss you. Not when he realizes how good it is with me. He's my angel, and now I'll finally have him."

I can't fucking take it anymore. I lunge at him, my fist connecting with his smug face, sending his head jerking to the side. He stumbles back a step, then brings a hand up to rub his cheek.

"Oh," Kyle chuckles darkly. "So you do have some fight in you. This just got more interesting."

I don't waste a second. I swing again, landing a solid punch to his ribs. He grunts, but before I can hit him again, he retaliates. His fist slams into my gut, knocking the wind out of me. I barely register the pain before he shoves me against my car. He's a big dude, but all I care about is Ryder, and I'll fight until I have nothing left to give to protect him.

"Let me guess," Kyle sneers, stepping closer. "You think you're the hero in this story, don't you? The one who gets to save him." His eyes are violent and dark. "But you're the one he needs saving from."

I shove off the car and swing again, catching him in the jaw and raising my fist again, but freeze when I see him reach inside his jacket and pull out a knife.

"I told you what would happen if you touched him again. But you didn't listen. Now you both get to deal with the consequences," he snarls. "This is your fault, Logan. The only person you can blame here is yourself for making me do this."

He lunges, and an explosion of pain tears through my lower abdomen.

I stumble back, gasping in shock as my hand flies to the wound. Blood seeps out around the knife still embedded in my gut, and I see it spread through my shirt. *How could I have been so stupid?* I should have been more prepared, but instead, I keep fucking up and breaking my promises to Ryder.

Kyle steps closer, until he's practically on top of me. He leans in, so close I can feel his breath on me as he whispers, "You don't deserve him. But it doesn't matter now. I'll take care of him. The way you never could."

I want to rip his throat out. I want to grab the knife and

stab him until there's nothing left but a bloodied shell of the monster who tried to take everything from me. But my body betrays me—my knees give out, and I barely catch myself before I collapse onto the pavement.

Kyle crouches beside me, watching me struggle, like he's committing this moment to memory.

"You're pathetic," he spits and then, with a brutal twist, he yanks the knife from my body, and a scream tears from my throat as blinding agony rips through me. I can't breathe. I can't think. Everything fucking hurts.

I watch him pick up my keys, and panic fills me for Ryder. Kyle's going to go to the apartment and let himself in. He knows where I live. *Fuck!* He starts to walk away, but before he disappears to let me bleed out on the cold concrete, he turns over his shoulder with a smirk and says, "Ryder's mine now."

No.

Fuck no.

I can't let this happen!

I have to warn Ryder. I have to call him—tell him to run.

My fingers fumble for my phone, struggling to pull it from my pocket. Blood makes it slick, and my grip is weak and clumsy. My vision starts to blur, black spots crowding the edges.

If I can just press the right buttons. If I can just hold on long enough to make the call...

But the world keeps slipping, and the phone falls out of my hands.

And then—

Everything goes black.

22

RYDER

Logan was supposed to call me by now.

I stare at my phone again, willing it to light up with his name. The rational part of my brain keeps insisting his meeting is probably running late. He didn't know exactly how long it would be, just said 'lunch time' and that he'd call me when he's on his way home, but it feels like it should be over by now.

It's not like Logan to forget to check in. Especially not now, not with everything going on. I know he's as worried about me as I am about him.

His being at the office today has made me even more painfully aware of how much our dynamic has shifted. We used to go days—hell, even a whole week, Friday to Friday— without seeing each other, and it never felt like this.

Now it feels like someone's ripped a piece of my heart out, and I'm just waiting for it to return. I've never missed anyone like this. Never felt this kind of ache. And yeah, it's probably a little crazy missing him this much after a few hours apart, but I can't stop the emotions running through me.

Maybe if the stakes didn't feel so high, I wouldn't be this anxious. But the apartment is too quiet and empty without him, and all I want is for him to come home now.

"I'll check in," I mutter to myself, grabbing my phone and typing out a quick text.

RYDER:

> Hey, everything okay? Meeting running long?

I stare at the message, my thumb hovering over the send button. He should've called by now, so I hit send, then toss the phone onto the couch like it might explode—anything to keep myself from staring at it, waiting for those three little dots to appear.

It's not lost on me that when the emails started, I thought I could handle this situation on my own, and now I can't stand being alone for even a few hours.

I honestly thought it would be no big deal and that I was being overly dramatic by involving Logan. But, like always, he didn't act like it was an inconvenience at all; he just stepped right in and held me together when I didn't know how to hold myself. We've always been good at showing up for each other. That part hasn't changed.

But it feels different now because I'm *in* love with him. Not an *I care about you* love or *best friend* love. It's deeper. It's visceral and all-consuming and constant. Now it feels like something fundamental in me has shifted, and I can't imagine a world where he's not right here next to me, touching me, kissing me, calming me with nothing more than a look, and I miss that today.

Logan isn't just my best friend. Or my boyfriend. Or a part of my life.

He's my whole world.

My safe place, my constant, my home.

My everything.

My person.

I hear my phone buzz, and I grab it at lightning speed, but it's just a regular, non-stalkery email. I let out a shaky breath and remind myself that he will call when he's done.

Sitting here alternating between staring at the door and my phone isn't going to help, though, so I force myself to get up and try to focus on work. Taking my phone with me, I head into the closet but keep the door open so I can hear Logan coming home. There's no way I'm in the right headspace to record anything, but I can at least prep and take notes. I grab the book I've been reading all morning, which is the next one on my schedule to narrate.

About ten minutes later, I hear the front door close, and the relief that rushes through me is instant. It feels like for the first time all day, I can finally breathe again knowing Logan's back. I drop the book and nearly trip over my own feet running out of the closet, heart pounding as I hurry to the main living area, ready to collapse in his arms. The stress of being apart was too much.

I turn the corner, already halfway through a breath meant to say 'I missed you so much, never leave me again,' but the second my eyes land on the person near the door, the words die in my throat.

It feels like the floor drops out from under me.

My heart stops, and panic fills my lungs because it's Kyle. Not Logan. Kyle is here, standing inside Logan's apartment.

He's wearing a dark zip-up hoodie, and he looks...unhinged. Hair messy, eyes wild, and there's a smear of blood on his face that makes my stomach twist.

And he's smiling expectantly at me.

"Hey, Ryder," he says, far more calmly than he looks. "I thought we could finally talk," he says, stepping closer to me. "Just the two of us."

My body goes ice cold, and I step back until I hit the wall behind me.

Fuck, where is Logan? And why the fuck is Kyle here instead of him?

Panic coils in my chest, but I need to tamp it down. I need to breathe and get him the fuck out of here.

"Leave," I snap, finally finding my voice. "Get the fuck out!"

Kyle stands there, watching me. His gaze rakes over me slowly, and I feel so violated. "But I came all this way to see you, angel."

My chest heaves, and I need to get my phone. *Why the fuck didn't I bring it out here with me?*

"Get. Out," I force out, trying to make him understand just how much I don't want him near me or in Logan's apartment.

But as usual, he smirks at me.

"I'm here for you. We can finally be together now."

I react on instinct, moving toward him to slam my fist into his face with as much force as I have. Kyle stumbles back a step, hand flying to his cheek, and I swing again, but he dodges it this time and grabs me, ramming his shoulder into my ribs and slamming me into the wall. I grunt, twisting to get out of his grip, but he's strong and entirely fueled by his sick obsession.

"The fuck is wrong with you two punching me in the face?" he seethes, starting to get angry now.

Before I even have time to process what he said, I bring my leg up to kick him in the ribs since I can't get out of his hold. It's enough to make him flinch and gives me an opening to free myself so that I can tackle him to the ground. We hit the floor hard, and I scramble to recover on top of him, punching him repeatedly anywhere I can reach, and blood starts pouring out of his nose.

"You don't get to show up here!" I snarl, not stopping. "You don't get to fucking claim me! I don't want you."

Kyle bucks his hips hard and uses the momentum to flip us, slamming me onto my back. The breath wooshes out of my lungs as he ends up on top of me, pinning me to the floor. Then, he reaches behind him, and his hand comes back around, holding a knife.

The blade is covered in blood, and before I know it, it's pressed to my throat, and I freeze instantly.

"Stop," he breathes. "Don't make this harder than it needs to be."

"Get off me," I hiss, but my voice trembles with the threat of the knife against my skin.

He leans in closer, and I want to shove him off me, but I don't trust him not to stab me. "I didn't want it to be like this, but you're not listening. I'm trying to show you how good we can be. You belong with me, angel."

My mind is a chaotic mess of fear and fury, but my body's still frozen beneath him. I want to shove him off of me, but the bloody blade doesn't waver, and the look in his eyes tells me he's not bluffing. He's so calm, it's unnerving, almost like everything is unfolding exactly how he imagined it would.

I can't help but wonder if he'd slit my throat if he claims to want me, but I have a feeling that wouldn't stop him.

He shifts his weight, still keeping the knife steady as he reaches into the back of his waistband, and that's when I see a gun. He lifts it slowly, replacing the knife with cold metal as he presses the barrel against my side.

"Now," he says calmly, leaning over me, his face inches from my own. "You're going to get up and walk to the door. And you're not going to scream or try anything stupid."

I stare at him, barely breathing.

"I didn't want it to be like this," he whispers, repeating his words from moments ago. "But you made me do this. If you'd listened, none of this would be happening."

The tenderness in his voice makes bile rise in my throat.

He pushes off me and yanks me up by the arm, the gun now hidden in the space between us, pressed tightly to my ribs. I stagger, legs unsteady as the room tilts around me. My entire body is shaking as he drags me, step by step, toward the door.

I walk because I have no other choice.

"Shh, angel, not one fucking word," Kyle whispers, brushing his lips too close to my ear. "You're safe now. I'll take care of you."

I walk out the apartment door, even as my mind screams at me not to, because right now, surviving means waiting for a better chance.

I need Logan desperately. *Why isn't he here yet?*

A broken sob leaves me despite my best effort to hold it in, and Kyle's fingers tighten at the sound. "You'd better be quiet," he whispers. "Or what happens to you will be so much worse than your manipulative little friend bleeding out in a parking lot. Don't make me do that to you, too."

What?

"What the fuck did you say?" I choke out, my voice cracking as my feet stop moving. I'm stunned still because there's no way Logan is bleeding out in a parking lot right now while I can't do a damn thing to help him.

But, as usual, Kyle smirks at me without giving me an answer.

I feel sick. Is Logan bleeding out somewhere while I'm unable to get to him? Is that why he hasn't called? Is that why he's not here right now?

My vision blurs with tears I refuse to let fall while he's watching. My whole body is shaking, and I feel like I'm splintering apart from the inside out as panic floods every cell in my body.

Please be okay. Please be alive. Please. I need you. I love you.

23

RYDER

A sharp, splitting pain radiates through my skull. The pounding is so intense that each throb behind my eyes makes it harder to focus on where I am. Everything feels muffled and distant as I try to bring my surroundings into focus.

The last thing I remember is Kyle walking me out of Logan's apartment with a gun pressed to my side. I silently prayed for someone to walk past me and sense that something was wrong and help me, but no one did. Instead, he shoved me into the back of the car and then...I don't remember. But judging by the pounding in my head, he must've hit me hard enough to knock me out.

Everything hurts, and my body feels heavy. My shoulders ache from being slumped forward, and my legs and back are stiff like I've been sitting in this chair for hours. I need to move my body badly, but the second I try, pain flares around my wrists and ankles, and I realize I'm bound to a chair. Rough rope digs into my raw, chafed skin. I try to calm myself by taking deep breaths, knowing

I need to stay calm and alert if I want to make it out of here alive.

My vision slowly comes into focus as I take in my surroundings. It's dim—almost pitch black, except for a single light bulb hanging in the middle of the room, casting a yellow glow across the concrete floor. The walls are unfinished and lined with exposed pipes. The room is mostly empty apart from stacks of cluttered boxes, and it's damp.

I'm in a basement.

Kyle tied me to a chair in a fucking basement.

I need to get the fuck out of here, but the ropes dig in deeper with every twitch of my limbs. I flex and wiggle my wrists, trying to slip free, but it only worsens the burn.

I try to breathe through it, but I'm spiraling.

And that's when I remember what he said about Logan.

Oh god, is he alive? Is he bleeding out right now, alone, because I couldn't stop Kyle? He has to be. *Please let him be okay.*

I try to shove the alarm down somewhere deeper to focus on getting out of here, but it keeps clawing its way back up my throat. I've never felt this kind of fear before. It's not just terror—it's helplessness, and it's suffocating and consuming.

I have to get out of here.

Before I can attempt to make a plan, footsteps make their way down the stairs, and I brace for whatever's coming next.

"Morning, sleeping beauty," Kyle says, his voice like venom wrapped in sugar.

I keep my mouth shut, refusing to give him the satisfaction of speaking to him.

He comes around the chair, stepping into my line of view. He's got that off putting grin creeping across his face, and it's apparent he's thrilled I'm waking up in his fucking dungeon.

"You looked so peaceful sleeping," he murmurs, reaching out to brush a hand down my cheek as he crouches in front of me.

I flinch away from his touch, revulsion twisting in my gut.

"You don't have to be afraid," he says softly. "You're safe now, angel."

Safe? He thinks being tied to a chair in a basement is safe?

"Where the fuck are we?" I bite out.

"Somewhere no one can hurt you."

I don't look at him, letting the silence stretch between us. It must grate on him because his fingers clamp around my chin, forcing my face toward his. I jerk away instantly, shaking my head out of his grip. I don't want him anywhere near me, and I sure as shit don't want him touching me.

Kyle sighs like I'm disappointing him. "I don't want to hurt you, Ryder. Listen to me, and I'll show you how good we can be."

I clench my fingers into my palms, digging my nails in hard enough to hurt since it's the only thing I can do. The ropes around my wrists pull tighter with the movement, but I don't stop, and I don't give him the satisfaction of a response. If he thinks being tied to a chair in a dark, musty basement is 'good,' then he's somehow more delusional than I thought.

"You need to stop fighting this," he says, dropping his voice. "I know he brainwashed you, but you'll see how much he was bringing you down soon."

Everything he's saying is so far beyond insanity, I don't even know how to respond, so I don't.

He crouches lower, his face inches from mine, while I'm stuck in place, unable to get away. "Don't worry, angel," he murmurs. "We can finally be together now. Logan won't be a problem anymore. I took care of him like I promised I would. I always keep my promises."

Dread claws its way up my throat so fast I can't swallow. I try to hide my worry and school my features, but Kyle sees it, and his gaze darkens like he enjoys seeing me on the edge of panic.

Logan has to be okay because I can't exist in a world where he isn't. I'd rather die than continue to try to survive this nightmare with Kyle, but I can't stop trying. I have to keep fighting for him, for me, for us.

I let out a deep breath and force my expression to remain neutral, steadying myself before I speak.

"I don't know how to make this any clearer, but I don't want you, Kyle. I will never want you. The only person I want is Logan. So let me fucking go."

"No, you're mine now," he seethes. "I've been waiting so patiently for you. I'm saving you. From him. From yourself. You need me."

"Saving me?" I spit the words like they're poison. "How the fuck are you saving me? You tied me to a fucking chair in your basement after kidnapping me! Then you say you stabbed Logan? You tried to get rid of the *only* person I care about in this world. That's right, it's him. Not you, you sick fuck."

"Oh, I didn't try, Ryder," he counters. "I succeeded in removing that obstacle. Watched him collapse right in front of me, saw the blood seeping through his shirt. I know how to stab someone and kill them. It was all his fault. He didn't listen."

Everything slows down around me, but my pulse is sprinting. My brain tries to form logic, but all I hear is 'I succeeded.' Those two words seem like all that exists now.

He couldn't have succeeded. I refuse to believe it.

Logan is the love of my life—the only person who's ever truly seen me and stayed. And not only stayed, but loved me unconditionally, completely, and without hesitation.

He's the reason half the good things in my life exist at all. He knows how to calm me down without saying a word, and somehow also knows exactly when to push back and keep me on my toes. He makes me laugh in a way no one else ever has. He's undeniably the best part of me.

When things shifted between us, it didn't feel strange or sudden. It felt inevitable, like we'd always end up there.

He's the only person I want close. The only one I want wrapped around me at the end of the day. Even when we were 'just friends,' it was always him.

He's always loved me back the same way—fiercely, fully, and without fear. He believed in me when I struggled to believe in myself.

And if he's gone—if Kyle took him from me...

Then I don't know who I am anymore.

I refuse to believe the words coming out of his mouth because there's no version of me exists without Logan. None.

"You think I wanted to hurt him?" He shakes his head like it's justified. "I gave him so many chances, Ryder, but he just wouldn't let you go."

He actually believes every fucked-up word coming out of his mouth, and he thinks he's doing me a favor. That Logan's the villain and I'm supposed to thank him for 'removing the obstacle.' I want to vomit, cry, scream, but instead, I suck in a sharp breath, clinging to the rage I feel about Kyle and this situation because if I let myself spiral into the fear tightening around my ribs, I'll fall apart.

"You ignored me because of him, and I don't like being

ignored, Ryder," he cautions, and I can hear the calm in his tone start to dissolve.

"You're a fucking psycho," I snap. "Just like I said when we were at the station, I do not want you, Kyle." I drag each word out as much as possible so he can hear the utter disdain in my voice. I'm playing with fire, but in this moment, I don't care. Fuck him for talking about Logan like this. Fuck him for thinking he's doing me a favor.

He exhales sharply through his nose and starts pacing in a slow circle around me, dragging his hand across my shoulders, like he's the predator and I'm his prey.

"I'm going to give you a chance to apologize for that, Ryder," he says, his voice low and cold. "It's the conditioning from Logan. He made you dependent on him," he snarls. "But if you keep saying things like that, I'm going to have to show you how wrong you are."

Every single cell in my body is revolting at what he's insinuating. The idea of him touching me, forcing this twisted, sick fantasy, has me biting my tongue so hard I taste blood. He keeps saying I'm not listening, but he's the one refusing to hear me.

"I don't want to hurt you, Ryder. I never did," he sighs. "But you need to understand—"

He stops right behind me, his breath brushing against my ear, and I flinch before I can stop myself. Completely repulsed by him.

"You do not get to disrespect me like that," he finishes, his voice angry.

My fingers curl into fists as my entire body screams at me to fight, but I can't get out of these fucking ropes.

"I'll give you a chance to apologize. That's how nice I am,

angel," Kyle murmurs, his hands settling on my shoulders, giving them a light squeeze, and my skin crawls.

I ignore his request, wanting him to know I'm not just going to obey his command. "You really think this is going to work?" My voice comes out harsher than I expect. "That I'll ever want you? That I'll ever see you as anything other than the sick, delusional piece of shit you are?"

Kyle stills. His fingers twitch against my shoulders, and I know I've struck a nerve. He releases me and circles to the front of the chair, then a sharp, searing pain explodes against the side of my face. The slap echoes through the room, whipping my head to the side, building on what I already feel, and my skull is somehow throbbing more.

"You made me do that," he says almost sadly, shaking his head like I forced his hand. "I don't want to hurt you, angel, but you gave me no choice." He shakes his head. "I've heard the real you. The version of you that knows how to submit, how to be good. That's who you are—not this mouthy, ungrateful version pretending he doesn't need me. You need to respect me, angel."

I drag in a slow, shaky breath through the pain. My lip is bleeding, and I can taste the metallic tang on my tongue.

What the fuck is he—

Wait, angel?

"Angel?" I rasp. "Is that why you keep calling me that? Because of a book I narrated?"

Kyle tilts his head and hums. "Yes, angel. That's when I could hear the real you. The boy nobody else noticed. The one who needed someone to love him enough to stay, and that's what I'm doing."

Of course, I remember the book. One of the main characters, nicknamed 'angel' by his partner, lived with an abusive father who made him feel like he didn't deserve love. His character easily slipped into a relationship where all he wanted was to make someone else happy.

I could relate to his character because I had an asshole dad, too. I also know what it's like to want something steady and good, but the only person who's ever fully seen me is Logan. So I don't know where the hell Kyle gets off thinking I'm his, when I've made it abundantly clear I want nothing to do with him.

"That was fiction," I snap. "It was a fucking job, and you're the asshole in this situation. How don't you see that?"

"You're wrong," he bites out. "It was you. I heard the need in your voice to be safe and seen. That's when I knew I had to have you, had to save you. I could hear the ache behind every word."

"That wasn't me," I object because how does he not understand that? "It was a character that I didn't even write. I was acting!"

I don't know why I keep trying to reason with him. He doesn't even see me as a real person; he sees me as a fictional character who belongs to him.

Kyle shakes his head slowly. "No. You were honest for once. You let me in, and you've been mine ever since."

My gut twists. "You're sick."

"No, angel." He leans in close and grins at me. "I'm your salvation."

Then he turns and walks away.

24

LOGAN

There's so much beeping, someone make it stop. It's persistent and annoying, and I don't remember ever setting an alarm that sounds like this. My mouth feels like I haven't had water in days. *Why do I feel so out of it?* I swallow against the scratchy dryness, and I think my lips crack. The beeping doesn't stop; it's pulling me closer and closer toward consciousness.

I force my eyes open, and the horrible fluorescent lights overhead sear into my retinas, and I wince. There's a dull, throbbing pain radiating through my side. A creeping sense of unease claws its way up my spine as I realize I'm in a hospital, and reality begins to piece itself back together.

"Ryder!" I gasp, my voice hoarse and barely above a whisper, even though I try to yell out for him.

But instead of him being there, my mom jumps up and reaches for my hand.

"Oh, honey," she breathes, her face a mixture of relief and worry as she fusses over me, smoothing my hair. "You're awake. Oh, thank you, Jesus. Jim, he's awake!"

My dad walks over, and they both stare down at me in the hospital bed.

"How're you feeling, son? We've been worried sick about you," he says.

"Where's Ryder?" I ask immediately, ignoring his question. I know they're worried about me, but I'm fine. I'm far more concerned about Ryder—there's no way he wouldn't be here right now if he could be.

My parents exchange a glance, and instantly, my stomach drops.

"Logan," Mom starts cautiously, her voice tight with something she's not saying.

I push myself up on my elbows, pain tearing through my side, but I don't care. I need answers, and I need them now.

"Where is he?" My voice is laced with panic.

She hesitates again, and my dad clears his throat before stepping in.

"We don't know. We've been trying to reach him, but he hasn't been answering his phone."

"Something's wrong," I blurt the words out before I've even had time to think. "Ryder's in trouble."

It's a gut feeling. Ryder wouldn't ignore my parents, especially not after I didn't come home or call like I promised. He'd be here. I'm so sure of it, I'd bet my life on it. He would have been the first one through that door, gripping my hand, climbing into this small, uncomfortable hospital bed with me, muttering about how I scared the shit out of him and how I'm not allowed to die before he does because he can't handle that kind of grief.

He never would have left my side, which makes panic rise because…because the only reason he wouldn't be here is if he *couldn't* be…because of Kyle.

My chest tightens, and this sick, heavy feeling forms in my gut. I don't want it to be true, but something in me already knows it is. He has to be in danger because there's no way Kyle would try to kill me and not go after him.

Kyle thinks Ryder belongs to him, because to him, love isn't something you give, it's something you take. Something you own and feel entitled to. And I was the obstacle standing in the way of the fantasy Kyle had built up in his head. He probably hopes I bled out in that parking lot, and I can't wait until he sees my face again when I find Ryder.

Because I know Ryder's out there and I won't stop until I find him.

God, I knew this was coming. Something felt wrong, and I did nothing to stop it.

The thought makes something tear open inside me as panic claws its way up my throat like I'm choking on it.

I'm so fucking sorry, Ryder.

I can picture it so vividly—every horrible scenario flashing through my mind like a horror movie I can't shut off.

"Honey, we don't know that he's in trouble. Maybe he's sick or something," Mom says gently, and I want to scream. It's not her fault; we never told her about the stalking. I didn't want to worry her, but now she doesn't understand the severity of this situation.

"How long?" I croak. "How long have I been out?"

She hesitates. "About a day."

A day.

A fucking day?

"You don't understand," I say, frantic now. "If he's not answering and it's been a whole twenty-four hours, something's wrong." My body screams at me to move, to get up, to do something, anything. I try to swing my legs over the side of the bed, but my body betrays me with a fresh wave of pain that nearly knocks me out again. Fuck! I'm stuck here wasting time while Kyle does fuck-knows-what to Ryder. *My* Ryder.

"Logan—"

"No," I snap, gasping through the pain. "We need to go to my apartment. Now."

"Sweetheart, you're—"

"Mom, no, you don't understand!" I cut her off and she looks shocked, I've never raised my voice and spoken to her like this before, but I'm struggling to control my emotions after knowing I've been out for a whole fucking day. "I'm sorry, Mom, but this is an emergency. It's life or death for Ryder. Dad, please, where are my keys? We need to go."

They need to understand how serious this is, but instead of rushing through the room like I want them to, Dad's mouth flattens into a thin line, lips pursed likely at the way I'm speaking to Mom, but then finally, he nods. He knows I wouldn't be like this unless something is very wrong, and it is.

"Honey, you didn't show up here with any keys. They said you only had your phone on you," Mom soothes gently, like that'll calm me down.

What?

God damn it, I forgot Kyle took my fucking keys. After he ripped the fucking knife out of me he took the keys.

No, no, no, this is so much worse than I realized.

I barely register that my mom is still talking. It's all static in my ears as my mind goes into overdrive.

Ryder's alone.

Kyle has access to my apartment.

There's no way Kyle didn't go after him.

"Logan, you are not in any shape to—"

"Mom, I love you, but right now is not the time," I bite out. "If Kyle has him—if he's been gone for a whole day—I can't sit here. I have to find him. I have to. Who knows what Kyle did to him? I'm so sorry I'm yelling at you, but this is an emergency."

"I'm going to go, Logan," my dad says firmly. "You're not in any shape to move. You were stabbed and had surgery. I'll handle it. Promise, son. I'll see what I find when I get there, and I'll tell the nurse you're awake so she can come check on you."

I want to argue. I want to go because the only thing worse than being stuck in this goddamn hospital bed is the gnawing feeling that he's not going to find anything. There's no way Kyle would still be there. He's too smart, but I still need Dad to go to be sure.

"I'll call you as soon as I get there, okay? See if I can get in without your keys."

I nod, gritting my teeth. I know there's no way I'm getting out of this bed right now, but if he doesn't find Ryder, I will.

"Fine. Okay." I relent, my voice hoarse with desperation. "Go now, please."

Dad gives a short nod before turning toward the door. Mom steps aside, her lips pressed into a worried line, watching him leave. I'm not ready for the line of questioning I know is coming, but as soon as the door clicks shut behind my dad, she pulls up a chair beside my bed.

"Logan, honey," she says softly. "What the hell happened?"

I let my head fall back against the pillows, exhaling aggressively through my nose. My stomach screams in protest, but it doesn't matter. Nothing matters except getting Ryder back.

"Logan." Her voice cuts through my spiraling thoughts. "Talk to me."

Thankfully, a nurse walks in and stops this line of questioning. Even though I know I'll have to answer soon enough. "Good, you're awake," she says with a smile.

She checks the monitor, shines a penlight into my eyes, and asks a few quick orientation questions. I answer them all —name, month, where I am—and she nods approvingly at my answers. Then she checks to make sure I can move my arms and legs, which I can. It just really fucking hurts.

"Alright, you're alert and oriented. That's good. The police have been outside waiting to talk to you since you came in, but I wasn't about to let them near you until I did a neuro check and made sure you were alert first. Are you ready to speak with them now?"

I nod, ready to tell the cops exactly who did this. My hands are already sweating, and I can't stop flexing my fingers like it'll somehow wring the tension out of me.

A moment later, the door swings open and two police officers step inside. The older of the two men—a tall guy with graying hair and tired brown eyes, and a plain button-down shirt and slacks—nods in greeting. "Mr. Hart, I'm Detective Santos. This is Officer Donnelly, who I believe you've met since he's assigned to your case. We need to ask you a few questions about what happened yesterday."

I nod, we've met Donnelly. He's in a full police uniform, with a blue button-down shirt, black pants, and a fully equipped duty belt that's doing nothing to ease my nerves.

Mom tenses beside me, sitting up straighter, and I can feel her glance at me. Regret starts to creep in over the fact that I didn't tell them how severe the situation we're in is.

My stomach twists hard for another reason, too. *What if*

they don't believe me? What if they work with Kyle, and this somehow makes everything worse? But it's a chance I have to take. Trying to figure this out on our own got us nowhere, except stabbed and likely taken.

I sit forward, heart racing, and try to steady my voice. "Good," I say, with a confidence I don't fully feel. My throat's tight, but I force myself to say it. "Because I know exactly who did this."

Detective Santos pulls out a notepad, pen already in hand. "Alright, go ahead."

"Kyle Pearson," I state. "He stabbed me in the parking lot outside of my office. In the parking garage." I want them to know I'm fully aware of all the details and remember everything.

There's a flicker of something between the two officers as they eye each other, but I can't tell what it is. *Maybe they think Kyle's a creep, too.*

"And you're sure it was him?" Donnelly asks.

"Yeah. I'm sure," I say with as much conviction as possible.

Officer Donnelly frowns. "And what's Kyle Pearson's connection to you besides being the one working on your case with you?"

I can feel my blood pressure spike at the question because he knows every detail I've reported.

"He's the one stalking Ryder," I grit out. "He's the one who's been sending him emails. Watching him, or us now, I suppose. He broke into Ryder's house and left a fucking note inside his office, as you know. We first met him at Pine Bar in town weeks ago." My chest rises and falls too fast, adrenaline still burning through my system. "And now Ryder's missing."

My chest rises and falls too fast, adrenaline burning

through me like I'm still in that parking garage, bleeding out, trying to get to Ryder.

That makes Santos pause. He glances at Donnelly before flipping to a new page in his notebook. "Missing? How do you know that?"

"He hasn't answered his phone in a day. He'd never blatantly ignore my parents' phone calls. I had to go to the office yesterday, and he was worried about being alone. There's no way Kyle stabbed me and didn't go after Ryder. He stole my keys; that's one of the last things I remember before passing out. There's no world where Ryder wouldn't be here right now if he could. I know Kyle did something. I know it."

The detective's expression darkens. "And you think Kyle Pearson is responsible for that, too?"

"I know he is."

Donnelly speaks up. "Has Pearson made any direct threats?"

"Yes. His last email was the most threatening. He said that if we didn't stop 'being together,' we wouldn't want to find out what happens. That he'd hate to see either of us get hurt, and it was our last warning."

This isn't exactly the time or place I had planned to tell my mom about our relationship, but she'll interpret that however she wants.

Santos nods, flipping his notepad shut. "Alright, Mr. Hart. We're going to need you to walk us through exactly what happened yesterday. Every detail. And while we do that, we'll get officers over to Ryder's house to check whether he's there."

I exhale, my pulse still pounding, but at least someone is *finally* listening.

"Ryder's been staying with me since this whole thing started. He was at my apartment before I left, and I highly doubt he would've gone home. My dad is on his way to my apartment now to see if he's there, though."

I never should've left. I should've explained to HR how dire the situation was instead of thinking cameras would be enough.

Wait, the cameras!

"Mom, where's my phone? I need it."

"It's right here," she says, as she grabs it from the table beside the bed and hands it to me.

My fingers fumble with the passcode before I manage to unlock it. The hospital's shitty Wi-Fi crawls as I open the security app. I mutter under my breath, "Come on, come on..." like rushing the load screen will make the feed appear faster.

The dashboard finally appears, and it says, 'offline.'

Offline.

They're all fucking offline. He must have hacked into the system and shut them down so there'd be no proof of him at the apartment. I refresh the app, trying again, but nothing changes, no matter how many times I try.

"Motherfucker," I hiss, my hand tightening around the phone.

He heard the officer tell us to install cameras. He was standing right there. *Of course, he knew to check. I'm so goddamn stupid for thinking it would actually stop him or lead to the proof we needed.*

I knew Kyle was dangerous, and I walked right into his trap like an idiot...and left Ryder alone to deal with it. I clench my jaw so hard it hurts.

I don't know how I'll live with myself if something

happens to Ryder. I love him with every fiber of my being. I love him in a way that makes words feel useless. In a way that makes everything before him feel like a placeholder. I love him in a way that makes me ache for every second I wasted pretending I didn't.

He has to be okay because I have to tell him that. He has to know how much I love him.

I squeeze my eyes shut for a second, trying to pull it together, but the second I open them, the cops are still staring at me.

But before I can open my mouth to speak, Mom's phone rings.

She fumbles for it, answering on the second ring. "Jim?"

I watch her face closely, my entire body locking up as she goes silent for a moment, listening. I can't hear anything on the other end, but I can see the color drain from her face, and my heart stops.

She slowly pulls the phone away from her ear.

"Ryder's not there," her voice trembling as she speaks. "But his phone is."

25

RYDER

I don't know how long it's been since Kyle left, but he's back. My bladder is screaming at me with the pain of not being able to go to the bathroom. He sits right in front of me with an eerily calm expression and I want to get the fuck away from him, except I can't move. My wrists still burn against the rope that's been digging into my skin for hours—or is it days?

I've lost all concept of time being stuck in this dark, musty basement.

Based on our last interaction, I have no idea how this will go or what he has planned. I don't know how to handle this situation, either. I want him to know he's out of his fucking mind if he ever thinks I'll willingly accept this, but I also have no idea what he's capable of. The only thing allowing me to bite my tongue is the hope of seeing Logan again.

Kyle taps his fingers against my knees, and my body recoils. I loathe the way his touch feels.

"Do you ever wonder why I picked you, angel?"

I swallow the bile threatening to rise in my throat at the

feel of his touch and that question because I don't care. I don't want to hear whatever twisted story he's told himself to pretend this is normal.

"If you're about to start monologuing about how I'm your soulmate or whatever, save it. I've told you repeatedly—I'm not interested. And I'm not that character from the book. The only person I need saving from is you."

His smile doesn't falter, and that has my concern rising. What is his game here?

"You're perfect for me," he starts. "You *are* my soulmate, Ryder. I heard you and had to have you. The way you gave yourself over so completely. The way you said you wanted to be protected and cherished. That was *you*, Ryder. The *real* you. Not this hard-edged, defensive version in front of me now."

I stay silent, knowing nothing I say will help me in this situation.

"I'd been waiting for you, praying for God to bring you to me, even if I didn't know who you were yet. I was getting restless in my life, and then my prayers were answered." His voice turns almost wistful as if he's imagining it. "I knew the second I heard your voice and the words you were saying that you were meant to be mine."

I still don't respond.

"Your voice guided me and gave me purpose. I didn't even know what I was looking for until I found you. The way you begged for a chance to make him happy…I knew I could save you the same way he did." He closes his eyes and smiles. "I felt your obedience and devotion for your partner, and that was when I knew I had to have you for myself."

I stare at him, stunned, nauseated, frozen in disbelief.

"I knew you were talking to me. I knew you were waiting

for someone who saw you, and I did. Just like I told you, I see everything, Ryder. Every part you try to hide." He leans in, voice dropping to a whisper, then gestures between us. "This isn't random. I found you because I was supposed to."

My chest heaves as I struggle to process this. He doesn't think this is a sick obsession. He thinks it's *fate*. He thinks I exist solely for him, and there's no reasoning with someone who thinks God co-signed their insanity.

"It's like you wanted me to find you with how much you post online, too," he says, voice low and steady. "But those days are over now. No one else gets to see you or have you but me."

He leans in slightly, and I wish I could move away. "All I had to do was contact my uncle to get the job at the department. You have no idea how easy it was. And the fact that you lived here? It proved it was meant to be. That first night at the bar, when you looked at me, I thought maybe you'd recognize it too. But then I saw *him* and how he hovered around you as if he had some claim. I watched the way he twisted you up, made you believe he was the one you needed." His expression tightens.

I grit my teeth. Logan *is* the only one I need, and I *need* him to be okay. He'd be the only person who'd know Kyle took me and the only one who'd come looking. I'm positive he'd burn the world down to find me, so I need him to be okay.

I force myself to stay still and keep my face blank. I'll never be his anything. Not now. Not ever.

"It's okay that you're confused right now. I get it. I used to think *he* was the one, too," Kyle murmurs, almost nostalgic in thought again. "I gave him everything—my time, my patience, my love—but it wasn't real. I was trying to force something that didn't exist, just like Logan's been trying to do with you."

Who the hell is he talking about?

"He found me right after my mom died. I was angry and alone, and he was perfect for me at first. We were good for a while, but then he started pulling away, saying I was too much and that he needed space." Kyle's mouth twitches in anger. "He stopped answering my calls, blocked my number, and moved to a different state. He tried to date someone else, like I was something he could run from."

He looks at me, and this time there's nothing soft behind it.

"He couldn't see what was right in front of him. He fought me and denied what we had over and over, and it started to irritate me."

I don't want to engage, but I need to know what he's talking about. "What happened to him, Kyle?"

Kyle sighs, shaking his head like he genuinely pities the guy. "He made choices, Ryder. I warned him what would happen if he kept pushing me away, but he didn't listen."

The nausea rises so fast I nearly choke on it.

"You know, people like him...they twist everything. I gave him love, but he was too broken to see it. He pushed me until I had no choice." He sighs before continuing. "It's heartbreaking, really, what he did to himself. But actions have consequences. I warned him what would happen—begged him to stop running from what we had."

He leans forward slightly, voice softening like he's trying to console me. "But maybe that pain had a purpose because it brought me here to you. And I don't want you to end up like him. You still have time to learn, angel. Know that I'm patient —so patient—but even patience wears thin when someone keeps hurting you after you've done nothing but try to love them. You don't want to keep making that mistake, do you?"

I blink, unsure I heard what he's insinuating correctly. "What do you mean? What did you do to him?"

"He wouldn't stop fighting me. I gave him chance after chance, and he kept throwing my loyalty back in my face. He made his choice when he refused to stop. His death was his decision."

Oh god. Kyle killed someone because they didn't love him back, and in his head, it wasn't murder.

It was *their* fault.

He truly doesn't see anything wrong with this.

My heart slams into my ribs. "You...you killed him?"

Kyle shrugs, but his expression is calm. "He gave me no choice. I warned him, and he still chose not to listen. His death was his fault, just like Logan's was."

My stomach lurches, and this time, it doesn't stop. The nausea claws up my throat too fast to swallow down, and I vomit right onto Kyle's shoes and pants. My whole body shakes as I gasp for air, bile burning my throat, and tears threaten to fall. I hate how powerless I feel at this moment. I have no idea what to do or how to survive this, except to start complying. Even if he thinks I'm part of his divine plan, he just made it clear that he'd still be willing to kill me. He's done it before, and now I know, he'd do it again.

Kyle stares down at the mess, and for a moment, I can't tell what he's going to do—yell, shove me, snap entirely. *Kill me.*

But then he does something worse.

He smiles.

A small, eerie smile that barely touches his eyes. "You're overwhelmed," he says, almost tenderly. "I hate that it's so hard for you, angel," he murmurs. "But I'm doing this for us, and maybe now, you'll get that."

He crouches down in front of me again, totally unfazed by the vomit. "Can't you see how much I love you?" he asks, brushing a hand through my hair. "Once we leave this place, everything will be easier. I've built the perfect home for us. You'll be so good for me, won't you?"

The air in the basement shifts because he's serious. He's going to make me disappear, lock me away somewhere no one can find me, and call it love even though he has no idea what love truly is. His expression darkens slightly as he studies me, then he sighs. "I have to do this, Ryder. You'll understand when we get there."

Panic crashes over me as he reaches into his pocket. I jerk against the ropes, raw skin screaming, but it's no use. My heart races as I see the syringe.

"You're stubborn," he says, almost admiringly. "That's why I have to protect you from yourself. That's why you need me, Ryder. I'll save you."

He steps forward, and I thrash as hard as I can, but it doesn't matter because I can't move. My wrists feel like they're bleeding from the rope burn.

He uncaps the needle with his teeth and jabs it into my neck.

"Shh," he whispers. "You'll thank me for this. We'll be home soon."

26

LOGAN

M y heart nearly stops.

"What?" I croak.

Mom puts her phone on speaker. "I checked everywhere. There's no sign of him," Dad sighs. "His phone is here, his keys are on the counter, and the door was unlocked when I got here."

My chest tightens, and my pulse is erratic in my ears.

"He wouldn't have just left," I murmur. "You know that. He wouldn't have gone anywhere without telling me, without his fucking phone—"

"I know, which makes this next part harder to say, son."

I brace myself, unsure what he's about to say, but knowing it's going to be bad.

"It looks like there was some struggle. A few things are out of place and knocked over."

My breath picks up, and the air in this room feels like it's suffocating me. My chest moves erratically, and I can't calm down.

"Logan," Mom's voice cuts through, but I can't understand what she's saying. "Logan, honey, you've got to calm down."

I can't breathe, I can't think, I can't do anything except spiral. My chest stammers, rising and falling in short, uneven bursts. I can't slow it down. My hands tremble as my vision narrows, and everything around me feels louder and farther away all at once. I can't catch a single thought. Just flashes of Ryder, Kyle, the cameras, his phone. Him gone.

Gone.

The thoughts won't stop. The what-ifs. The fucking certainty that Ryder is gone and that Kyle took him. That he's alone and scared and I—

I wasn't there. I let this happen.

Fuck my job. It's never been worth more than Ryder, and yet I made him feel like it was—especially during the most stressful, terrifying time of our lives.

A gasping sob tears out of me. Fuck. What do I do? My lungs refuse to expand, my chest caves in, my head is too fucking light and—

"Logan."

I barely register Mom grabbing my face, forcing me to look at her. Her hands are warm, steady, but it's not helping. "Breathe, honey," she urges, her voice shaking. "Slow down. Breathe."

But I can't. Doesn't she get that? I can't calm down. I can't. The panic has its claws too deep in me now, its grip tightening with every second that ticks by.

The heart monitor beside me starts to beep faster, and a nurse bursts through the door a moment later, already moving toward the bed.

"What's going on?" she asks sharply, glancing between Mom and the screen. She adjusts the oxygen tubing near my face and raises the bed slightly. "Logan, I need you to slow your breathing, okay? You're safe. You're in the hospital. You're okay."

But I'm not okay. Ryder is missing.

Kyle has Ryder, I know it with every fiber of my being. I don't even realize I'm saying his name over and over until Mom grabs me and pulls me into a hug.

"You have to calm down," she pleads. "We will find him, Logan. I promise you, we will, but you need to breathe. You can't help him like this."

The nurse is still beside me, monitoring the screen, her hand firm but gentle on my shoulder. "That's it," she says softly. "Deep breaths. In through your nose, out through your mouth. You're doing good. There you go."

I squeeze my eyes shut. Try to force air in, then out, even though my lungs feel like they're made of cement.

In.

Out.

In.

Out.

I can't continue to fall apart. Not when Ryder needs me. Not when he could be out there fighting for his life.

My breath finally starts to even out and the monitor slows with me. I sit up straighter, grounding myself, and find my voice again.

"I need to go," I say, already throwing the blanket off me. Pain shoots through my side once again, but I don't care. I shove myself up, my vision tilting, black spots dancing at the edges. Mom is by my side in an instant, her hands pressing down on my shoulders.

"Logan, stop," my mom demands. "You are not leaving this hospital."

"I have to!" I snap at her, feeling horrible. I take a breath and continue. "Mom, if Kyle has him, then every second we waste is another second he's in danger—"

"I understand," she says, her voice breaking. "I know, Logan, I do. But you're still in pain and they haven't discharged you yet, honey. You can't help him like this."

"You want to help him?" The nurse cuts in, clearly taking my mom's side. "Then stay here long enough to gain your strength back. You can't walk out of here right now and help anyone. You just had surgery."

Fuck, she's right. I hate that she's right because what if I collapse somewhere? What if I find them and end up putting Ryder in more danger because I can't fight back? I know I'm being reckless, but the only thing I want is to get Ryder back.

Finally, I remember Santos and Donnelly are still here. I turn to Santos, who's still standing nearby, watching everything unfold with a tight expression.

"Send a team to Kyle's house," I demand. "Right now."

There's a beat of silence as Santos exhales through his nose and glances at Donnelly. "Pearson...he's one of ours," he says finally. "Well, sort of."

My stomach twists. "And that's supposed to mean what?"

He lifts a hand, like he's trying to tread carefully. "It means this isn't going to be as simple as just knocking on his door and dragging him in. He's connected; his uncle is the Chief. If we're wrong..."

"I'm not," I snap. "I know it's him. He stabbed me, and he took Ryder. I don't give a shit what kind of access badge he has, he's dangerous and he's got Ryder. And if you wait too long, it's going to be too late."

Santos hesitates for a moment longer, then nods slowly.

"Alright. If you're sure—and it sounds like you are—we'll do everything we can."

"I am, please, just get Ryder back," I grit out.

Santos nods again. "Okay. We'll do everything we can."

I HATE FEELING SO COMPLETELY USELESS. THE WAITING AND not knowing is killing me. It hasn't even been that long, but it feels like every second without news is an eternity. Finally, about twenty minutes later, my phone rings and I answer before the first ring even finishes.

"Please tell me you found him," I beg without any preamble.

There's a pause, and somehow, my gut sinks even more.

"No one's here. We searched the whole place," Santos confirms. "There's no sign of Ryder at all."

Goddamn it.

I squeeze my eyes shut and force myself to think, but Kyle is always calculated and careful. He never mentioned a location in any of his emails or anything that could give him away.

But that's what makes it click.

"There's got to be somewhere else," I mutter. "He's too careful. He wouldn't bring Ryder to his own house. He knew we were on to him, and I don't know if he thinks I'm dead or not, but if I woke up, he'd know I'd be able to ID him."

Think. Think. Think.

Would he go to Ryder's place? No. Too obvious. And he wouldn't risk somewhere public, like a seedy motel, because he wouldn't risk the chance of being identified or heard.

"Does he have access to any discrete locations from being

a consultant on the force? Anything remote, but within driving distance?" I ask, desperation creeping back into my voice. "We need to exhaust every possible option."

"We're looking into that now," Santos confirms. "We're also sending officers to your place to talk to neighbors."

"Please look into every possible location he could have gone. Please."

I hang up before he can say anything else.

My mind keeps reeling. Nurses come in and out to check on me, saying I can likely be discharged in a day or two, depending on how I'm doing, but it still feels too long. Time stands still in this bed, and it feels like this waiting will be my downfall.

Until my phone rings again.

I snatch it up and hit the green button almost as fast as last time.

"Yes? Did you get something?" I ask.

Santos's deep voice fills the line. "A neighbor heard noises around one yesterday afternoon. Said it sounded like an altercation, but they didn't check."

I sit up so fast that the pain slices through my side again. "They didn't fucking do anything?" I hiss.

"No," he says, "which, unfortunately, is very common. A lot of people hear a commotion but don't want to get involved, or they second-guess themselves. Sometimes it feels safer to do nothing, which is a sad reality." He sighs. "They said they were scared of calling the cops over nothing or starting an issue with their neighbor."

Someone heard him. Someone was right there, feet away while Kyle was dragging Ryder out of our fucking apartment and they didn't do a goddamn thing. They just sat there, afraid to call the cops over nothing.

Nothing.

I squeeze my eyes shut and let out a deep breath, but that only makes it worse. My brain's already filling in the gaps—picturing Ryder fighting, yelling, maybe even begging for his life—while some fucking neighbor sat on their couch, debating whether it's worth dialing three fucking numbers.

And they didn't.

And now Ryder's gone.

Rationally, I know I shouldn't be upset with them. Maybe I would've done the same thing in their position. I'll never know, but right now, being rational isn't on my list of concerns.

"Did anyone else see anything? Outside, even?"

"No. We're sorry, Logan. It was the middle of the day—seems most of your neighbors weren't home."

This doesn't give us anything, but I know Kyle was the reason for the altercation, and I know he took Ryder.

"I know he took him. Even without any eyewitnesses, I know. So, how are you going to find him?"

"Well," Santos says slowly, "here's the other thing. There's been pushback from a higher-up."

My stomach twists. "What? From who?"

He hesitates. "The guy who brought Kyle in as a consultant. He's—well, he's not happy about this."

"You're telling me some asshole who hired Kyle is more worried about his reputation or his relationship with a stalker and kidnapper, oh and not to mention the person who fucking stabbed me than finding Ryder? The innocent person they're supposed to serve and protect?"

"He's vouching for Kyle," Santos admits. "Calling him a 'professional' and claiming you're making baseless accusations. Just between us, he knows Kyle personally—and he wants us to stop looking."

"Are you fucking kidding me?" I yell out in rage.

"If you're positive Kyle's the one who stabbed you, we'll keep searching. We're on your side, Logan," Santos says, voice firm. "But they're trying to slow this down. They don't like this at all, but we do want to help you."

I let out a bitter, humorless laugh. "Well, tell him to go fuck himself."

"Logan," Mom warns gently from the chair in the room.

I ignore her, my patience snapping clean in half. "No, I'm serious," I bite out. "Tell him to go fuck himself, because Ryder is gone, and I know exactly who took him. So either he gets his head out of his ass, or he can watch while we take legal action against your entire department for letting a goddamn stalker have free reign. Oh! And let's not forget attempted murder so he could kidnap my fucking boyfriend."

"Look, we're on it, okay? We're on your side, Logan," Santos huffs. "I just wanted to update you. I'll call you again as soon as we have more."

This time, he hangs up, and my head is clouded with frustration. I need to get the fuck out of here.

And if Kyle so much as lays a finger on him—

I'm going to kill him. And it won't be an attempt.

27

RYDER

I slowly blink, forcing my eyes open. My head throbs with a dull, rhythmic pulse, and there's a metallic taste on my tongue.

Once again, I'm disoriented.

And once again, I'm tied to a fucking chair.

My limbs feel sluggish and unresponsive. Whatever Kyle jabbed into my neck before I blacked out is still working its way through my system—everything feels foggy.

My back aches like I've been stuck in this chair for hours, and my muscles are sore in ways that don't make sense. There's pain in my shoulders, and my ribs hurt.

How the fuck does he keep moving me?

He must be carelessly hauling my limp body around like I'm dead weight. It feels like he dragged me by the arms.

But then my nose catches a scent. It smells like food, and I realize just how hungry I am. I feel like I've been passed out or drugged for days.

My stomach twists, both from the scent and the brutal

realization of how long it's been since I last ate at Logan's apartment. I don't even know how long ago that was anymore. *A day? Two? More?*

My stomach clenches painfully, a hollow, cramping reminder that I'm running on nothing. I feel weak and shaky, and so deeply uncomfortable as I notice the other sensation.

My face flushes with shame before I even register what it is.

I shift slightly, and the feeling confirms it—my jeans are damp and cold against my skin. Somewhere between being drugged and waking up here, I must've pissed myself, and humiliation hits me hard and fast.

I squeeze my eyes shut, hating how my body feels like it's no longer mine and he's stripped away every bit of control I had, right down to my basic dignity.

I force myself to hold back my emotions and figure out where I am.

It looks like a house. At first glance, anyway.

Despite it looking like a semi-normal studio apartment with furniture, lamps, and even a fucking fake plant, I'm still tied to a chair like a prisoner. And through the smell of food, I catch a hint of fresh paint.

The space seems clean and semi-nice, and that somehow makes it worse than the dark basement. It's like he's trying to disguise a prison as a home, and that's when I realize what's off about this space.

There are no windows. I can't see a single one, and I've never been in a house without windows. It's like he built this space to look lived in, but it feels more like he constructed a cage to keep us trapped in this room together.

Kyle walks over in my direction, holding a plate of food.

"Oh, good. You're awake," he says, as he walks closer and sets the food on the table near me.

"I figured you'd be starving," he says, like we're roommates or friends.

He's right, I *am* starving, but I don't want to give him the satisfaction, so I clench my jaw and swallow the hunger down as best I can.

"Where the fuck are we?" I force out.

"Our new home. We needed a fresh start," he says casually. "The basement was always temporary. I knew you wouldn't be comfortable there forever. But this..." He gestures vaguely around the room. "This is where we really begin. I built it for you, angel. This was my construction project."

A cold sweat breaks across my skin. *Built it?*

"I tried to make this place our home. I even decorated it for us. Look," he says, pointing to a spot behind me. I try to turn my head, but I don't even need to move that far.

There are pictures. So many pictures. A collection of photos he's printed out of me. Some are grainy—he must've taken them at the bar, while I was walking, even one from inside my house, probably from when I heard the noise in the bushes. Others are clearly from my social media; he even has the picture from my narrator profile. My face is everywhere—it's something out of a nightmare. He even photoshopped us together in some, and placed his face over Logan's.

"It's nice, isn't it?" he muses. "I wanted this place to feel like you. We can add more pictures of us soon. I bought one of those home printers for us."

I'm trapped in a fucking shrine to myself with a psychopath.

I force myself to breathe evenly, keeping my voice flat. "This is fucked."

"Oh, Ryder," he hums. "You don't mean that."

"I do," I bite out, feeling like maybe death is the best option after all.

"Remember what I told you about the last person who fought me?" He sighs. "You remember, don't you, angel? I thought we'd come to an agreement. I'd move you here and you'd be happy. We'd be happy together, angel."

There's no way I agreed to that. Even drugged out of my mind, I wouldn't have promised something so insane. There's no world in which I'd ever willingly agree to this.

I see him move and I freeze for a moment, worried he's going to pull another needle, or knife, or something out of his bag, but no, it's almost worse.

It's a book.

One I recognize immediately, and I have an idea of where this is going.

Kyle runs his fingers along the cover. "This is where it all started."

I say nothing.

"This is the first book I heard you read," he murmurs, flipping it open, tracing a finger down the first page. "The book that brought us together, angel."

I keep my expression neutral. For the first time in my life, I curse my profession, even though I know that's not the problem.

He is.

"Now, here's what's going to happen, angel," he rasps. "You're going to eat this meal I made you, and then you're going to read this book to me."

I stay silent again, but he must disapprove of my lack of

response because he leans forward and kicks me in the shin, and I flinch back hard.

Instantly, Kyle's voice softens. "See? I don't want to have to do that, angel, and I won't have to if you listen."

"Okay," is all I manage to say.

He stabs some of the food on the plate and feeds it to me, forkful by forkful. It feels so manipulative, but the chicken and broccoli taste incredible. I almost don't care if he's poisoned me again through the food, and I wake up in a new place. I'm ravenous and I need this.

"Drink," he grunts, holding a cup of water with a straw in his hand. I try to slow down, but I chug the entire thing, and he chuckles.

"Thirsty, huh? I'll get you some more. Don't eat without me," he says with a wink, like I could move.

As he turns to go, I force my throat to work. "Bathroom," I croak.

He pauses in the doorway and looks at me like he's considering this.

"Soon," he decides, and disappears before I can say anything else.

After he gets back and continues feeding me until he's satisfied with how much I've eaten, he dabs the corners of my mouth like he's proud of me and there's nothing I can do.

He hasn't let me go to the bathroom, and he's immediately ready to move on to the book. He picks it up and holds it open for me like it's reading hour at the library.

"I listened to you reading every night after I first heard your voice," Kyle admits. "Your voice was the only thing that helped me sleep."

Jesus fucking Christ.

He lifts the book, holding it out toward me. "Read it to me, angel."

My throat tightens, and I flinch, dragging my gaze away from the book. I don't want to do this. Every cell in my body is screaming at me not to, but what choice do I have? Sitting here tied up, weak, and worn down, my options are limited—and Kyle doesn't seem to handle disobedience with grace.

As much as I want to refuse, I can't keep pissing him off.

Before I start, Kyle tilts his head, studying me. "You must be exhausted, angel. I'll let you sit on the bed if that helps. It's very important to me that you give this your all, Ryder. I'll know if you don't. I've listened to you hundreds of times."

I almost laugh at the sheer insanity of that statement.

"Oh, wow," I say dryly. "A bed? That's so generous of you."

"Ryder," he scolds.

Right, Logan.

Logan, Logan, Logan.

I need to bite my tongue for Logan and hold onto hope that he's going to find me. I have to stay alive, despite wishing I didn't have to live through another minute of this.

My jaw tenses, and with every ounce of self-control I have, I mutter a quiet, "Fine."

His face lights up, and he reaches for my ankles. "Before I untie you, let me make one thing clear, angel. I am in charge here, not you. If you try anything, I will have to hurt you, and I don't want to. Just listen to me, that's all you have to do. Okay?" He waits for me to respond so I nod. "Okay. Now, I will untie you and you will go straight over to the bed." He speaks clearly, so there's no misunderstanding between us.

I nod again.

"I want you safe, angel. Don't make me do something we'll both regret."

I know he's not fucking around, but if I see an opportunity for escape, I'm going to take it. If not, I'm going to make him think he can start trusting me. It's the only option I have left, even though the thought of doing that makes my skin crawl, but if I have to, I will.

He unties the knots at my ankles before reaching for the ones at my wrists. I force myself to stay completely still as his fingers work at the rope. The second my wrists are free, blood rushes back into them. I curl my fingers, my nails digging into my palms to keep from trembling.

He pulls me up and drags me to the bed as I stumble over my feet. "Go on, get comfortable."

I make my way to the bed before collapsing against the pillows. I don't feel strong enough to keep myself upright from the lack of usage of my body, so I pick up the book Kyle has selected as he settles in too close for my liking at the end of the bed, even though there are a few feet between us.

Then, without another choice, I open the first page and begin to read.

28

LOGAN

I stand looking around the room. It isn't much—a single couch, a coffee table we found on the curb, and a mattress and dresser for each of our bedrooms. But none of that matters because this is our home, and we'll build it up more with time.

It's just me and Ryder now—no more roommates.

Ryder flops onto the couch, stretching out with a groan. "Man, I don't even care that we don't have a TV stand yet. This is perfect."

I chuckle, setting down a box labeled KITCHEN SHIT and grabbing a beer from the barely-stocked fridge. "I give it a week before you start bitching about the lack of furniture."

He grins, cracking open his drink and clinking it against mine. "Nah, this place is perfect. You, me, and the rest of our lives. We're living the dream."

I snort. "Oh yeah, the dream of being broke as shit while we figure out what to do with our lives. I hope my internship will lead to a job offer. Yours too."

He takes a sip of his beer, then sits up. "They will, I know it. And, seriously, Logan, this is everything I want. The fact that we're doing it together makes it even better."

I feel something in my chest tighten, but I don't let it show. So I do what I always do with my best friend—I keep it light.

"Yeah, yeah," I say, knocking the rim of my bottle against his again. "Here's to us. Two dumbasses figuring it out together."

He beams at me, and his smile is the last thing I see before I slowly drift back to consciousness. For a few perfect moments, I'm back in our first apartment, preparing for the rest of our twenties as college graduates with the world at our fingertips.

Never once did that version of me imagine we'd be nearly thirty, living separately, and in the situation we're in right now.

Once I get Ryder back, I'm never letting him go. Ever. I'll fucking glue him to me if I have to, but we're doing everything together moving forward. The pain of being without him right now—of the not knowing—is so much worse than my stab wound.

I finally open my eyes and am once again blinded by those horrid fluorescent lights. The fucking endless beep, beep, beep of the machine I'm hooked up to immediately starts to grate on my nerves. Both of my parents are in the room now, and I assume there's been no update, or they would have woken me up, but it doesn't stop me from asking.

"Is there any update? Has anyone called?"

"No, sweetie. Not yet," Mom soothes.

"When can I leave? It has to be today, right?"

"It should be. Now that you're awake, we can call the nurse and double-check."

I'm fine, I don't even know why I'm still here. Part of me feels like they're only keeping me here so I don't go out and murder Kyle myself. Although I think that would be too easy of a way out for him. I think rotting in prison would be worse, and I need to remind myself of that, so I also don't find myself there for murder. I've lost Ryder once, and I refuse ever to lose him again.

"Yes, get the nurse, please. I need to make a call," I grumble. I'm not trying to be an asshole, but I don't know how not to be when the love of my life is somewhere out there with a lunatic holding him hostage. We have no idea what Kyle is capable of, which is why every minute feels so overwhelmingly stressful.

I grab my phone and call Santos first.

"Anything?" I bark when he answers.

"No, not yet. The warrant we've requested to search Kyle's work files was denied."

Rage burns through me at those words. They're protecting a kidnapper over us. Apparently, being stabbed isn't enough evidence for them to do what's right, which is why neither one of us let on that we *knew* it was Kyle last time we were at the station with him. I had a feeling we wouldn't be believed over someone they hired.

I let out a cold, cruel laugh before I speak. "He stabbed me, and now Ryder is missing, and they don't think the man I identified is worth looking into?"

Santos still doesn't reply, probably letting me process my rage.

"I'll do it myself then."

"Logan, we're going to continue to do everything we can. We'll see what other resources we can leverage since we weren't able to obtain the warrant. We'll keep working and be in to—"

I hang up, not caring to hear the rest of that sentence. The same words he's been repeatedly telling me, even though nothing is getting done.

I pull up the one number I have in my phone that could possibly help me with this—Matt. He couldn't do much with tracking the emails, but that has to be because Kyle is some crazy cybersecurity hacker. Well, he's probably not, but if he can fix it, he can hack it, right? He knows exactly how to be untraceable.

He can't be that stealthy with public records, can he?

It rings once before Matt picks up. "Logan, are you okay, man? I heard—"

"I need your help," I cut him off. "Kyle took Ryder. The cops are looking, but I need more. They're dragging their feet on this, and I need to know where he could have taken him."

There's a pause. "Shit," Matt mutters. "Alright. What do you know?"

"Not enough," I admit. "They searched Kyle's place and found nothing. There was an altercation at my apartment that a neighbor heard around one in the afternoon, the day I came into the office, and Kyle stabbed me in the parking garage. The cops are moving too slowly because some higher-up has a personal relationship with Kyle and doesn't think he could be involved in something like this. Kyle's a cybersecurity consultant for them. That's all I know. I need to know where else he could've taken him."

"Fuck, man," Matt exhales. "That's a lot, and I'll do what I can, but Logan, I don't have access to confidential information."

Of course he doesn't, this isn't a fucking movie. He's a guy who works in tech and has a personal interest in true crime, but he has to have something he can use to help, right?

"I'm not asking you to hack the Pentagon, Matt," I plead. "I just need a lead. Public records, property listings, old addresses—anything that could tell us where the fuck he's hiding. Any old work buildings in the surrounding area? Anything." I'm begging at this point, but I don't care about the desperation bleeding through my voice. This feels like the closest I've gotten yet, and we haven't made any progress.

"Okay, okay. Give me some time, I'll see what I can do."

The line goes quiet except for the sound of Matt's fingers on his keyboard for what feels like an eternity. I try to be patient, but I want to know what he's finding. I'd do anything for Ryder, and yet, I still let Kyle get what he wanted. I let Kyle take him, and I don't know how to be okay with that. I won't be okay with that if Kyle has touched even a single hair on Ryder's perfect body.

Matt curses under his breath, dragging my attention back to the phone. "Logan? Kyle doesn't own much outright. Doesn't own his home, no rental properties apart from the one he's in now, no campers or anything tied to his name. But I did find one thing."

"What is it?"

"There's an address listed as a secondary location on a business registration for a short-lived consulting LLC he created a couple of years ago. It's not listed under his name now, but it popped up when I cross-referenced some of his old data from public sites."

I perk up at that. "Where is it?"

"Looks like a warehouse in town that's close to the lake,

and I can't figure out why he'd list that address unless he had access to it somehow. So be careful, Logan."

A warehouse on the harbor that's probably abandoned. *Of course.* No one goes down there since they no longer use that port. Now it's a place that's isolated, a place where no one would hear Ryder cry for help. Dread pools in my stomach, but so does a tiny flash of hope because this must be where Kyle took him.

"Send me the address," I demand.

"Logan," Matt protests. "Man, I know what you're thinking—"

"I have to go, Matt. If the cops won't take this seriously, I will. I have to. I love him. I can't let him spend another minute longer than he has to be trapped with Kyle. I can't, please."

"You were just stabbed and you're in the hospital, you're not invincible, Logan."

"I appreciate your help in all of this, but there's nothing you can say that'll change my mind," I confirm. "Please, please send me the address. I need it."

Another person who actually gives a shit about me and my safety, and I'm snapping at them like an asshole. At this rate, I'm going to owe everyone in my life a stack of apology cards once Ryder is back in my arms. But right now, I don't fucking care. How can I care about my safety when I don't know what condition Ryder is in? I want to set the whole goddamn world on fire for him and I will tear through every roadblock, every hesitation, and every bureaucratic bullshit excuse until I find him.

And I will.

Nothing will stop me.

I have to get to him, and if no one is going to help me, I have to do it myself.

Matt is silent for a long moment. Then, finally, he exhales. "I'm texting you the address. But Logan, don't be a dumbass, okay? You can't help him if you're dead."

I hang up before he can say anything else.

29

RYDER

"Get in the shower."

Kyle's voice is firm and has an edge to it. I can hear his patience fraying even though I've done everything he's asked since he demanded I read him that book.

I need to stay alive, so I've been cooperating.

Stripping out of my clothes in front of Kyle makes me more uncomfortable than anything that's happened up to this moment. Every one of my instincts screams at me not to do it, even though I desperately want a shower. I know better than to think he'll leave me alone to rinse off in private.

The thought of being naked anywhere near him makes me feel exposed in a way I'm not prepared for because it's a reminder that my autonomy is gone.

"Ryder," he says again. "I won't say it twice. I'm trying to help you here. I'm being nice and giving you what you want."

I swallow hard, knowing I don't have a choice because I'm a prisoner who can't fight or resist at this moment. After I read to him, he let me walk around the confined space freely, but I know he's only testing me.

It's also probably because the door is padlocked from the inside, and I haven't seen a key anywhere. He obviously locked us in when he first brought us here, and I was still unconscious, but at some point, he'll need to leave. At some point, we'll run out of food or supplies, or he'll get called into the station, and then I can try to find my escape.

I have to be smart, and this isn't the time to make my move yet, which leaves me with only one option at the moment.

Slowly, I move toward the shower. Kyle follows close behind me, and I can feel his breath against the back of my neck. My shoulders involuntarily hunch up to try to protect myself.

"Turn it on," he instructs.

I reach out and twist the barely working knob of the shower. The pipes groan, and the water comes out brown at first, and I can't help but gag. The repulsion is too much, but after a few seconds, the water runs clear and steam rises, which is a silver lining if there ever was one. *At least I won't have to take a cold shower.*

I stare at the water, but feel his gaze burning a hole in the back of my head. It feels like he's undressing me without even touching me.

"Strip."

I reach for the hem of my shirt with shaking hands. My fingers tremble as I pull it over my head, and Kyle's eyes darken at the sight.

I force myself to breathe and don't look away as I unbutton my jeans. I shove them down and step out of them. Awareness prickles at my skin, knowing that I'm fully exposed now, standing in front of him in my underwear. Every nerve in my body is on high alert as he tilts his head slightly to look at me, his eyes flickering over my torso, making their way down my stomach. It's disgusting.

I step back, trying to walk into the shower, but Kyle's voice stops me.

"You're not ready yet, angel. You forgot something." He smirks at me. "Remember what we talked about? About listening?"

Kyle's voice is expectant, like he knows I'll listen to him now because he threatened me with death.

But fuck him, I'm done. I'm not stripping and losing the last bit of dignity I have to appease him. I'm not giving him that. At this moment, I'd rather die than hook my thumbs under the waistband of my underwear and give him what he wants.

I turn without a word and step into the shower, knowing I'll pay for that later, but unable to find it in me to care. I grab the bottle of shampoo and start washing, and it feels like the first moment of relief since he barged into the apartment.

30

LOGAN

The second I have the address from Matt, I'm done waiting. I'm not trusting the cops to handle this. I'll only call them when I know for sure that Ryder is there. Right now, my only priority is getting there.

I'm going to get him back, if it's the last thing I do.

I strip to put on the fresh clothes Dad brought back from my place, barely noticing what he packed until I see one of Ryder's shirts in the pile. It makes the need to get out of here even more pressing.

The nurse cleared me, but even if she didn't, I wouldn't stay here another minute. I'm not feeling one hundred percent, but I'm good enough. I can rest more after I get Ryder back in my arms.

I grab my keys, turning toward the door, but Mom steps into my path.

"I know you're going after him, and I know nothing I say will stop you." She inhales sharply, her hands twisting together. "But Logan, we love you. Your dad and I—you're our whole world."

The words hit me like a gut punch, and I feel like a horrible son. I know she's scared I'm walking into a death trap, but she doesn't know what it's like to love someone so much that you'd tear apart the entire world to save them. Or maybe she does, and I'm breaking her heart right now.

"I love you too, Mom," I say, my voice thick with emotion. "But I have to do this. He's *my* whole world."

She nods with unshed tears in her eyes, and she steps out of my way.

"I'm coming with you," Dad says, clapping a firm hand on my shoulder.

And that does it. Mom breaks out into an uncontrollable sob, and *now* I officially feel like the world's worst son. *At least they have Michael. The worst thing he's done is move to Baltimore.*

"Dad, no," I say, shaking my head. "You can't. You need to stay with Mom."

"I can't let you go alone. We have to swing by the house first. I have to get something, then we'll go."

I have a feeling I know what he's getting, so I nod. We both hug Mom and tell her we love her before we make our way out of the hospital and to the car.

After a quick stop at my parents' house, we pull up a block away from the address Matt sent. As expected, the place looks dark and abandoned, with dozens of broken windows, and it's right near the old harbor. It feels eerie. All I want is to get Ryder and get the fuck away from here as fast and unharmed as possible.

I swallow hard and look at Dad after taking in my surroundings. His face is set in stone, and I'm grateful he came with me because my nerves are at an all-time high. When I reach to open the door, he stops me. "Wait."

Dropping my hand away from the handle, I turn to him and watch as he pulls a gun from his jacket. Then he shows me a second one tucked in his waistband.

"Just in case," he says, handing me the one from his jacket. "I need you to be protected this time. Do you remember how to use it?"

Shit, do I?

It's been years since I've been to a shooting range with him. It was something he insisted on when I was probably around twenty-one—one of those 'just in case' lessons. He always said it was better to be prepared and never need it than to need it and not be prepared. Turns out, I'm glad he took me, even if I feel a little rusty.

I wrap my fingers around it, and the weight of it makes my stomach sink with the reality of this situation.

"I think if it comes down to it, it'll come back to me. Right? Like riding a bike?"

He hesitates, then nods, eyes serious. "It's loaded and the safety's off, so don't touch the trigger unless you mean it. Keep your finger outside the trigger guard, not on the trigger, until you're ready to use it."

I nod. Finally, we open the car doors and step out.

We move slowly and cautiously toward the building. I wouldn't put it past Kyle to have this place rigged with cameras, but I don't see anything. We creep around the first corner of the building, doing our best not to draw attention to ourselves.

An unmistakable scream comes from somewhere inside, and my entire body stops dead for a second before I lunge forward without thinking, but Dad's arm shoots out, stopping me before I can rush in.

"Wait," he demands. "We don't know what's inside. We

need to call Santos first and tell him to meet us here. We need all the help we can get because we don't know what we're walking into."

I fumble my phone out of my pocket, my fingers shaking so badly I nearly drop it as I hit his name.

Pick up, pick up, pick up, I chant to myself.

"We're still looking, Logan."

"Well, stop. We found him. I'm texting you the address. Get here now. Bring backup. We heard screaming."

"Copy that," he says without hesitation.

I hang up and immediately text the location. Seconds later, his reply comes through: *Ten minutes out. Wait for us. Don't do anything stupid.*

Ten minutes.

Fuck, that's too long.

"What do we do?" I ask, turning to my dad.

He contemplates for only a second before saying, "Let's keep going. Maybe we'll be able to locate them if we keep moving."

We continue circling the perimeter of the building, my entire body humming with adrenaline. Everything looks empty and lifeless, but we don't stop moving. This must be where he is, based on the scream we heard.

When we first came around the other side, it was hard to see inside. The windows were too high, and what we could see was just scrap wood, busted concrete, and old office walls collapsing in on themselves. There was no clean line of sight across the whole building. But now, as we move around the back side, we can see in and when I notice it, I suck in a breath.

Dead center in the otherwise empty space is a single, jarring structure. A room that looks like it's under construction—the only part of the entire building that's new. It's made of plywood, with no windows, but it does have a door.

But that has to be it.

That's where he is.

Dad and I both look at each other now, and then back to the makeshift structure where we hear muffled noises reach us from inside.

Please let that be Ryder.

Please let him still be alive.

I yank out my phone and fire off a text to Santos, giving him our exact location. They should be about three minutes out now.

That's when I hear Ryder's voice yell, "Fuck you!"

Three more minutes isn't something I can wait for, so I quickly text Santos again: *Going in. Ryder's hurt.*

Dad meets my eyes again, and I'm so grateful he isn't trying to hold me back; he just gives me a nod. I nod back, gripping the gun in my hand tightly as we move up to the plywood door. There's no time for being quiet, we're going in and we're going in now.

Dad raises his gun and fires at the handle. The sound shatters the air. I don't hesitate for another second before I slam my shoulder into the door, and it swings open—

And what I see makes me stare, wide-eyed in horror.

Kyle is standing inches from Ryder with a knife pressed to Ryder's throat. He's got his disgusting fingers in Ryder's wet hair, and there are cuts all over his torso, arms, and legs. He's naked, except for his boxer briefs, covered in goosebumps, and he's bound to a chair. I want to shoot Kyle right then and there.

I lift my gun back up and point it at Kyle's head, but he's so close to Ryder. Ry's eyes are terrified and glassy, but he's still breathing and conscious, even if he looks like he's barely hanging on. His body must be crashing after fighting for so long, and there's so much blood pooled on the floor underneath him.

"Thought you'd be six feet under by now," Kyle sneers, tightening his grip on Ryder's hair. "Guess I'll just have to fix that."

"Let him go," I say, my voice low with rage. *God, I fucking hate him.*

"You're not going to shoot me," Kyle says, like he doubts how much I love Ryder. He doesn't understand that I never want to see his face again—never want him to take another breath of the same air Ryder breathes. "You don't have it in you."

Ryder doesn't speak, but his eyes lock with mine as a single tear slides down his cheek, and with a voice so soft it almost breaks me, he whispers, "I love you."

His eyes close, and his body sags slightly in Kyle's grip, like he's stopped fighting.

And that's when everything inside me goes still.

He can't be saying goodbye, not when I'm this close. I can't take it anymore.

"I heard that," Kyle says, voice eerily calm, pulling Ryder's head back more. He presses the blade into his neck enough to draw blood. My whole body panics watching a thin crimson line dripping down his throat.

"Stop fucking touching him!" I yell, enraged at seeing his grimy hands on *my* Ryder.

A faint wail of sirens cuts through the distance, and while the sound fills me with relief, it's enough to send Kyle into a panic.

"No," he growls, the blade pressing deeper. "They're not

taking you from me. I won't let them. No one gets to have you but *me*."

That's when I realize he doesn't care if he kills Ryder because if he can't have him, then no one can. All it takes is one wrong move, one flick of his wrist, and Ryder's gone before I can even take a single step forward.

I need to end this.

My heart is pounding so hard I can feel it in my teeth. I look to Dad quickly, and he gives me one curt nod, telling me to do what I need to do. My vision tunnels, every detail sharpening into high definition. I haven't fired a gun in years, but I remember him telling me that if I ever had to hold a weapon, it had to be with purpose. That I couldn't afford to hesitate. That if you're going to take the shot, you better know in your bones what you're aiming at and why.

And I do. I do. I know exactly what I'm aiming at and why.

Kyle's standing to the left of Ryder, so I need to aim as far away from Ryder's head as possible. I keep both hands on the grip, squeeze tighter, try to control my breathing, but I can feel myself unraveling from the inside out because if I miss, I'll never recover. My stomach churns, and I hear the approaching wail of police sirens, close enough now that I know backup is seconds away.

And for a second, I think maybe I should wait.

Maybe I won't have to be the one to pull the trigger.

Maybe if I wait one more minute, the cops will burst through the door and handle it.

Maybe I won't have to be the one who—

Then Kyle chuckles, and I decide it's time to put a bullet in him and knock that smug smirk off his face once and for all because his hands are still on Ryder. *My* Ryder.

I take one final breath and pull the trigger.

The sound is deafening in the small room—a single, brutal crack rips through the air and echoes off the plywood walls. The recoil jolts up my arms, but I don't flinch, and I don't breathe until I see the impact.

Kyle jerks violently as the bullet tears into his shoulder, his grip on Ryder releasing all at once. The knife clatters to the floor, spinning across the concrete as he stumbles backward, shrieking in pain, both hands flying to the wound.

But then he snaps, lunging forward, blood pouring down his arm.

"You fucking ruined everything!" he howls at me, eyes wild. "He was mine!"

He staggers toward us, fury overtaking pain, and I should've known he wouldn't go down without a fight.

Dad steps between us, raising his weapon and planting himself in Kyle's path.

"Take one more step, and I swear to god, I will kill you," he growls, his voice low and deadly.

Kyle stops dead in his tracks, panting hard, hatred burning in his eyes as he clutches his shoulder. "Fuck you! You don't get to have him."

I know Dad's got this, so I rush forward and drop to my knees beside Ryder, heart pounding so hard I can barely hear anything else. My fingers fumble at the ropes, shaking so badly I can't get a grip, can't work fast enough, can't think past the desperate, all-consuming need to get him out, get him out, *get him out.*

Dad comes to help, keeping his weapon raised and eyes locked on Kyle like he'd already made peace with pulling the trigger if he had to.

He crouches down beside me, handing me the knife Kyle

dropped, and starts slicing through the ropes. His calm focus is the only thing holding me together as my lungs burn, my hands tremble, and every part of me screams with one singular thought: *Ryder needs to be free* now.

When the last rope falls away, Ryder falls forward from the chair into my arms, like he doesn't have the strength to hold himself up anymore. I catch him, wrapping my arms around him, one hand braced behind his head, the other gripping his waist. I need him anchored against me, need him to know he's safe, that I won't ever let go again.

The police storm in seconds later with guns raised, shouting commands. I turn my head and see Dad lower the gun he had pointed at Kyle as Kyle starts screaming nonsense. I hear the sharp bark of an officer telling him to stay down, and hear the clink of handcuffs closing around Kyle's wrists as they start to read him his rights, "You have the right to remain silent..."

The words drift somewhere past me as everything else in the room fades into the background. Because all I can see is Ryder. He's clinging to me, shaking and crying, as the warmth of his blood soaks into my shirt.

We're holding on to each other like a lifeline, and I pull him as close as I possibly can.

He's alive.

He's breathing.

He's here.

And I am never letting him out of my sight again.

I hold him through it, whispering, "I love you," and "I've got you," and "you're safe," on repeat until the paramedics rush in and we're loaded into the ambulance together.

31

RYDER

The last few days were strange.

Sitting here, safe, warm, with clean clothes on my back and Logan beside me, doesn't feel real. It feels like I'll blink and wake up back in that plywood room. Or worse, I'll open my eyes and realize I'm still there, tied up, waiting for Kyle to decide what comes next.

After they arrested him, they brought me straight to the hospital. The cops had questions. The doctors had concerns. A psychiatrist stopped by for a session, though I barely remember what I said to him. I think I stumbled over the words, trying to figure out how I'm supposed to explain what happened.

Physically, I'm fine. I only needed seven stitches total, four on my forearm and three on my side from the knife. The rest of the wounds on me are superficial. They said I have bruised ribs, and I was dehydrated and exhausted.

It's the rest of me that's not fine.

Logan knows it, too.

I don't think either of us is okay, not really.

The whole time we were in the hospital, he refused to leave. Not even when the doctors wanted to keep me overnight. I told him he could go home to sleep in a real bed, and take a goddamn break because he had found me, and saved me, and brought me home. Now he needed to rest because he was recovering, too.

Logan looked at me in the hospital room like I'd said something insane and said, "Not happening, baby. I just got you back, I'm not going anywhere."

My mom made the drive, and she was at the hospital, worried sick. She fussed over me nonstop, which is understandable, but all I wanted to do was sleep.

Now, we're finally home—just the two of us. My mom's staying at my house while we're back at Logan's. She wants to hover and take care of me, I can tell, but she understands we need space and time to decompress with each other after what happened.

Even though everyone saw Kyle get dragged out of that warehouse in handcuffs, and logically I know he's behind bars, it still doesn't feel real. It still feels like Kyle is going to turn up at the door or break in again.

Santos assured us we wouldn't have anything to worry about, but I still hear Kyle's voice in my head, so fucking smug telling me I need him when I don't. I never did. Shutting my eyes, I press my knuckles to my temples, as if I can physically force him out of my mind.

Logan must notice because he shifts closer, stroking my hair back from my forehead, lips pressing gently to my skin. All I want to do is break and fall into him, so I do. I curl into him, pressing my face into his neck, inhaling his scent deeply. He's the only thing capable of grounding me. His arms tighten around me instantly, and his fingers trail along my back. For a moment, it's just us, breathing and holding each other.

Then, before I can stop myself, the words spill out.

"I keep thinking," my voice is hoarse as I speak. "What if I didn't get out?"

Logan stills beneath me.

"I mean, what if you hadn't found me in time? Been so persistent? Would the cops have even done anything?"

"Stop, baby," Logan cuts in. "I don't want to do 'what ifs' because I found you and you're here. You're safe now, and that's the only thing that matters."

I blink rapidly, trying to shove down the emotions threatening to choke me whole. I let out a shuddering breath, sagging into him completely, letting him take my weight, take the fear, take everything because I know he will. I know he'll carry it for me if I let him.

So I do. Everything pours out of me, and I cry into his neck, "You could have died."

"But I didn't, and now we're both okay. We're both right here, and I'll never go anywhere without you again, baby. I promise. I'll quit my job if they tell me to come in again. Nothing is as important as you."

Logan moves, pulling me into his lap, looking down into his beautiful blue eyes. His hands splay wide against my back, holding me together as I bury my face into his shoulder, breathing him in as tears start to streak down my cheek.

"I'm right here," he murmurs, pressing his lips against the side of my head. "You're safe. You're home. He's never getting near you again, Ry. Not ever."

A few moments stretch between us before I pull back just enough to look at him.

The last few days have been overwhelming, but now that

we're finally home, I can say what's been stuck in my head. There was one loud thought that plagued my mind when we were apart—the thing I knew I couldn't leave unsaid if I ever got the chance.

"I love you, Logan," I proclaim, voice thick with emotion, as I pull back to look him in the eyes. "I'm so *in love* with you. You have always been my person, and now you're my everything. I love you so much."

I swear I see his breath hitch at my admission before a slow smile creeps across his face. He leans in, resting his forehead against mine.

"I love you, too, Ry," he says with so much awe in his voice. "You're it for me. Always have been, always will be. I'd do anything for you, baby. Anything. I love you so much."

I don't even hesitate. I pull him into me, kissing him like I'll never get enough because I won't.

He cups my face when we pull back. "I loved being your friend and was happy to be around you. Being near you always felt right. But then a few weeks ago, something flipped, and I couldn't stop falling for you even if I tried."

I smile, my heart so full it hurts.

"Honestly, I thought I was losing my mind after the whole...shower incident," I admit with a sheepish laugh. "I couldn't even tell you why I walked in, or why I stayed so long. I'm pretty sure I spun out for a full twenty-four hours trying to figure out what the hell that meant for us. I just knew I really liked what I saw, and I thought about joining you in there."

"That makes two of us," he laughs. "I've always loved you," he whispers. "But it's different now. I want you. I need you. I choose you. You're it for me."

My chest tightens at the weight of those words. They're so

simple, but they hold so much weight. I want to bottle up this moment and savor it for a lifetime. His fingers slide into my hair, his lips brushing over mine so gently it barely counts as a kiss, but it feels like everything. I didn't think I could love him more than I already do, but somehow, he keeps proving me wrong.

"Me too," I say, my voice thick with emotion. "You're my world."

And when he kisses me again—deeper this time—I know we're safe.

We're home.

And this time, nothing's tearing us apart.

32

LOGAN

I wake up to the warmth of Ryder cocooned around me. His steady breaths ghost over my chest, and his hand rests around my arm. I breathe him in and let the reality of this moment settle—that he's here in my arms again.

Thinking back, I should've killed Kyle. That piece of shit doesn't deserve to still be breathing, but I'm sleeping much better knowing he's behind bars and I hope prison is worse than death. We haven't heard anything about his sentence yet, but I do know he survived the gunshot wound, which I have very mixed feelings about. I don't care if that makes me a bad person.

I still meant every word I said about never letting Ryder out of my sight again, though. Wherever he goes, I go, and vice versa. If I have to quit my job, I'll quit. It's not like it's my dream job, and even if it were, *he* is my dream. My life with him by my side until we're old and gray is my real dream.

My arms tighten around him, and I pull him even closer. I don't want even an inch of space between us, and despite trying not to wake him, I feel his body stretch out against me, and a smile instantly takes over my face.

"Mmm," he hums. "Morning."

I smile, tipping my mouth down to kiss him softly. "Morning, baby."

He inhales deeply and smiles up at me when I pull away.

"I slept," he murmurs, sounding surprised. "Like, actually slept. All night."

I let out a sigh of relief that he wasn't up all night tossing and turning with fear and nightmares. "Good, baby," I whisper. "You needed it."

Ryder nods against my chest. Then slowly, he tips his head back to look at me. His beautiful brown eyes are still sleepy, and his brown hair is disheveled in the way I love so much. It makes my heart fucking ache and I can't help but lean down and press another kiss to his lips. His beard has grown a little longer than the short length he usually keeps it at, since he hasn't been able to take care of it properly, and I love the burn against my skin.

"I love you, Logan," he promises.

My heart kicks into overdrive at his words. Even though he told me last night, I can't help but cup his face, tracing the line of his scruffy jaw with my thumb, thinking about what eighteen-year-old Logan would say if he could hear those words now. He'd be stunned speechless, because he has something he never let himself dream of.

Almost a decade ago, I met the most beautiful man I'd ever seen, who had a personality that clicked with mine perfectly. But I told myself being his friend was enough when I'd found out he was straight, and every time those feelings of *more* tried to surface, I shoved them back down, convinced that wanting more would ruin everything. But now, he's said those words out loud. For a second time. Confirmed what I've always wanted to exist between us. Every part of me wants this.

I swallow the emotion in my throat and look him in the eyes.

"I love you, too, baby."

I kiss him again, slow and sure like a promise of more. Because that's exactly what it is—a promise of forever. He's it for me. When we finally pull apart, we're still tangled in each other, reluctant to let each other go.

"Alright, come on, let's get up and make breakfast. We can't spend all day in bed, unfortunately," Ryder says, pulling away with a kiss to my forehead.

After a few more minutes of cuddling, we drag ourselves out of bed and make coffee and eggs together. We work around each other in the kitchen, each with a signature mug. Ryder's says, *'Don't talk to me until I've eaten this mug,'* and mine says, *'Actually, this is my first rodeo.'* It's such a small, silly little thing, but being in the kitchen, pouring coffee into our mugs, feels like home.

After we finish eating and washing the dishes, Ryder turns to me while drying the pan. "As much as I wish we didn't have to go anywhere today, I think our parents will start pounding on the door if we don't get over there soon, *boyfriend.*"

The word should make me feel giddy and proud, but all it does is bring back the weight of what I did.

I let it slip at the hospital by calling him my boyfriend without thinking or knowing if he was ready to share that with anyone yet. I outed him in front of a room full of people while he was tied to a fucking chair in some warehouse, fighting to survive. He didn't have a say. I took that moment from him, took his choice.

Even though he teased me for it, even though he swore it didn't matter and that he was just grateful I found him, I can't shake the guilt. He's been through enough, had enough taken from him, and I hate that I added to it.

My face must give away my inner turmoil because Ryder's smirk is quickly replaced by a look of concern.

"Logan," he says gently, turning to face me fully. "Stop beating yourself up, babe."

"I just…" I hesitate. "I wish I hadn't said it before you got to. I hate that I took that choice away."

He's quiet for a moment before he reaches up to cup my jaw, his thumb brushing over my cheek. "Logan, I meant what I said—"

I cut him off, "But—"

"No, Lo." He shakes his head. "Listen to me. Did it happen the way I expected? No. But, honestly, it's a relief. Now we don't have to sit everyone down to make a big announcement while they all wait for me to share my sexuality with them. I never really wanted to *have* to come out in the first place," he says, and I understand that. "I just want to be your boyfriend and live our life without having to explain it to everyone. And I don't want that to sound like our relationship isn't important to me, because it is. You're everything to me, Loge. I just want to love you without a preface."

"I get it," I tell him, because I do. I treated my coming out pretty much the same way. My parents have always loved me unconditionally, and when I told them in high school, I knew they'd be okay with it. It also wasn't some big sit-down announcement. I simply told them I thought a boy was cute, and they smiled at me with so much love in their eyes, then asked questions about him.

"You said it, and they accepted it, just like we knew they would," he continues. "It's honestly so much better this way. Trust me on this. You did *me* a favor. I don't plan to come out to anyone. I plan to hold your hand, and kiss you, and love you publicly without making an announcement every time. But, if you could do me one more favor and tell your brother so I don't have to deal with that when we see him later, that'd be great," he laughs, and I feel my guilt start to ease. I shouldn't keep pushing this on him when it's my own thing to work through.

After everything that's happened, my brother drove to my parents' house yesterday, knowing we'd be coming over today.

"You want me to do it now or wait until we get there and be the one to tell him?" I ask.

Ryder smiles at me. "You can tell him when we get there."

I nod and start to pull away, but Ryder lets his hand fall from my chin down my arm as he laces our fingers together. "Hey Logan?" he says, keeping my attention on him. "You've always been my choice. Now it just means we can show up in front of all of our family as boyfriends, and I can't wait for that."

The words leaving his lips fill me with so much love. I let out a sigh, and he leans in to kiss me slowly. It tastes like reassurance, and it silences every ounce of guilt in my body.

When he pulls back, he smirks at me. "Now, come on, boyfriend. Let's get moving."

I let out a quiet laugh, shaking my head, grateful for him breaking the tension. I know things are nowhere near 'normal'—we're both carrying so much we still have to unpack and process, but this morning Ryder seems a little bit more like himself. I think waking up in my bed after a full night of sleep gave him a little sense of safety that he's been craving and didn't get at the hospital. Being together at home, just us, has always been our space where we could be our neediest, most vulnerable selves without judgment.

We finally start moving, getting ready and hopping in the shower—together, obviously—before locking up and heading out. We stop at the store on the way to pick up a bouquet of flowers for our moms. I was an asshole in the hospital; it's the least I can do. Ryder's mom is meeting us at my parents' place so we can all spend the day together, as one big unofficial family.

"You okay?" I ask, reaching over to lace our fingers together after we get back in the car with the flowers.

"Yeah. Still feels like a lot of pressure, though, for some reason. I don't even know why—maybe because it's the first 'normal'," he emphasizes with air quotes, "hangout we've had since the first email before we even knew what was going on. I still feel kind of guilty for not telling them about anything that was happening."

I watch as he wets his lips, his gaze flickering away for a second before he lets out a dry laugh.

"It's not every day your son's best friend-slash-boyfriend gets kidnapped, and falls in love mid-crisis. Real high-stakes romance shit. Oh, and let's not forget the part where your dad stormed a warehouse with you with guns like he's Liam Neeson."

I snort. "Yeah, good thing for his military background. He was dead set on coming with me though, and honestly, I'm so fucking glad he did. My nerves were at an all-time high, and I probably would have done something reckless because you were the only thing I could think about."

Ryder huffs, shaking his head, looking at me with a genuine smile now. "Alright, alright. Let's go get fussed over by our parents."

I lean over and give him a quick kiss. "C'mon, baby."

Ryder groans but climbs out of the car with me, holding the flowers for his mom. I take the ones for mine and keep his other hand in mine. We walk up the front steps, and before I can even knock, the door swings open and Mom is standing there with red-rimmed eyes like she's been up all night crying over us. She steps forward and pulls me into a crushing hug, squishing her flowers in the process.

"Oh, honey," she whispers against my shoulder, squeezing me so tight I wince. "I'm so glad you're okay."

"Mom," I grunt. "Ow. Still healing."

She releases me, then her gaze lands on Ryder, and she makes an entirely different sound. A soft, heartbroken noise as she reaches for him, gripping his face like she's making sure he's real.

"Ryder," she breathes.

His throat bobs, but he doesn't pull away. "Hey, Mrs. Hart."

"Oh, sweetheart," she murmurs, cupping his cheeks before pulling him into a hug. "We were so worried. I've been worried sick about you both."

Mom holds him for a long moment, then finally pulls back, brushing her hands over his arms like she's checking him for injuries herself. Then she turns over her shoulder.

"Jim, Michael, they're here!"

"Mom, these are for you. I'm sorry I was an asshole in the

hospital, I was so scared and I was taking it out on everyone in the room, including you. You didn't deserve that."

"Oh, honey, no. I get it. I am so glad you pushed so hard and you're both okay."

I smile at her, and Ryder does the same, as my dad comes into view. His eyes flick between me and Ryder, like he's checking to make sure we're actually okay.

"Hey, boys," he says.

"Hey, Dad."

"Mr. Hart."

"Oh, Ryder, sweetie. Call us Jim and Anne, please. We've been through enough for the formalities."

Dad nods, then moves toward Ryder, pulling him in for a hug before doing the same to me.

Michael comes bounding out of the house in jeans and a gray hoodie. He looks so much like me, just a couple of years older with shorter, neater blonde hair that's a little darker.

"Little bro, you had me so worried!" he exclaims as he walks over and pulls me into a bone-crushing hug.

"Missed you, too. But you gotta loosen your grip."

"Oh, shit! My bad, I didn't mean to squeeze you so hard," he looks apologetic.

"You and Mom," I laugh, shaking my head.

He turns to look at Ryder now and pulls him in for a loose hug, probably aware Ryder also has some stitches.

"Michael, we just want to tell you something quick," I say when he and Ryder break apart. I walk over to Ryder and take his hand in mine. "We're together."

A big smile takes over my brother's face, as expected. He gives us both a long, knowing look. "So, you two finally figured it out, huh?"

Ryder immediately groans, burying his face in his hands.

Dad just shrugs at this interaction. "I've been calling that since, oh, I don't know. Years. You always were like an old married couple."

"Jesus Christ. Maybe a little, 'happy for you both' first?" I deadpan.

Ryder groans, turning to me. "See, this is why I didn't want to have to come out. Told you, you did me a favor."

"Ryder, you know we love you. We are so happy for you two," Mom coos, while Dad just nods alongside her, and everyone's smiling at each other, right in time for Ryder's mom, Emma, to pull up. She barely stops the car before she comes rushing over to him.

"Ryder!" she yells as she pulls him into a big hug, her face a mix of relief and exhaustion.

Ryder sinks into her hug, and she murmurs something I can't hear into his shoulder. He nods in response, eyes squeezed shut, and I let them have their moment. He hands her the flowers he bought for her, and she smells them. "They're beautiful, thank you, Ry."

Then her gaze shifts to me.

"Hi, Emma," I greet.

"I'm just so happy to see your faces again," she exclaims, pressing a hand to her chest.

"You do know it's been, like, not even twenty-four hours since you last saw us, right?" Ryder says with a teasing tone, though I can still hear the emotion beneath it.

Emma's eyes snap to him, fire immediately returning to them, and I have to bite back a laugh. "I don't care how long it's been, you were kidnapped, Ryder! Kidnapped by a lunatic!" she reminds us, throwing her hands up. "Of course I'm going to act a little out of my mind every time I see you!"

I watch Ryder try—and fail—to hold back a smile at his mom.

Mom claps her hands once the moment settles. "Who's hungry? I made a ton of food."

It turns out the day is mostly about them checking in on us, making sure we're okay in every possible way—physically, mentally, emotionally. There are a lot of hugs, a lot of reassurances, and while it's exhausting, it's also healing.

We talk a little about Ryder and me—our relationship, how it happened—without mentioning the mutual jack off session that turned into 'sharing' lube, or how I kind of accidentally came out for him.

Ryder's mom, of course, already figured it out based on our behavior at the hospital, but even with the teasing, everyone is unbelievably supportive. We've been inseparable for a decade, and if anything, it seems like our parents have been waiting for us to figure it out. So while their acceptance of our relationship isn't surprising, it still feels really good.

When it's finally time to say goodbye, Ryder's mom pulls him in for one last hug before she prepares to head back home, her arms wrapping around him tight, like she's holding onto him for both of us.

Then she pulls back slightly, her eyes meeting mine as she says, "I'm so glad you're okay. I'll come back soon, okay? You come visit me too."

Ryder nods at her and promises he will.

Then she looks back and forth between both of us as she says, "I'm happy you both have each other. It makes me feel better about leaving, knowing you won't be alone, Ry." He swallows hard, and his eyes get a little glassy as he smiles.

"Me too," I say softly, taking Ryder's hand as he separates

from his mom and steps back toward me. I give his hand one last squeeze, then lead him to the car, so we can finally go home.

33

LOGAN

It's been a week since Ryder got home from the hospital, and our stitches are healing nicely. Kyle loved that fucking knife, but at least we're here, *together*, and he's in prison, rotting.

"C'mere," I murmur, holding out a hand as Ryder walks around the bed toward me, pausing to double-check that the curtains are closed tightly.

Today has been exhausting, and I know he feels it as much as I do. We spent half the day with my family again, and my parents made sure we both knew just how much we are loved, again. They want to spend every moment with us they possibly can after everything that happened, and I do think it's been good for Ryder to be surrounded by so much love.

Once we're both in bed, he scoots back against me, his body fitting against mine in a way that feels so natural. His ass presses against my dick, but I'm not hard and it's not sexual.

I don't want to make him feel pressured to do anything he's not ready for. I'll let him take our physical relationship at the pace that works for him. So far, it's been lots of snuggles, hugs, and kisses, and it's been perfect.

Instead, I lean in and press a gentle kiss behind his ear before whispering, "I love you, baby. I had such a good day with you."

He scoots back even closer and lets out a big sigh. "Mmm, I love you too."

Something in my chest aches, but it isn't pain—it's love. Love so deep and consuming, that I don't know how we were ever just friends. I smile against his skin, loving this moment with him.

"Who knew we'd be so mushy when we became boyfriends?" I tease.

Ryder flips over fast, his grin so big it's almost ridiculous. "I knew," he says, propping himself up on his elbow, smug as hell. "I've seen you cry over commercials, so this isn't exactly shocking."

I roll my eyes. "Once. I cried over one dog commercial," I emphasize, even though I'm pretty sure he was also wiping his eyes.

He gives me an exaggerated look. "Mhm, okay, we can say that."

"Okay, first of all," I say defensively, even though it's all in good fun, "you've cried over plenty of things so don't give me shit."

"Yeah, but I'm not the one pretending to be so surprised that we're sappy together," he shoots back, pulling me into his arms, and I wrap mine around him even tighter.

I bark out a laugh. "Well, I like us sappy, baby. Almost as much as I like you clinging to me like this."

"Me too," he laughs softly. "Especially since you're physically restraining me from escaping your arms," he teases, but he isn't moving away—he's somehow shifting even closer, his fingers brushing low over my stomach.

His gaze locks onto mine, and in that moment, I feel completely done for. His caramel-brown eyes are dark with need, and the intensity of it sends a shudder rippling down my spine. He looks at me like I'm the only thing that exists. The only thing he's ever wanted. It's the kind of feeling that makes me weak while simultaneously lighting up every inch of my body in anticipation.

I still wait, though. If he wants more, I want him to be the one to take the lead—and as if he can read my mind, he moves. His lips crash against mine, and there's nothing slow or hesitant about it. Just desire and need and urgency, like he's starving and I'm the only thing that can satisfy him. I groan into his mouth, tilting my head, drinking in every perfect sound he makes. Our kiss is all tongue and teeth and passion, his hands are everywhere they can reach.

And god, I'm more than willing to lose myself in him completely.

I'm already hard, and I can feel his erection pressing against me, before he starts grinding his hips into mine. The friction has my whole body aching for more, but I don't push. This is whatever he wants it to be, nothing more.

But I can tell he's just as needy as he gasps into my mouth and snaps his hips forward, like he can't hold back. He presses his thigh between mine, thrusting his hips forward as his hand trails lower, gripping my ass with a tight squeeze that makes me moan.

We haven't explored any anal play yet, but fuck do I want to. I groan at the thought, tipping my head back, and he takes the opportunity to mouth at my throat—licking, biting, sucking like he's trying to mark every inch of me, and I don't want him to stop. I'll proudly wear him on my skin every day for the rest of my life.

"Logan, fuck, I need you," he breathes, voice desperate.

I love him like this, all wild and needy and uninhibited. I want all of it—his want, his urgency, his craving. However he wants me, whatever he gives me—it's always enough.

"Tell me what you need, baby," I whisper. "I'll give you anything you want."

"Logan, please," he begs, and fuck if that isn't the hottest thing I've ever heard, even if he didn't answer my question. "I don't care if you fuck me or if I fuck you—I just need you, need more." The desperation is evident in his tone as he rolls his hips into mine, and I want more, too. "I need it, please," he begs, fingers digging into my ass. "I don't want any more space between us."

I groan, heat flaring through my body at the way he's begging for this. For me. I'd give him anything he wants, no questions asked, but I need to be sure this is what he truly needs.

I cup his jaw, brushing my thumb along his cheek, tilting his face until our eyes meet. "Baby, are you sure? I don't want you to feel rushed or pressured if you're not ready," I murmur, brushing my lips over his slowly before pulling back. "We have time. We have forever."

His gaze burns into mine, and he leans forward to kiss me deeply. His tongue slides into my mouth as he rolls me onto my back, climbing on top of me on the bed. His weight holds me down as he rocks his hips against me again, and fuck, the friction is everything. It's so good, I feel like I can barely breathe as I try to resist bucking my hips into him. Ry breaks away to drag his tongue down the column of my throat, and I gasp, fingers digging into his back, arching into him as he licks over my pulse point, then bites down. The sensation is so intense, yet not enough.

"I love you for checking," he pants against my skin, his lips brushing over the mark he made. "But I'm ready. I want this. I can't think of anything but this, Lo."

Fuck, Ryder.

I sit up, capturing his lips, kissing him deep, filthy, slow. I let him feel everything I want to give him, and I'm positive I normally wouldn't care who fucks who, but I know what I want right now. I bite his bottom lip, then whisper it right into his mouth. "Fuck me, Ryder. I want you to fill me with your cock. Stretch me open, fill me up, claim every inch of me. I'm all yours, baby."

His breath shudders, his whole body going still for a moment. Then I feel his cock twitching hard against mine, his fingers digging into my waist and I know he loves the idea of filling me.

"I'm versatile, baby, so I'm always good with either," I murmur, licking over the edge of his jaw, feeling his pulse pound beneath my tongue. "But tonight I want you inside me. Do you want that?"

His brown eyes darken with hunger, and his breathing grows more erratic as he nods. His mouth goes back to my throat, sucking deep and biting hard enough to make me whimper. I don't care that I'll have marks tomorrow—I don't care about anything except how fucking desperate he is to take me, to claim me, to finally make me his.

I can feel Ryder's breath coming faster, the weight of him pressing me down into the mattress, the heat between us almost unbearable. His hips jerk forward, and fuck, I can feel his cock throbbing against me, the precum dampening his boxer briefs.

"Take these off," I say, pulling against the fabric. He slides off me and rips them down while I do the same, stripping out of the only piece of clothing we got into bed with.

His mouth claims mine when he's back next to me on the bed, facing each other on our sides, and I let him take everything he wants, let him devour me.

I pull back slightly. "Want me to play with your hole? Let you see how good it feels?"

"Fuck yes," he breathes, his forehead pressing to mine, his eyes wild and blown-out with need.

I smirk, fingers trailing a little lower, dragging through his crack until I pause at his hole. But, I don't press in, just tease him there to get him used to my touch for now. His breath catches, but he doesn't pull away, and I take that as a good sign.

"You like that?" I ask, my lips brushing against his in a quick kiss.

Ry swallows hard, his voice shaky. "I...I think so."

I grab a pillow from behind my head. "Lie on your back and let me put this underneath you," I say, as I guide the pillow where it needs to go.

He's sprawled out below me, and I push his legs up a little. I tease the tip of his cock with my tongue before sucking him into the back of my throat and he groans. While he's focused on that sensation, I let my finger drift back down to his hole and continue exploring with his cock in my mouth.

His hips start to jerk the more I touch him there, and his reaction is so hot. I hum against his silky cock, loving how receptive he's being, how open he is to my touch. I pop off him, letting my tongue lick and tease his head before taking him in my hand while my other fingers still play with his hole.

"You want to feel my fingers inside you? Want to be stretched open while I let you fuck me, baby?"

His body's reaction is instant and cock twitches in my grip. "Jesus, Logan," he gasps. "Fuck, I had no idea you'd have such a filthy mouth."

I grin at his response, letting my fingers continue to circle his puckering hole.

He groans, arching into me now before whispering, "Yes, more."

I could keep teasing him forever, and I can't wait to show him how much we have to explore together. I reach for the mostly full bottle of lube and a condom in the nightstand. But then an idea strikes me, making my whole body thrum with anticipation because I think he's gonna *really* like this.

"Don't move," I murmur, pressing a quick kiss to Ryder's lips before jumping off the bed and heading to the bathroom. I rummage through my toy box I keep tucked away in here, and find exactly what I'm looking for.

When I return, Ryder's breath hitches when he sees the medium-sized black silicone plug in my hand.

"Logan," he gasps. "What…?"

He doesn't have the words, and I love that he's speechless. I climb back into bed, straddling his thighs, leaning forward to press a quick kiss to his lips.

"Do you want to try, baby?" I ask him, dragging my fingers over his stomach, teasing him with barely-there touches.

I see his throat bob before he nods his head, and I lean forward so my mouth is next to his ear. "Want to have my plug in your ass while you fill my hole with your cock?"

His body flexes underneath me and I suck his ear lobe into my mouth.

"Fuck," he whimpers. "Yes. Oh fuck, yes."

My heart is pounding over how willing he is. How open and eager he is to try more with me. I shift off his lap to grab the lube, coating my fingers before settling between his legs. I push his legs up and circle his rim, teasing him again for a moment before finally pressing in with one finger, and Ryder lets out a grunt as I slowly push past the initial resistance. I let him adjust to the stretch, focusing on making this as good as possible for him.

"Fuck, baby," I soothe, watching him come undone beneath me. His cock twitches as precum leaks from the tip, and I grin at the sight. "You look so fucking good like this," I praise, moving my finger slightly, letting him get used to the pressure.

He lets out a shaky exhale, hips shifting as he groans. "I— fuck, Logan—"

I kiss and suck my way down his inner thighs, trying to let him get comfortable with the new sensation.

"You like it, baby?" I ask as I slowly get him used to the feeling, and he nods. After a few minutes, when he's writhing on my pointer finger, I pull out before pushing two back in. I work him open carefully, and his whole body shakes as he lets out a soft, breathless moan.

"So good, Lo," he says, voice raw and needy.

I smile to myself, knowing he's only going to become more desperate as I continue fucking my fingers into him. Once again, he starts rolling his hips.

"More, Loge, please."

Groaning, I pull my fingers out to grab the plug and cover it in lube. "Let's see how much you like the plug, baby." I bring it to his entrance, rubbing the tip against his hole, but not pressing it just yet.

"If you don't like this or it hurts, let me know and I'll stop. It's supposed to feel good."

He nods and spreads his legs a little more for me, and fuck, the sight of him spread out and willing to try this with me makes my whole body thrum with need. I press the plug in slowly, watching the way his face shifts and mouth parts as he adjusts to the feeling.

He sucks in a breath. "Feels...weird."

"Good weird or want-me-to-stop weird?" I check, sliding my hand down his thigh.

His cheeks flush red, and he bites his lip. "Keep going," he says, and I wait a few more moments before I press the rest of the way in. Trailing my hands over his skin, I try to distract him, kissing him slowly before guiding his hips up a smidge more and letting him feel how good it is to move with it inside of him.

The groan that leaves his mouth is sinful. I know that's the moment he understands how good it feels to have his ass stuffed, and I can't wait for it to be my cock inside of him one day. I grin, dragging my hands up his back and pressing our foreheads together.

"You ready to fuck me now, baby?" I tease in a low voice.

He licks his lips, his hips rolling slightly, and I feel how much he wants it. Feel how much he likes the plug inside of him.

"Yes," he breathes, his voice hoarse and filled with need.

I grab the lube and coat my fingers, ready to work myself open quickly for him while I straddle his legs, but he stops me, wiping the lube from my fingers the best he can.

"I want to do it," he says, and I swear the air is knocked out of my lungs at Ryder's desire.

I don't hesitate. I climb off his lap and bend over on all fours for him on the bed so he has easy access to my hole.

"You wanna stretch me, baby," I encourage, and I hear him let out a little moan. "That's so hot. Go one finger at a time to get me ready for your cock."

He circles my hole at first, just like I did to him, before he presses the tip of his lubed-up finger in. "Fuck, you're tight," he exclaims, and I can't help but chuckle against the bed at his reaction.

"I love being your firsts, baby. You have no idea how much I love it."

That must encourage him, because he pushes in deeper. The stretch is tight but familiar, and fuck, I still can't get over the fact that Ryder's finger is in my ass. The intimacy of this moment makes my whole body tense with anticipation for *more*.

"Shit," Ryder breathes. I turn my head and see him watching his finger disappear inside of me so intently. His eyes are locked onto it like he's memorizing every detail, and I can't help but smile at him in awe. *God, I love this man so much.*

"You good?" he asks me, and I nod, pushing back slightly on his fingers.

"More, baby. Give me another finger."

He pulls his finger out and squeezes more lube on them before pushing two in this time. He lets out a breathy groan. I can tell he's loving this, and he doesn't let up. He keeps fucking into me with his fingers and I moan, letting him hear how much I want this.

"Fuck, you sound so good like this," he rasps, shifting so he can kiss down my back, biting lightly at my skin.

"Yeah?" I pant, rocking against his fingers.

I feel him twist his wrist, opening me up more until I'm fully ready for him. I reach back, gripping his cock, stroking him the best I can from this position as he preps me, and his hips jerk into my hand.

"Ryder," I groan. "I'm ready, baby."

He slowly removes his fingers from me and grabs the condom from the table, rolling it down his dick and slicking himself up with lube.

"Flip over," he says. "I want to see your face."

I almost melt as I do as he asks, shoving a pillow under my hips. When he scoots closer, I wrap my legs around him. He guides his cock to my hole and I feel him there, eagerly waiting. Dragging my fingers down his back, I grip his ass, pulling him closer. His breath is ragged, his whole body tight, but his eyes never leave mine.

"Fuck me, Ry," I whisper, leaning up to press one last kiss against his lips before I start to guide him inside.

He pushes into me slowly, stretching me open inch by inch, and fuck, the sensation is so deep and full and perfect. Ry's breath is ragged as he pushes in. I can tell he's still holding back, like he's afraid to hurt me or lose control too fast, so I rock my hips up, taking him deeper, grinning when he lets out a deep moan.

"Ryder, baby," I moan, dragging my hands down his back. "You're not gonna break me. Promise."

I smile up at him, and that seems to spur him on. He jerks his hips forward, deeper into me, and his face crumbles as he lets out a low, broken moan.

"Oh, shit, Logan. I—I forgot…about the plug."

I can't help but let out a little laugh, knowing he'd love the dual sensation. The combination of the stretch and pressure is perfect yet overwhelming, making everything more sensitive. I decide to add even more to the intensity by tightening my legs around him and squeezing enough to make his cock pulse inside me.

"Yeah?" I grin. "You like it, baby? Like knowing you're stuffed full while you're filling me?"

He huffs as he keeps thrusting into me, and his hips start rolling against me like he can't control himself anymore. Watching him come undone like this is my new favorite form of ecstasy.

"Fuck," he pants, biting at my throat. "I—this is—I've never felt anything like this, Logan, oh my god. I'm not gonna last."

I laugh again, completely loving this as I grind up against him, making us both groan.

"You're doing perfect, Ry," I murmur, leaning up, licking over the shell of his ear, and biting lightly. "Fucking me while you're stretched open for me. God, I can't wait to get inside that ass."

His whole body is shaking at this point, and he's thrusting into me so good that my eyes roll back. I reach around to cup his ass and lean slightly to the side so I can press against the base of the plug, pushing it just slightly, but it does what I want. Ryder shouts, and his whole body jerks.

"Fuck—Logan—holy shit, what the—" He's nearing his breaking point, I can tell. His thrusts are getting sloppier and more out of control as he tries to finish his sentence. "I don't know where to focus—I wanna fuck you forever, but I also wanna—"

I pull his face down for a filthy, messy kiss, our tongues licking into each other's mouths, moaning into the heat of it.

"Baby," I whisper, rocking against him to meet him thrust

for thrust. "When we're done, I'm gonna spread you out and fuck you while you're still loose from this. You want that?"

Ryder whimpers, actual fucking whimpers, and I know he's seconds away from coming. His rhythm falters, and his whole body is shaking. He's gripping me so tightly that I know I'll have bruises tomorrow.

"Yes. Fuck, Logan—"

"Yesss," I gasp. "Come for me, baby, fill me up."

He buries his face against my throat and his whole body spasms as he moans my name, filling me with his cum. I wish he were bare so I could feel him leak out of me. His grunt is so deep and feral, I can't help but stroke myself, and all it takes is three pumps before I'm following him over the edge, my orgasm ripping through me, covering us both in my release.

Ryder slumps against me, both of us panting and sweaty and tangled up in each other. For a long moment, neither of us moved, completely boneless in the best way.

Then, I let out a small laugh into the crook of his neck. "So much for me filling you up, huh?" I chuckle, pressing a quick kiss to his shoulder. "I couldn't hold back when you came—it was so sexy, baby. You're perfect."

Ryder lets out a groggy chuckle, shifting slightly but still too blissed out to move much.

"That good, huh?" he teases, smirking against my skin. "Guess I do have a magic dick after all."

I roll my eyes, dragging my fingers lazily up his spine, my smirk matching his, loving that he's in a teasing mood after that.

"Don't get cocky, baby. It was the whole thing—your desperate noises, the way you lost your mind when I clenched around you, the whimpering—"

"Whoa, whoa," Ryder laughs, cutting me off with a half-hearted glare, his cheeks flushing deep pink. "First of all, I did not *whimper.*"

I grin, shifting my hips slightly, extracting a groan from him because he hasn't pulled out of me yet.

"Oh, baby," I murmur, smirking as I nuzzle into his jaw, pressing a teasing kiss there.

"You so did, and I loved it."

"Yeah, yeah," Ryder groans again, before finally pulling out of me, rolling off the condom, and heading to the bathroom. He comes back with a wet washcloth for me, cleaning me up and throwing it into the laundry basket in the corner, then pulls me back into him like he hates the space between us.

I chuckle, dragging my fingers through his hair, tugging just slightly.

"How did the plug feel?" I ask, noticing he must've taken it out in the bathroom.

Ryder lets out a slow breath, like he's considering the question. "Yeah. It was kinda hot."

"Just kinda?" I arch a brow at him, dragging my nails lightly down his spine, and he relaxes right into me.

"Okay, really hot," he admits, grinning and pressing his forehead against mine. "But after tonight? I think I'm gonna want to fuck you a lot."

I laugh, shifting to pin him beneath me again, my cock already trying to rally at the thought.

"You won't hear any complaints from me," I murmur, pulling him into a deep kiss.

34

RYDER

"What is going *where*?"

I nearly choke on my coffee because that doesn't sound right. Logan just told me we're going on a date today, but it involves getting our dicks swabbed.

"Yeah," he says, completely straight-faced. "They shove a Q-tip in your dick."

I continue to stare at him because there's no way. He's got to be fucking with me.

"I've been tested before, and they've never done that."

He finally caves and bursts out laughing. "Alright, alright. Yes, I'm fucking with you. They'll just take a urine sample. Maybe get a little blood drawn, a throat swab if you're lucky. We'll see what they recommend."

I shake my head at him because even though we're boyfriends now, he hasn't stopped giving me shit, and I love him more for it.

"Date of my dreams. How did I get so lucky?" I deadpan.

"What's more romantic than confirming we're clean so we can fuck raw?" he says, right before taking a bite of his bagel.

———

WITH OUR BODILY FLUIDS SUCCESSFULLY COLLECTED, I HALF expect our 'date' to be over, but of course, Logan has other plans. The second we walk out the door, he grabs my hand and pulls me down the street like a man on a mission.

I realize this is the first time we've ever held hands in public, and I can already hear everyone who knows us saying something along the lines of, 'about time!' just like our parents did. *Was it really that obvious to everyone else?*

Regardless, I can't wait for everyone to see us together. I don't care what their reactions are, I just want them to know Logan is officially *mine*.

"Where are we going?" I ask, giving his hand a squeeze.

Logan glances at me with eyes full of mischief. "I did promise you a cheesy date, didn't I?"

"Oh god," I laugh. "I can only imagine."

"Don't worry, it's not an overpriced restaurant where the portions are tiny. We can do that another day. Today, I figured we'd go to our spot, but it'll still be *cheesy*." He emphasizes the word, and I'm not sure what he means, but I let him lead the way.

We veer off into a tiny sandwich shop where Logan heads over to the register and tells the cashier he's here to pick up an order. The man behind the counter hands Logan the bag, and he thanks him. Then, we turn to leave for our next destination.

"Let me guess," I say, peeking at the bag. "Meatball sub?"

"Yep, with extra *cheese*. Just how you like it."

I pretend to wipe an imaginary tear. "You really do love me, huh?"

He nudges me toward the door, chuckling. "You know I do."

We walk back to the car and get in, and Logan drives us toward the lake. When we get there, he grabs the blanket we always keep in the trunk and a backpack from the back seat. I smile as I imagine what he could've brought as he takes my hand and we walk toward the water. Once we get to our favorite spot, he drops my hand to spread out the blanket, before plopping down and dragging me with him.

"I might have done a few other things to cheese this date up, but I wanted to come here with you. I've really missed it."

Everything melts inside me at that as he starts rifling through the backpack, pulling out a speaker, two bags of chips that seem like mostly air, and two beers already in koozies. He hands me the one that says, "World's Best Boyfriend" and takes the one for himself that says, "World's Okayest Boyfriend."

I squint at them, confused. "Uh, Logan, why did you declare yourself the okayest boyfriend?"

Logan cracks his beer open and it hisses and sputters out of the top.

"Well, if letting you get kidnapped isn't enough of a reason, let's go with the fact that this is the first real date I've planned for you, and that makes me mediocre at best."

He says it like a joke, but there's still guilt underneath it that he hasn't managed to let go of. I see it in his eyes, how he's still blaming himself for something that was never his fault. But, I get it, if the roles were reversed, I'd probably be doing the same thing. He didn't invite Kyle into our lives. He didn't put that darkness in Kyle's head that made him think and do the most awful things. And yet, he still carries it.

Adjusting to life again has been challenging, not because of Logan, though. He's been the only thing that's felt solid and grounding, and I'm so grateful his company decided to let him work remotely indefinitely. I'm sure getting stabbed in the parking garage after a mandatory meeting made them rethink their policies. But part of me still feels like I'm waiting for something to go wrong whenever we're in different rooms. It's why I decided to take time off work until further notice. I want to go back because I love narrating, but I also need to feel safe while doing it. Sometimes, all it takes is a shadow shifting in the corner of my eye that sends me spiraling.

The fear doesn't ever truly leave. It just quiets down enough that I can forget for a while, and Logan being around all the time makes forgetting easier. Being with him, wrapped in his arms or listening to him breathe beside me at night, always helps remind me I'm safe.

I haven't figured out how to feel fully like my old self again. I don't even know if that version of me still exists, but we're working on it in therapy. I started earlier this week and already had my first two sessions. We agreed to twice-weekly meetings online until we feel I'm in a good place to transition to once-a-week sessions.

What we talked about this week was finding joy in little things—like Logan insisting this is our first real date, even though we've been inseparable for a decade and have had a scheduled date night for basically half of it—even if we told ourselves it was platonic.

We also discussed how healing isn't a linear process, and that being safe doesn't always mean I feel safe. But being with Logan is the one thing that always feels right. Because Logan isn't just my person, he's my home, and I know I'm his, too. So I reach out, threading my fingers through his and squeezing gently.

"You're not mediocre," I promise him. "You were the only person who fought like hell to find me. I'm here because of you, and I don't need you to be perfect—I just need you to be you. That's more than enough, babe."

He squeezes my hand back and nods once, like he's absorbing the words and trying not to let guilt consume him.

"Okay," he murmurs, finally managing a small smile. "Then I'm gonna start working toward being the world's best boyfriend. Like, award-winning levels. I want a trophy. Or at the very least, a custom mug. Maybe one of those stupid koozies, too, declaring it for everyone else to see and be jealous of."

I snort as we slip back into our normal rhythm. "I'll add it to the list. You can earn it."

He nods solemnly like it's his sole focus now, then hands me my sandwich and grabs his own. I unwrap mine, the smell of marinara and melted cheese hitting me all at once, and I realize how hungry I am.

Logan clinks our beers together like it's a toast we both need.

"To surviving," he says.

"To learning to be okay again," I add.

Then, he pulls out his phone, scrolling for a moment. "Serious question now. Do we go full cheesy first date and listen to a shitty love songs playlist? Or do I queue up something decent?"

I narrow my eyes. "Do you *have* a shitty love songs playlist?"

His smirk widens, and then suddenly, "*I Wanna Dance with Somebody*" by Whitney Houston starts blasting from the speaker.

"Logan," I wheeze, nearly choking on my beer through a laugh.

He grins, already eating his sandwich. "Alright fine, not shitty because this song is an absolute banger. Tell me I'm wrong."

He's not wrong, so I let it play, grinning as I dig into my food, and letting the warm spring sun soak into my skin. For a while, we eat and exist together, stretched out on the blanket, our fingers brushing without thinking as we lie next to each other. It's quiet and simple, and normal. It brings me back to so many days we've done this over the years. This is what our relationship has always felt like, but now we get to live it. *In love.*

But there is one more topic that I've been meaning to bring up, and now feels like the perfect time.

Logan's apartment is familiar, and I'd follow him anywhere, but his place and mine both feel weighed down by bad memories. I want something new. A completely fresh start for both of us. Not necessarily to erase what happened, because *we* started there, but to choose what comes next. To build something that's ours without trauma hanging over it.

"Do you want to buy a place together?"

Logan doesn't move, and for a second, I think I might have broken him. Then, slowly, he turns to look at me.

"You really want that?" he whispers.

"Yeah, I do," I nod, shifting to face him. Most people would probably say this is bad timing and we should wait, let the trauma settle before making any big decisions, but this doesn't feel fast to me. It feels inevitable.

"Your lease is up soon, and I think I want to sell my house. I want a place where we can start fresh together. I don't want to make a home out of either of our places," I say quietly. "Yours still feels like…like where *it* happened, and mine just doesn't feel like home anymore. I want to be together permanently in a place where we can start fresh. A place where we can choose what's next, and what's next for me, is us."

Logan reaches for my hand and laces our fingers together. He looks so overwhelmed, I almost laugh. Like, somehow, he never thought this would be a possibility. His eyes are shining a little, but he shoves me before I can say anything about it.

"Ryder!" he nearly yells, grinning like an idiot now.

"So…that's a yes?"

Logan huffs a laugh, then launches himself at me, rolling me onto my back and tackling me in a full-body hug.

"Baby," he murmurs against my neck. "That's a hell fucking yes!"

I grin, threading my fingers through his hair. "Good. Because I plan on christening every room in our new house— and I fully expect you to keep your flip fuck promise."

Logan snorts, shaking his head as he pulls back. "Jesus, Ryder."

I smirk, rolling us so I'm on top now. "What? You said you're vers and I gotta try bottoming somehow."

His fingers curl into my hips, his voice low, amused. "You think I'd say no to that?"

I laugh, rolling off him, and he immediately pulls me back, arms wrapping tight around me. "I already have every-thing I want with you. All that's left is a front door that's ours to walk through."

35

LOGAN

"Fuck, your tongue feels so good."

Ryder's mouth is hot and wet and perfect around my cock, and I have zero control over the noises I'm making. My fingers are gripping his perfect brown hair as he hums around me. I nearly choke on the vibration that shoots through me before he pulls off with a pop. His lips are wet and his pupils are blown out, and he looks so sexy on his knees like this for me.

"You like that?" he asks with a smirk.

He doesn't even wait for a response before he's swallowing me down with no hesitation. Ryder has become insatiable for my cock and I'll never be one to deny him what he wants.

He hollows his cheeks and I feel his throat constrict around me as he sucks me as far back as he can. I'm so close, and my whole body is tensing beneath him.

"Baby—gonna—"

Ryder groans around me like he was waiting for those words and it sends me over the fucking edge. My hips fuck into his mouth as I come hard down his throat. He sucks me through it, not wasting a drop, and when he finally pops off, he licks his lips and looks so pleased with himself.

"Jesus, baby," I breathe, still catching my breath.

Ryder grins, crawling up my body to press a slow, teasing kiss to my lips. "Told you I'm getting good at that."

I hum, still half-dazed. "Not gonna argue with you, even if you are so damn cocky since realizing you like dick."

Ryder laughs and I feel his hard cock press against me.

"Need some help with that?" I murmur against his ear, my hand already slipping between us.

"Yes," he groans and pulls off his underwear.

I slide down his body, pressing kisses down his chest and stomach, until I'm exactly where I want to be. He shifts his hips like he can't wait another second, so I give him one teasing lick from base to tip before taking him into my mouth. The sounds he makes are my favorite as I suck him slowly, teasing him, even though I know how badly he needs to come. I pop off briefly and his cock slaps against his stomach as he groans in frustration.

"Logan—" he starts to huff.

I grin at his protest.

"You know I got you, baby," is all I say before I take him to the back of my throat and swallow around him. I bob my head up and down, adding my hand to really send him over the edge, and in no time, I feel his fingers tighten in my hair.

"Gonna—come."

I moan around him until he's shooting down my throat. I swallow everything he gives me, taking every last drop, giving him one last suck before I finally pop off.

"Damn," he chuckles. "That was fast. Guess I really was pent up from you."

I crawl up his body and claim his mouth, letting him taste both of us on our tongues. He groans, but before we can go another round, I break the kiss.

"Shower," I whisper against his lips.

"Mmm, fine," he reluctantly agrees.

We hop in the shower to get ready for the night, even though with how much he's touching me, I can't understand why we have to leave the house in the first place.

"Do we have to go?" Ryder asks, echoing my thoughts.

I chuckle, running my hands down his back. "That's up to you, this was your idea, remember?"

His face twists into something between regret and exhaustion. "Fuck past me for making plans."

I laugh, reaching past him to shut off the water. "Come on, let's get dressed. We'll save round two for after the bar. Maybe that flip fuck I've been promising, huh?"

Ryder grumbles under his breath, but lets me pull him out of the shower anyway and wrap a towel around his shoulders.

"Be honest," he says in a low voice. "You think this is a terrible idea, don't you?"

I glance up, meeting his gaze.

"No," I say simply. "I think it's a big deal for you, but I also think you're ready. You've been doing so well in therapy, and you know I would never push you. If you don't want to go, we don't have to go yet. It's that simple."

Ryder swallows hard and nods his head.

I am so proud of him and the work he's been doing in therapy. It's only been about a month, but the shift is already there.

I've been going to therapy too. At first, it was to deal with the guilt and feeling like I failed Ry, but I've been learning that I didn't cause what happened. Kyle did. And even if I'd seen every sign, I couldn't have predicted what he'd do. Therapy helps me process it all, so I don't weigh Ryder down with my guilt. He's got enough to process on his own, and I'm so proud of him for doing the work.

Tonight will be our first time back at Pine Bar since everything happened. I don't know exactly how much people know, but I know it's enough. I'm sure there'll be whispers, sideways glances, speculation from people trying to fill in the blanks. *That's one of the downfalls of small towns; everyone knows everyone's shit.* But we're not going to survive all of this only to shrink away from the world. So we're going.

The case was all over the news, and what happened to us isn't a secret. At first, the headlines started vague, "*Local Man Hospitalized After Stabbing,*" and "*Local Man Kidnapped, Suspect in Custody,*" but it didn't take long for everything to unravel publicly.

Enough people know what Kyle did and what Ryder and I went through. I can't even count how many calls, emails, and messages I got from coworkers, especially after Sierra, who found me bleeding out and called the ambulance, shared what she'd seen. I know she was scared and panicked and needed to process, so I don't blame her for talking about it. I'm just glad she called 911 before it was too late.

Still, I can see Ryder's mind moving through all the possible scenarios and conversations before they happen, so I move behind him, sliding my arms around his waist and pressing my lips to his bare shoulder. "We don't have to go," I murmur against his skin. "If it's too much, say the word, and we'll stay in."

Ryder exhales, tilting his head to the side, giving me more space to kiss down his throat.

"I want to go. I want to get our life back to normal," he

says. "It's just…we haven't really seen anyone yet. Not outside of family. It's gonna be—"

"A lot," I finish for him.

"Yeah," he nods.

I pull back just enough for him to see me in the mirror. "We'll go in, have a drink, let people be weird for a few minutes. And if you want to leave at any point, we leave; we don't owe them any answers. I don't care where we are as long as we're together."

"Yeah. Okay." He exhales, then shakes himself off, turning around and grabbing me and pulling me in for a quick kiss. "But if anyone says some dumb shit, I fully expect you to cause a scene so I don't have to."

I grin. "Oh, baby. You think I'm capable of subtlety at this point?"

Ryder laughs, pressing a quick kiss to my lips before stepping back. "Alright. Let's go."

36

RYDER

"Ready?" Logan asks as we stand outside Pine Bar. I exhale and turn to look at him. "Guess it's now or never."

He lets out a little laugh. "You sound like we're about to step onto a battlefield."

"Have you met the people inside this bar? That's exactly what it'll be like," I say as I raise my eyebrows because he knows exactly what I'm talking about.

Logan laughs again. "Okay, okay. But if anyone gives you shit, remember, you asked me to cause a scene. I'll gladly tell them to fuck off."

"I feel like I'm gonna regret that, huh?" I question, even though I love his protectiveness.

"Nah. I won't do anything too embarrassing, I promise," he grins before reaching for my hand and slotting our fingers together and using his other hand to open the door.

I don't know what I was expecting, maybe the whole bar to fall silent as everyone turned to stare at us, but only a few people even turn to the door and see us when we walk in.

Most people are still engrossed in their conversations, and it's not like we know *everyone* in the bar. But there is the standard Friday night crowd, like us.

The one person who does see us immediately is Mia. She's got her red bandana tied around her black curls, a black tank top, and jeans. Instead of calling out to us, though, she raises an eyebrow, smirks, and nods her head toward the table we usually sit at.

Logan leans in. "That was very cryptic."

I snort, tugging him toward our table.

Mia is already seated at the table we usually claim, two beers in front of her, looking entirely too pleased with herself. She gestures at the drinks. "Sit. Drink. Prepare yourselves."

Logan slides in first, giving her a suspicious look. "For what, exactly?"

She leans forward, resting her elbows on the table. "I wanted to talk to you two before you got ambushed by everyone else."

I pause, beer halfway to my mouth. "Ambushed?"

Mia shrugs like we should expect more attention. "You're kinda a hot topic right now."

Logan rolls his eyes. "Oh, come on. The news cycle has moved on."

"Not for the people in this bar," Mia says, looking at me now. "The ones who've known you forever—the ones who've been waiting for you to finally get your shit together."

I set my beer down, looking around and seeing a few people looking our way, but nothing crazy. Wait, is she talking about—

"I'm so happy you're finally together!" she manages to squeal at a low volume. "I feel like I've been waiting forever for this day."

I let out a little laugh, grateful she wasn't bringing up the Kyle situation, only the fact that Logan and I just walked in holding hands.

"I'm really happy, too," I say, looking at Logan with a smile.

Mia studies me for a second, then nods. "Yay! Then let's drink and celebrate! First rounds on me, bitches!"

Logan snorts a laugh. "Thanks, Mia."

The night goes smoothly. As expected, there are a few offhand comments—some version of 'knew it,' or 'about time,' but no one's shocked or treats it like it's a big deal. Most people avoid bringing up what happened with Kyle; a few want to make sure we're okay, but no one truly pries or crosses any lines. It feels good to be able to breathe normally again in one of our favorite places.

Pete doesn't even beg us to play darts tonight, which feels like a win on its own. Though I know I will need to keep my promise to him and play soon. Maybe next Friday.

Throughout the night, I lean into Logan, letting his arm slide easily around my shoulders as we cuddle into each other at the table.

Yeah, we've turned into 'those people' who sit on the same side of the table now. I can't help it, I just want to be close to him.

"You good?" he checks.

I nod, knocking my knee against his. "Yeah, I really am."

Logan grins. "So, does this mean I'm finally allowed to make out with you in public?"

I snort. "Yeah, lover boy, it does." And he leans in.

BY THE TIME WE STUMBLE THROUGH THE APARTMENT DOOR, I'm drunk off Logan. His hands have barely left me all night and the way he looked at me at the bar has got me ready for this flip fuck he keeps teasing me with.

We've fucked multiple times since our first time a few weeks ago, but he's bottomed every time. He keeps getting me ready for him with his fingers and toys, and *damn*, do I love that plug. But I'm ready, I want his cock inside of me, and I'm going to make sure tonight's the night it happens.

I go to open my mouth, but the only thing that comes out is a grunt because next thing I know, Logan's mouth is crashing into mine as he pins me against the door. His fingers grip my hair, his body presses into mine, and he slides his leg between mine, giving me something to grind against.

"Mmm," I moan against his lips.

I feel Logan's lips curl into a smile against my mouth, all filthy and knowing. "You had me hard all night at the bar, couldn't wait to get back here."

He steps back from me, and I hate the space between us, but I love how quickly he strips out of his clothes. He's hard and naked in front of me, and he's a sight to see.

He comes to stand on the side of my body, grabbing my hand and positioning it right at his ass. I give him a squeeze and let my finger explore until my mouth drops open as I notice the snug end of a plug in his hole.

"You—" I swallow. "You put it in before the bar?"

Logan smirks at my shock. "After our shower. Figured since I've been promising you that flip fuck, I would be prepared."

Fuck, that's hot. My cock throbs instantly and I can't wait to feel him inside of me. I've been waiting for this, too.

"You are so sexy," I groan, already reaching for his straining dick.

But Logan grabs my wrists, stopping me. "Not yet, baby. Tonight's about you first."

"But—" I begin to protest, but he cuts me off.

"Let me take care of you," he murmurs, kissing me slowly. "I want to taste you first. You want me to rim you, baby?"

I shudder, nodding before I can even form a thought. Logan guides me toward the bed with a look in his eyes that makes my knees weak. His hands are on me, stripping off every layer of clothing until I'm bare, and he rakes his eyes appreciatively over my body before licking his lips like I'm his favorite snack.

"On the bed, on your stomach," he commands.

I do what he says, and as soon as I'm down, I feel the mattress dip as he leans forward to press a trail of his kisses down my back. Once he gets to my ass, he spreads me open and hums to himself.

"Damn, Ryder. You are so sexy." He already sounds breathless, and I love that he reacts like this to me, especially since I still can't help but feel vulnerable spread out like this.

Logan wastes no time. His mouth is on me instantly, licking a long, wet stripe up my crack, and I jolt forward with a gasp. His tongue is hot and wet and purposeful, teasing over my hole in slow, maddening circles. It feels so good as he grips my thighs and spreads me even wider, groaning against me like I'm the best thing he's ever tasted, and I can only hope I am.

The sounds we're both making fill the room in the hottest, most sinful way, and every flick of his tongue sends sparks racing through my body. He licks and sucks and presses the tip of his tongue into me as I cry out in pleasure. I'm panting, writhing, and desperately trying to push back deeper on his tongue as my hard cock rubs against the sheets. Him tongue fucking me is easily the best thing I've ever felt and torture all wrapped into one. It's so damn good but not enough. I need more. I always need more when it comes to him.

"Logan," I gasp, my voice breaking. "Oh my god, please. More."

He hums against me, and the vibration sends a fresh wave of heat through my core. He doesn't stop lapping at me before pressing his tongue even deeper inside me this time. I'm moaning his name and begging for more as he feasts on me.

He pulls back slightly to blow cool air against my hole, and I squirm beneath him from the contrasting sensation. "You like that, baby?" he rasps, his voice so low it makes me shiver. "You taste so fucking good. I love this ass, *mmm*," he hums.

All I can do is moan and press back, chasing more of him. I'm shameless and needy and completely coming undone under his touch. The way he's eating me out feels like he's praising me.

Like I'm his favorite sin.

And fuck, do I want to be.

He pulls back, and I hear the snap of a bottle of lube opening up, then he's pressing a slick finger inside of me. I moan into the pillow and start fucking myself on his finger. I've never felt this desperate before, and I'm pretty sure his mouth is to blame. He's devouring me tonight, and I'm not above begging for his tongue every day for the rest of my life.

He pulls out and adds a second finger, and my thighs tremble as he twists his fingers just right, pumping them in and out, making me needier and needier.

"More," I beg. "Please, more."

He stills his fingers inside of me, and drapes his body over mine as he leans in against my ear to whisper, "Tell me what you need, baby."

I shiver at his words and push back against his hand, more than ready for his cock. "Your cock. Need your cock in me."

His breath catches and he licks behind my ear and, fuck, I like that. "Yeah?"

I nod, shaky, gasping, completely lost in him. "Yes, please. Fuck me."

Logan curses under his breath, sucks the lob of my ear in his mouth and then pushes himself off me. His slick fingers leave me, and I feel empty without him inside of me.

"Turn over, baby."

I flip over in time to see him coating his cock in lube. I lick my lips as I watch him, feeling strangely jealous of his hand. He's gorgeous as he kneels between my legs and pushes my knees back. I watch as his thick, flushed cock moves toward my entrance until I feel him against me. "Relax, baby. I got you. Breathe out when you feel me press in."

I do as he says. The stretch burns slightly, and I can't help but tense a bit at the much fuller sensation as he presses in.

"Remember to breathe, Ry."

I nod, trying to breathe through him filling me up inch by inch. *He's fucking huge.* I groan as he bottoms out and grip his shoulder, pulling him closer to me.

"Fuck," Logan groans against my neck. "You're so tight. Feels so fucking good."

I gasp, feeling overwhelmed with emotions and sensations right now. This is everything. His first time inside me, my first time bottoming, and it's with the one person I love more than anything in the world. We both breathe each other in for a moment, and I whisper the only thing that's repeating in my mind right now. "I love you."

He smiles at me, leaning down to press a gentle kiss to my lips. "I love you, too, baby. More than anything. You don't know how much this moment means to me."

But I do. It's everything. After everything Kyle tried to take from me, the fact that I still want Logan to take the lead in bed proves just how much I love and trust him. We've discussed trust and choice, and I trust him enough to listen to me, no matter what I request. And that's why I feel safe letting him take control.

All I can do is look up at him and nod, and he starts slowly rocking into me, letting me feel all of him. The burn subsides and it feels a little strange, but so damn good.

He picks up his pace, thrusting deeper and harder, and the sensation makes me whimper. *Just like he says I do.*

"You feel so fucking good," he grits out, gripping my hips, fucking into me harder, and making me lose my goddamn mind. His hands roam over my body as he keeps snapping his hips forward, and I'm positive nothing has ever felt this good in my—

"Holy fuck!" I yell out in ecstasy as his cock thrusts against what must be my prostate and sends a violent shudder through me.

I take back what I just said because that *was the best thing I've ever felt in my life.*

"Oh—fuck," I gasp, writhing beneath him.

Logan lets out a heady groan. "Yeah? That the spot?"

"Jesus, yes—right there."

He grinds into me just right, over and over. He's so deep inside of me, I feel him everywhere. My body is shaking and I'm so damn close.

"Logan—"

He grabs my wrists and pins them over my head, and I love that he's once again taking the lead.

"Not yet, baby," he murmurs, leaning forward to kiss me hard. "You've still got to fuck me, remember? I'm almost there."

I whimper into his mouth, telling myself to hold out for his ass. I'm throbbing and desperate and know it'll only take me two minutes max before I'm coming inside of him.

Logan thrusts his hips hard a few more times before I see him break. He groans deep, his hips jerk, and I feel his cum filling me up. He's right, getting tested was so worth the feeling of knowing his cum is inside me right now, and fuck, I can't wait to do the same to him.

Logan stays buried inside me for a moment, forehead pressed to mine. His lips brush his before he pushes himself up and pulls out of me. Before I even have time to clench to keep his cum in me, he's reaching for a new plug in his bedside table and coating it with lube. He pushes it inside me, and I gasp at the new sensation, loving that I'm not empty. Logan licks his lips, his blue eyes hungry and dark.

"So you don't spill a drop," he says in a low voice before leaning in closer. His lips brushing my ear as he adds, "Your turn, baby. Fuck me."

He reaches behind him to take his plug out and sets it on the table before dropping back on the bed beside me and spreading his legs open for me.

Goddamn.

My orgasm is building from that alone, and I need to be inside of him now. My body is already thrumming with anticipation at the sight of him all spread out for me like this. I groan because this is the hottest moment of my life. I can't believe Logan is so filthy, and I still can't believe I get to experience this side of him.

"This is going to be over quick, holy shit, Logan. You're so sexy, this is so hot."

I grab the lube, coating my fingers before pressing two fingers inside him, feeling how open, how wet, how fucking eager he already is for me.

"Fuck," he breathes. "Ryder, I'm ready for you, baby."

I slide a third finger in, just to be sure, and then I move closer in front of him. I lift his legs and line myself up with his hole. Pressing the head of my cock against him and pushing in slowly. I watch every bare inch of my cock disappear inside his tight little hole, and Logan groans as I fill him up, his fingers digging into my arms, and I let out a shaky breath as I grip his hips.

"You feel so good. You're taking me so well, Lo," I say as I bottom out inside of him.

"Move, Ryder, please," he begs immediately.

I pull out halfway, then slam back inside of him, giving him exactly what he asked for. Logan chokes on a moan, and I love watching him come apart beneath me. I keep the pace slow at first, making him feel every inch before I give him more.

"Fuck, Ry—"

"Yeah?" I grip his hips, angling my thrusts just right, dragging another wrecked sound from him. His whole body shudders, and his muscles are tensing. I lean over, pressing a kiss to his sweaty, flushed skin. "Feel good?"

He lets out a broken laugh. "So good. Holy fuck."

I grin, fucking him faster and harder now. I lose myself in him, between him and the plug inside me, I'm getting so close.

319

"Logan, I'm gonna—"

His hands clutch my back as his legs wrap tighter around me. "Come in me, baby," he demands. "Fill me up. I want it all."

I thrust hard into him one last time, burying myself deep as I come hard, shaking as I fill him with everything I have. My orgasm rips through me until I collapse against him, both of us shaking, panting, utterly fucking ruined.

When Logan catches his breath, he chuckles. "So flip fucking is totally gonna be a thing now."

"Yeah, babe. It is. Fuck, that was hot." I grin, leaning over to press my lips to his.

"You're so fucking mine," he whispers against my lips.

"I always have been."

EPILOGUE: LOGAN

The house is small, but it's perfect for us. I look around the empty living room and feel so much gratitude. It has hardwood floors, big windows, and an actual wood-burning fireplace surrounded by brick. And best of all? It's ours.

Ryder steps up behind me and places his hands on my shoulders and squeezes.

"So?" he asks, tilting his head. "Think we can make it work?"

I laugh, shaking my head. The affection I feel for him is so deep it almost hurts. "It's a done deal, dumbass. We signed the papers this morning."

He grins—no, beams—at that. He's emitting so much joy right now, it's like it's bursting out of him. He comes to stand next to me and bumps his shoulder against mine, just enough to make me sway a little. "Then, I guess we're officially homeowners together, love of my life."

I love hearing those words from his mouth. Part of me still can't believe we made it here, but at the same time, I can see our future mapped out so clearly in this space—lazy weekend mornings with coffee on the porch. Nights curled up in front of the fireplace while we watch reruns and bad comedies. Our mixed and matched furniture from both of our places until we find our style.

In some ways, it reminds me of when we got our first apartment, but it's also so different. We aren't those same twenty-two-year-old kids who just graduated from college. This feels so much *more* than that. This feels like the forever I didn't dare let myself dream of.

But we're here, and we did it. And now we get to do this forever.

It's been a whirlwind few months of coordinating with realtors, getting Ryder's house ready, dealing with a lot of paperwork, scheduling photos, showings, and conversations about budgeting and neighborhoods. I wanted to bash my head against a wall by the end of it, but now it all feels so worth it, standing in the middle of our new empty living room.

Ryder wanders into the attached kitchen, and I watch him with so much awe. We really have been through hell, but we survived the worst of it, and now we get to do everything together.

We finally have news on Kyle's case, too. He pled guilty, so it meant no trial and no lawyers picking apart our trauma like it was a theory on a whiteboard. I don't know how we would've handled questioning from lawyers who were trying to poke holes in what we survived or question our experience on the stand. We were told it was the best-case scenario because it spared us the worst of it, and maybe they're right.

Instead, we sat through a quiet sentencing hearing while they read the charges like a grocery list. Kyle was convicted of kidnapping, attempted murder, aggravated assault with a deadly weapon, stalking, false imprisonment, obstruction of justice, and tampering with evidence—each one spoken so clinically, it barely sounded like the nightmare we'd lived through.

The last one they read was murder in the second degree, and that one gutted me to hear.

I knew what he'd said to Ryder in that basement, but hearing it read out loud and confirmed shook something loose in me, because that meant there was a very real chance I could have lost Ryder after Kyle had previously killed someone who rejected him. He confessed it, right to Ryder's face, and now it was proven. The prosecutor said Kyle's confession and the location of the victim's remains had lined up, and he'd been a missing person for two years, but now there was enough evidence to close the case. I can't help but wonder about his family and how they must be feeling. It's awful, but I'm glad Kyle won't be free to hurt any more people.

He was sentenced to thirty-two years in prison, with no possibility of parole for at least twenty-five.

The judge said justice had been served, and the prosecutors nodded like the math worked out. And in some ways, maybe it has. Kyle's rotting in a jail cell, Ryder is safe, and while no amount of time will ever be enough for the hurt and pain he put Ryder through, he's been working so hard on healing to the point he only ended up taking five weeks off of work before he went back.

And Kyle's uncle, who hired him as a consultant, the same one who wouldn't put the warrant through for Santos and tried to shut the investigation down because "Kyle's a good man"? Yeah, he stepped down as Chief. He's now under investigation for obstructing justice, thanks to Santos.

Santos has had our backs through it all, and I'll always be grateful for him taking me seriously, despite his superior telling him to back off. He risked a lot for us, but he did what was right by the law. Maybe, one day, he'll be the Chief.

My company has continued to let me work from home. I'm sure it's probably more out of guilt than anything, but I don't care what their reason is. Being home with Ryder helped both of us, and it also gave me a sense of clarity. I started taking freelance design clients, and I'm going to keep building my client base so that I can eventually work for myself full-time. Especially now that we've signed the mortgage papers, it's just a matter of *when*.

It feels right to branch off and take the leap. I only want to work on projects that excite me, rather than watered-down, play-it-safe designs for clients who are unclear about their vision. I'm excited to build something for *us*.

I follow Ryder into the kitchen and wrap my arms around him from behind as he sinks into my embrace. He leans his head back on my shoulder, and I breathe him in.

"Hey, Ry."

He turns, eyebrows raised curiously. "Yeah?"

I don't say anything, just close the distance between us, grabbing the front of his shirt and kissing him so hard he stumbled back against the counter with a surprised grunt before kissing me back like he's starving for me. When we finally break apart, he's panting as his lips form into a big grin.

"Well, damn."

I smirk. "What? Never been kissed by a homeowner before?"

His grin widens. "No, but I'd like to do it again. Preferably forever."

I laugh, and this time when I kiss him, it's softer and slower. I linger, pouring every ounce of affection into it as we stand there for a long moment, bodies pressed together in our empty kitchen, in our new house, in our new life.

Ryder pulls back slightly, his eyes darkening as they flick to my mouth. "So," he murmurs, voice dipping lower. "Are we gonna break in the bedroom first, or should we start right here?"

I chuckle as his breath hitches, and it only makes me grin harder.

"Living room," I decide. "Then the bedroom. Then the kitchen. Then the fucking garage, if we make it that far. Might have to defile every square inch just to be sure it's really ours."

Ryder groans, his fingers tightening on my hips. "I can get on board with that."

I smirk, dragging my teeth along his bottom lip before nipping at it gently. "I love you, always. You're home, baby."

"I love you, too," he replies, eyes soft even as his body practically vibrates with want.

Then, without another word, I lace our fingers together, turn on my heel, and tug him with me, laughing, as we head straight for the living room floor like two idiots too in love to care about furniture.

Because that's the thing about fresh starts—they're whatever the hell we want them to be.

And we want this. All of it. Together.

EPILOGUE: RYDER

The air smells like salt, sunscreen, and something tropical, and I feel completely free.

Logan doesn't know exactly where we're going yet. All he knows is we landed in Mexico this morning, after I dragged him through customs, then stuffed him into a shuttle with tinted windows. He's been trying to get it out of me since we left the house this morning, but I held my ground. I didn't even tell him we were coming to Mexico. I packed his bag, his passport, and a few other items for him, so he had no idea.

Now, we're walking down a winding stone path lined with palm trees, heading toward the private villa that comes into view just as the ocean does. It has whitewashed walls, a pool on the terrace, and a view that looks like it was ripped straight from a honeymoon brochure. As soon as we get there, he stops walking and stares with parted lips. His sunglasses tip down slightly as he turns back to look at me. "Is this where we're staying?" he asks in disbelief.

I shrug, biting back a grin. "Yup, only the best for the World's Best Boyfriend."

"Holy shit, Ryder!"

"You don't know this, but last year, when things were bad, I promised myself I'd take you to a resort in Mexico when it was all said and done to thank you, and now, here we are."

"Holy shit," Logan breathes, tugging off his sunglasses. "This is incredible!" He turns and stares at me for a beat, like he's not sure if he wants to kiss me or cry, before he pulls me into his chest and buries his face in my neck.

"I don't deserve you."

"Well, you've got me anyway, and I'm not going anywhere."

We stay there like that for a long moment, wrapped in each other with the ocean in the background and the sun warm on our skin. Eventually, we wander inside, hand in hand, exploring the villa that'll be ours for the next seven days. There's champagne on ice. A king-size bed draped in sheer white fabric. A tub big enough for two. And on the table by the window, a note: "Welcome, Mr. Stevens and Mr. Hart. Congratulations on one year together."

It's perfect.

Logan snorts. "I can't believe it's only been a year. It feels like we've lived a dozen lives in that time."

He's not wrong; so much has changed in twelve months.

Logan quit his job four months ago—finally. It took him longer than he expected, but he did it after spending most of the last year working remotely and building his freelance business on the side. Once he got to an income point he felt truly comfortable with, he took the leap, and now he's fully on his own. His work is incredible—just like him. Watching him build his business from the ground up and light up over client projects has made me unbelievably proud of him.

We also adopted a dog last fall, a mutt named Beans, and

it's ironic because as much as Logan hates beans the food, he loves Beans the dog. We take her on long walks and argue about who's better at training her—me, obviously. At night, she curls up at the foot of the bed while we curl into each other, and I love that she makes our family feel complete.

Logan walks out onto the terrace, tugging his shirt off as he stares at the pool. "Private pool. You went all out, huh?"

"I figured we earned it," I say, smiling at him.

"You packed my swim trunks, right?"

"Nope, you're going in naked," I smirk at him. I did pack them, but he doesn't need them right now.

"I can get behind that."

"And I can get behind you," I say as I waggle my eyebrows at him.

He laughs and turns to face me fully. Sunlight spills across his chest, and I'm struck all over again by how much I love him. How beautiful he is. How much softer his eyes have become now that stress isn't living behind them.

"I love you," I say.

He softens immediately, walking toward me until he's standing so close I can feel the heat of him. "I love you, too. Thanks for bringing me here, Ry."

"I'd take you anywhere."

He smiles, and I could live inside that look forever.

So I take a breath, reach into my pocket, and say, "Actually, there's one more thing."

He watches me curiously until I pull out the small box I've been carrying all day and drop down to one knee. His lips part, eyes wide as they flick down to the ring inside. It's black and sleek, with a textured center and polished edges.

"I know it's only been a year of us dating," I start. "But after everything we've been through, after all the ways you've loved me and held me and helped me come back to myself, I don't want to waste another second not calling you mine in every way I can. You've been my best friend since the moment we met, and I feel like we were always supposed to end up here. You're it for me, Logan. You're everything, and I can't imagine a future where we're not husbands." I swallow hard, eyes locked on his. "Will you marry me?"

He blinks at the tears forming in his eyes, and he nods fast. "Yes," he breathes, pulling me up off one knee and into his arms. "God, yes. I love you, baby. I want forever with you."

When I break away, I slip the ring onto his finger, and he kisses me with so much passion. I can feel his dick start to get hard against my leg, and when we finally break apart, breathless and grinning, he says, "So, should we break in the bed first as an engaged couple?"

I laugh at that. "I was thinking the pool, actually."

Logan hums thoughtfully. "Then the bed. Then the shower. Then the balcony."

"Then probably the floor because you'll be too weak to make it anywhere else," I add and waggle my eyebrows.

He shoves me. "You are such a cocky little shit."

"Only because I know it's true," I beam. He's right, though, I have become cockier since I realized I like dick.

We both laugh before I take him in my arms and tackle him into the pool. We both pop out of the water laughing before he jumps into my arms and kisses me senseless.

This time last year, we were fighting for our lives. And now, we're fully living them.

And we're not done yet.

There's so much more I want with him—more places, more quiet mornings, more days where the only thing that matters is the way he looks at me across a room, and I forget how to breathe.

We've already survived the worst. Now we get to build the best.

Together.

THE END.

ACKNOWLEDGMENTS

THANK YOU for reading my debut novel! I woke up one morning and thought, "what if someone stalked a narrator for his voice?" At the time, that was my whole idea and probably the reason I rewrote this book three times before my betas even saw it, but I love its final form almost as much as I love Logan and Ryder.

Massive thank you to my beta readers Alyssa G., Bryoni H., Em R., Ronan M., Jenny B., Charley H., Rissa J., Sabrina R., Crystal K., Narissa J., and Cath V! You all helped shape this book and made me feel far more confident sharing it with the world. Thank you so, so much for all your feedback, suggestions, support, and love for these two!

Brittany, you've gone above and beyond for me! Thank you for answering all my questions about how indie publishing works and for proofreading this book twice. You've been such a huge support system for me throughout this journey. I seriously can't thank you enough!

Lexi, thank you for everything since we started writing! Thank you for encouraging me to set dates for everything, or who knows if this book would've ever been published! I am so glad we connected. You've made this journey so much more fun and helped keep me sane! And I can't wait for all the co-writing we have ahead of us.

ABOUT THE AUTHOR

Bec Benson is based in the Northeast, lives for the first sip of hot coffee in the morning, genuinely believes emo music can make you happy, and is obsessed with mgk (but not in a Kyle-obsessed way). *Straight to You* is her debut novel.

Want to read about the first time Kyle heard Ryder's voice? Sign up here for the bonus scene: https://becbenson.com/straight-to-you

Come hang out in Bec Benson's Book Besties here: www.facebook.com/groups/becbenson/

THE REALITY OF WANTING HIM

Book one in the *Love Without Label* series, co-written with Lexi Amber, is coming July 23, 2025

Blake

When my parents threatened to cut me off if I wasn't married by the time I turned thirty, I thought finding a wife would be easy. But apparently, I'm not the best at dating, and almost two years later, I'm still very single.

My birthday is coming up fast, and unless I want to give up the comfortable lifestyle I'm used to, I need to find someone willing to settle down with quickly. I'm desperate and out of ideas, until my best friend suggests I apply for a new reality dating show.

Now I'm a contestant on the first season of *Love Without Labels*, a completely blind reality dating show where we talk to each other through distorted voice technology and texts. No photos, ages, genders, or even names will be revealed until we decide to move in together.

I knew all of this when I signed up, and even though I'm straight, I assumed it would be easy to tell if I was talking to a woman.

Apparently, I was wrong.

Liam

It's my final season working for the family farm before I take over for my dad. I'm ready to find someone to build a real future with, but I know they aren't in my small hometown.

Love Without Labels feels like the perfect chance to find my person. I've never cared much about labels anyway. All I want is someone who's loyal, honest, and I can share my dreams with.

As we narrow down our matches, there's only one person I can imagine a future with. Someone who listens, makes me laugh, and feel wanted in a way I haven't in a long time.

But while I've kept my mind open about who I'm falling for, apparently, he's been convinced I was a woman this entire time.

Will he still want to continue building on the connection we have now that he knows the truth? Or was this relationship doomed before it could really even begin?

PRE-ORDER HERE: https://books2read.com/u/mv8vaV

www.ingramcontent.com/pod-product-compliance
Lightning Source LLC
Chambersburg PA
CBHW020931260626
47169CB00006B/1674